THREE COUSINS

A NOVEL

JESSICA LEVINE

SHE WRITES PRESS

Published 2025

Printed in the United States of America

Print ISBN: 978-1-64742-868-6
E-ISBN: 978-1-64742-869-3
Library of Congress Control Number: 2024920492

For information, address:
She Writes Press
1569 Solano Ave #546
Berkeley, CA 94707

Interior design and typeset by Katherine Lloyd, The DESK

She Writes Press is a division of SparkPoint Studio, LLC.

In memory of
Floss and Laurie

CONTENTS

1

THE LETTER

(Anna)

Anna needed to get the futon from the garden room, but her mother was there, drinking. It was a warm day on the North Shore of Long Island in late August 1976, and she was flushed from loading the old Buick station wagon Doug had borrowed to move her to New Haven. Sweat beaded on her forehead, and her wavy auburn hair, which she'd put up in a bun earlier, fell around her face. Doug was rejiggering the boxes in the back of the car as Anna went back inside the white clapboard house.

Stepping into the living room, she heard her mother on the phone. Normally, her mom spent her days in the backyard studio, but she'd come inside to make a call. Her chatter was more than an annoyance; the wild swings in the rhythm of her speech—from staccatos down to hushed tones then back up to shrill laughter—triggered the apprehension Anna had always felt around her. It started in her chest, then crept up the back of her neck and over her skull to her forehead. Anna had a love/hate relationship with her mother. Yes, Linda was an amazing sculptress, a force of creativity, a whirling goddess of clay and stone who'd inspired her daughter to draw and paint. But decades of disappointment had turned her into an alcoholic of the abusive, histrionic variety, and Anna preferred to avoid her. Still, she needed that futon. Moving to the threshold, she saw a coupe glass on the wicker side table. Probably a corpse reviver. Her mother was having her weekly "long-distance cocktail" with her sister in California. The smoke from her cigarette floated out through the porch screens, over the rhododendron border, and into the garden.

"You're right, it won't necessarily be a disaster," Linda said. "Uh-huh. Uh-huh." The utterances suggested she truly listened to her sister, perhaps the only person she ever did listen to. "We did get along, didn't we? So why shouldn't they?" Linda glanced at Anna, who pointed at the futon. "Listen, I have to get off. Anna's about to leave. I love you."

Linda stood up.

"You and Sarah taking bets about whether the three of us will get along?" Anna asked. She looked forward to getting away from her mother and living off campus with her two cousins. Her senior year at Yale would be special. She'd do art in her own space and focus on her other passion—languages. The plan was to start Mandarin and continue with French. She hoped to live abroad one day, maybe even travel around the world.

"Of course. Cousins are different from sisters. But you have to admit, it's an experiment, three cousins moving in together. Anyway, she sends her love. And hopes you'll transmit news about Robin."

"Robin can transmit her own news."

"She can, but she won't. She never does. Your generation just doesn't share. Do you need lunch?" Linda asked.

"We'll get hot dogs on the boat." Anna and Doug would take the ferry from Port Jefferson across the Long Island Sound to Bridgeport, then get on the highway to New Haven. "You still okay with my taking the futon?"

"I don't see why you have to go up a whole week before school starts."

"Because the apartment is available, and I want time to settle in."

"Aren't you hot with all that hair? Don't you know how to make a bun that stays up?" Linda smashed her cigarette in a gold-rimmed ashtray, strode over to Anna, and pulled her hair back away from her face.

"Ouch, stop that!" Anna cried out. She smelled gin on her mother's breath.

"You're so beautiful and you do everything possible to make yourself ugly, the way you always have. You eat too much, you pick your skin, you don't take care of your hair—"

"Enough already! And I haven't picked my skin in years!"

"I'm glad you're leaving," Linda said. "Just watching you every day all summer fills me with sorrow and disappointment."

"And I can't wait to get out of here!" Anna screamed. "Because guess what? I'm disappointed in you too!"

"You're an ungrateful pig!"

"Guess where I learned that from!"

Anna stormed out of the house to the driveway, and there he was, her man, so willing to be helpful, still shoving the easel, boxes, and lamps into the back of the car.

He looked up. "She drinking already?"

"You heard us fighting?"

"Her voice carries."

"I hate her."

"I get it. But you gotta let it go."

"I just wanted to strip the futon in the guest room," Anna said, "and we had a fight." She undid her bun and redid it, tucking a rebellious lock behind one ear. "I hate it when she touches me."

"I don't understand why you want the futon. Why not buy

a real mattress and throw it on the floor?" Doug asked. He was a tall, athletic guy who'd want a big bed to thrash around in.

"I'll be in the living room," she said. "I need something that folds up."

"Why? What about when we want privacy?" Hooking a thumb through the belt loop of her jeans, he pulled her closer and, in a caressing gesture, brushed the hair off her cheeks.

"I hate having to go to the campus studio all the time. I want the living room so I can paint at home. Julia and Robin are taking the bedrooms."

"Robin needs her own room, okay, I get that, but why Julia? She doesn't even have a boyfriend. It doesn't make sense," Doug said.

It was true. Julia, the youngest of the three cousins, was also the shyest. She'd probably never even been kissed, though she'd come of age in Manhattan in the early 1970s.

"It's true she doesn't have a boyfriend, but that's exactly why she needs her own room. So she can get one and get laid."

"The three of you had a cousinly meeting about how to help Julia lose her virginity?" Doug let go and stepped back.

"Not exactly—"

"You're saying we can have sex when you come see me in New York but not when I come up to New Haven."

"I'll be coming down to see you most weekends, but you'll be coming up maybe once a month because there's nothing to do in New Haven, and you know it. And the bedrooms are too small for me to paint in. Come on, please don't take this as a rejection."

"Why shouldn't I?"

They'd been together since freshman year of high school. They fought often, but she knew how to settle an argument quickly. Moving her hand up and down over his pants zipper, she kissed him lightly on the lips. "Because I like your bod." She slid her fingers inside his pants.

He returned her kiss with pressure. "All right then. I'll try not to feel rejected."

"Come on, let's go take that futon apart."

They found Linda still sitting in the garden room.

"Oh, Doug," Linda said, gulping the last of her cocktail, "how lovely you're helping Anna." Her wrathful, loathsome expression had become soft and smiling. She was a quick-change artist, able to behave when Doug was in the room. "I'm so appreciative." She looked at Anna. "Honey, I hope you find the futon comfortable."

"Thanks, Mom." Anna grimaced.

The two young people rolled up the futon, carried it outside, and fastened it to the roof of the Buick with ropes and bungee cords. Doug took the frame apart and shoved it into the rear of the car.

"Okay, we're leaving now." Anna took a few steps back toward the front porch; her mother came forward to hug her, then kissed her on the mouth, turned her back, and went inside. Anna wiped her mouth with the back of her hand. She didn't like hugging her mother, and she hated the mouth kiss, some Russian-Jewish thing passed down from her grandmother Iris. It was okay when Iris did it, but when Linda did it—yuck. That tiny bit of love right after the hatred and contempt made her feel unclean.

Fuming, she slid into the front seat where Doug was already at the wheel. Having been subjected to the tortures of art critique groups, Anna guessed her mother's critical streak had started with her early training. The quest for perfection fostered the habit of thinking, then saying, it's too dark, it's too light, it should be a little to the left, a little to the right. The head is too large, the paint is too thick, the composition is off. Artists who got into that frame of mind were bound to extend the criticism to the people around them. Linda thought her husband worked too hard and ate too much. Her older daughter, Evelyn, was flighty, remote, and unreliable. As for Anna, her hair was a tangle, her waist too thick, her academic interests unfocused, and her art lazy.

"I overheard everything before," he said.

"She always stops when you come in. I don't know what I'd do without you."

"You'd find some other tall, tough guy to keep her under control." He gave her a big grin, and she couldn't help smiling back. He turned on the radio—"Don't Go Breaking My Heart" was on—and they were off.

They drove the car onto the ferry, then climbed the narrow metal staircase up two flights to the top deck, where they stood at the railing. The mood was festive when the big boat pulled away from Port Jefferson with its quaint little marina and ramshackle houses climbing the hill. They stayed at the stern and watched the town grow smaller as they moved out between the sandy cliffs that jutted forward like two arms embracing the bay. Halfway across the Sound, they walked to the prow to enjoy the approach to Bridgeport.

This sea was a neutral space, a safe, watery middle where they could discuss dangerous questions.

"I've decided I'm definitely applying to MIT for architecture," Doug said.

Anna nodded. "That makes sense. I thought you would."

"Maybe it's vain of me, but I'm sure I'll get in. How about you come up to Cambridge to live with me after graduation? Or you still thinking about Europe?"

"I am," she said. "I'm still thinking about it."

He put his arm around her waist. "I don't want you to go away again."

"But I have to. I have to get away from *her*. And I want to live abroad again. Junior year wasn't enough for me. You could put off graduate school for a year and come with me."

He shook his head and gazed toward the shore. "I don't feel drawn to Europe the way you do."

She put her arms around him. "I do love you, but I've got to get away."

He said nothing.

"Doug—"

"You don't expect me to be happy about it, do you?"

"No, I don't," she said. "But I expect you to try to understand."

When they reached the apartment near Orange Street, Robin, who was settling into the bedroom at the end of the hall, came out to greet them. Anna thought she looked robust and healthy. They hugged, the New Yorker and the Californian, and took stock of each other. Anna liked Robin's style, the headband over her curly hair, and the big earrings made of brass and enamel, probably from India; she worshipped her older cousin, whose fearless attitude she hoped to emulate one day.

"When did you get here?" Anna asked.

"Just yesterday. I shared the driving with Gloria again. We took a week to drive cross-country."

"Gloria was your best buddy at Wellesley, wasn't she?"

"Yeah, I'm really lucky we got into the same graduate school. She's fun to hang out with."

"You still going up to Boston before school starts?"

"Yes, I am, tonight," Robin said. Her girlfriend lived in Cambridge. "I just wanted to drop Gloria at her place and unload my stuff here. How was your mother over the summer? Did she behave herself?"

"Don't ask," Anna said. "Thank God Doug was with me today."

"You still her knight in shining armor, huh?" Robin asked him.

"Yup, serving my lady with love and grace." He smiled and went downstairs to bring up another box.

"Really," Anna said, "I'd like to have nothing more to do with her. This morning she was awful. She says mean things. She— she insults me. It's unbearable." Tears came to her eyes, maybe because Robin was not only older and family but also a student in psychology interested in female "patterns" who had witnessed Linda's drunken rages more than once. The three cousins had always helped each other survive their difficult mothers: Anna's was alcoholic, though the word carried so much stigma at the time it was never spoken, Julia's was narcissistic, while Robin's was crazy in some undefined way.

"You should write her a letter," Robin suggested, "and give her an ultimatum."

"I've thought of doing something like that. But what kind of ultimatum?"

"I don't know. Something that would set boundaries. What would you like to say to her?"

"I'd like to say, 'If you don't stop drinking when I'm around, I won't come home to visit.'" Anna's heart pounded with rage.

Doug came in with another carton and set it down. "Sounds good to me," he said. "I'd support you in that completely."

"I think it's a great idea," Robin agreed.

The younger generation was ready to put the older in its place.

"I'd say to her, 'If you ever get drunk and harm me again, then I'll never, *ever* have *anything* to do with you *ever* again.'" She unpacked with quick, angry gestures. "'Because this time I've really, really had it.'"

Anna stopped, thinking of how her father might react. "It's ridiculous. I can't," she said, suddenly deflated.

"Why not?" Robin asked.

"It's not so easy—"

"Just look at you. As soon as you said, 'I can't,' you started to shrivel, like you were going to collapse."

"I *am* about to collapse," Anna said. "She's trying to kill me with her hatred."

"She's jealous of you because she feels like a failure, and you're ten times more talented than she is, and you have your whole life ahead of you."

It sounded so true, Anna had to pay attention. "You're right. I have to write her."

"Let's finish up so you can do it."

The three of them brought up the rest of the boxes and the easel. Setting her art supplies down, Anna's rage at her mother softened at the prospect of getting back to painting. It would be her year to master the human form; she'd signed up for figure painting and had a male friend willing to pose for her.

They dragged the futon frame and mattress up the stairs, made the bed, and flopped onto it. Robin brought out a joint. They smoked one, then a second. Anna, who didn't smoke pot often, flew high as she wrote her mother a letter longhand on a pad of yellow paper.

I've had it with the way you insult and criticize me when you drink. You don't realize how you harm me when you're intoxicated and how it damages our relationship. Any future contact between us will be conditional on your sobriety.

It was paradoxical to write such a letter while stoned, but maybe she needed to be stoned to find the courage to write it; however, she stopped short of telling her mother how much she loathed her.

I advise you strongly to agree to these terms if you wish to remain in contact with me, she concluded. *Your daughter, Anna.*

When she was done, Robin went to her room to dig up a stamp and an envelope, then sealed the letter inside.

The three of them got in Doug's car, and he drove until Anna saw a mailbox and yelled, "Stop!" She jumped out and stuck the envelope in the mail slot. Then they continued on their way to Brother's Pizzeria, one of the few spots where they liked to eat in New Haven. Doug drove slowly because he was stoned too.

✺

Robin left for Boston late that night. The next morning, Doug returned to Columbia, leaving his car with Anna. She set to painting the living room and organizing the art corner that would save her schlepping to and from the campus studio. She hated the competitive atmosphere there and wanted to avoid being distracted by other art students.

A few days later, the walls had been repainted, and she made a list of supplies she needed to buy: some canvas, paper, a few new brushes to replace old, damaged ones, and more paint, of course. The letter she'd sent her mother was far from her mind when the telephone rang.

It was her father.

"Anna, is that you?"

"Hi, Dad."

Anna's amicable relationship with her dad was facilitated by his minimal appearance in her life. A professor and research scientist at SUNY Stony Brook, Carl Stark spent seven days a week at the lab to escape his wife. The more absent he was, the more Linda drank, and the more Linda drank, the more absent he was. This arrangement lubricated the nominal cohabitation of two people enslaved to a joyless marriage by history, property, and children.

"How's school going?" Carl asked.

"Fine. How are you?"

"I went to the post office to pick up the mail," he said, "and I saw a letter from you to your mother." He cleared his throat.

"Did you give it to her?" She imagined him, white lab coat buttoned over his protruding belly, sitting in the university office on the same linoleum hallway as his smelly lab.

"Not yet. I haven't opened it, but I can guess what's in it," he said. "I know you had a rough summer."

"I can't stand it anymore, Dad."

"You can't understand. She's had so many failures and frustrations—"

"That's no excuse for the way she treats me—"

"You need to think this through, Anna. If you fight with her, I'll be forced to choose sides. You're my daughter and I love you, but she's still my wife, and she runs my home . . . in her erratic way . . ."

"Daddy!"

"Where and how would I see you if you break with her? It's absurd, Anna. You can't do this."

"I'd come see you at the lab."

"And where would you stay? At a motel?" he asked.

"I'd stay with Doug and his parents."

"Anna, I'd still have to make a choice. The most likely upshot would be that I wouldn't be able to see you anymore."

Anna clenched her teeth. She had launched the letter in self-defense, like an arrow, and her father had intercepted it in midair. He was aware of Linda's verbal abuse but had never stepped in to defend his daughter because his instinct was to side with his wife. Since Linda had always reserved physical violence for when no one else was around, he didn't fully understand the harm she'd done, and Anna couldn't explain it to him now because the habit of not speaking was old and deep.

"Anna," he said, "you still there?"

"I'm still here." She contained her fury in order not to alienate the only parent she had.

"Can I tear up this letter?"

"Okay," Anna conceded, "tear it up."

She felt trapped and betrayed as she heard the faint sound of paper being ripped.

"It's done," he said.

Maybe one day, with a little imagination, she'd be able to

do something different and more constructive with her anger, like tap into it as a source of strength and momentum to propel herself far away.

"Okay then," she said.

"It's for the best. You'll see."

Frustrated but relieved, she hung up. Maybe her father was right. She had wanted to excommunicate her mother, but the drama would have been a huge and draining distraction from school. Her mind turned to fantasies of escaping to France or China or some other land. One day she would set out bravely and maybe not return.

Anna picked up the list for the art store and looked at it again. Brushes, paints, and canvas. For the moment that was all she really needed to make herself fresh and clean.

2

WANNA BE
CRAZY FREE

(Robin)

R obin left for Boston late, after having pizza with Anna and
Doug, and it was around midnight when she arrived at
Stephanie's apartment in the three-story brownstone on Com-
monwealth Avenue. She wore jeans, a folded red bandanna that
kept her short, dark curls off her face, and a pair of beat-up
Frye boots. Stomping around in those boots during her years
at Wellesley College, she'd kicked through mounds of leaves in
the fall and crossed snowdrifts in the winter and puddles in the
spring. She'd even worn them under her graduation gown. Now,
in the summer heat, they made her feel powerful and confident,
the graduate of a women's school that had given her the sense of
being the first sex and no longer the second. And enough of an
adult to be in a relationship with her professor.

Robin let herself in with her key, put her bags down, and saw
Stephanie asleep on the couch with a manuscript on her belly.
That was what Steph did: she worked until she couldn't keep her
eyes open anymore. Robin sat down beside her.

"Steph," she whispered. "I'm home."

Stephanie stirred, opening her eyes, and Robin leaned over and kissed her lightly on the lips.

"Where have you been?" Stephanie asked. "I thought you'd be here for dinner."

"I wanted to help Anna unpack a bit. Then it made sense to eat with her and Doug. And . . . well . . . we had a smoke, so I had to wait for it to wear off."

"Why would you get high when you knew you'd be driving up?"

"I said, I waited for it to wear off."

Stephanie propped herself up a bit and glanced at the clock. "You could have called. I don't have your new number and couldn't call you."

"There was a lot going on." Robin chafed at the cross-examination.

"I was dozing, longing for you. And remembering our first kiss. You remember it?"

"Of course I do." Robin felt her irritation softening.

Robin had become involved with Stephanie, who'd been her teacher in a class on feminism, in the fall of her sophomore year at Wellesley. Robin had been drawn to her without realizing it at first; she simply accepted the open invitation to come to office hours as often as she wanted. The two women were opposite in a way that created attraction. Robin: young, a little lost, and more than a little wild. Stephanie: mature, in control, and seemingly wise.

"Tell me what you remember."

Robin laughed. "I said to myself, 'What am I doing getting into my teacher's car, going to her apartment?'" One evening, after a meeting of the feminist circle on campus, Stephanie had invited her back to her apartment for dinner.

"That whole drive into Boston, all I could think about was how I wanted to kiss you."

It had been a little expedition for Robin as Stephanie lived in Boston, almost an hour from the suburban Wellesley campus.

The drive had given them the time and privacy they needed to shift from their teacher-student relationship to a more intimate rapport.

"I was so nervous," Robin admitted.

"But as soon as we got here . . ."

"Our clothes came off." Robin shifted uncomfortably on the couch. She had to decide whether to tell Stephanie about the hetero adventures she'd had that wild summer in San Francisco. When they'd parted lovingly in June, Steph had given her permission to step out.

"Be free, don't let me tie you down," Steph had said. But who knew what her reaction would be when faced with the facts of Robin's recent escapades.

"You want something to drink?" Robin asked. "I'm parched."

"Water."

Robin went into the kitchen and flipped on the light. She saw clean dishes in the dish rack and on the windowsill, the plants she'd given Stephanie over the years: a little African violet, a spider plant, and an ivy. Robin liked taking care of people, animals, and plants, and she liked giving gifts. But the plants looked dry and neglected. The African violet was burned by the sun; Stephanie hadn't kept it in indirect light as instructed. Filling a couple of glasses with water, Robin stared out at the low buildings on the other side of the avenue. They were partly blocked by the dense foliage of trees growing in the wide median, but lights shone through, and a piece of the triangular, neon Citgo sign floated above in Kenmore Square. Sounds from stereos and TVs came in through the open windows from neighboring apartments, and voices rose from the sidewalks.

Back in the living room, she saw Steph was gone. Robin found her lying naked in the bedroom, the sheet kicked down. The streetlight filtering in through the flimsy curtains illuminated her skin. Steph's blonde hair, long and wavy with reddish tints and a bit of frizz, made her think of Botticelli's Venus. Robin was ashamed that she had a thing for blonde women because she thought it made her sexist. But blondes were the light to her dark. They ignited her passion for the female body—made her want to bury her face in the nook of a woman's head and shoulder or in the crevice between her thighs. Some of Steph's hair was braided; the rest lay loose on the pillow. Robin put the water down on the night table and lay down next to her. There was a soft eroticism in lying fully dressed next to her naked lover. She caressed her breasts, leaned over, and sucked on a nipple.

"I missed you," Steph murmured. "Take your clothes off."

"You're not too sleepy?"

"Not for something simple." They had code words for their different routines. "Simple" meant stopping after a single climax—just a bedtime release to wind down.

Robin was soon naked. They intertwined, moving together like waves. Steph's skin felt silky, both cool and warm against hers. She felt Steph's hands stroking her face, then moving down between her thighs. There were kisses, caresses, exploring fingers. There were words of love.

Afterward, Stephanie quickly dozed off, but Robin felt restless in her arms and bothered by the light coming in through the curtains and the music in the street. Her eyes open, she measured how her summer adventures had breached her emotional attachment to her partner. Yes, Stephanie had given her permission to have other lovers, but there were consequences to infidelity: Robin had diluted her feelings for Stephanie, thinning the broth as it were, and the intensity of her early passion was gone. She'd made love to her partner fueled by ritual horniness, not the joy of reunion.

Disconnection came over Robin as she wondered how much her infatuation with Stephanie had been fed by a need to escape the fishbowl life of Cazenove, or "Caz," the dorm that lesbian students favored. Certainly, it had been a relief to commute to Steph's Boston apartment, where she did homework while her lover prepared classes. On campus, the two women had to be discreet. At the time, there were no official rules against a professor getting involved with a student; nonetheless, either because theirs was a same-sex relationship or because of their age difference, they had the sense of doing something risqué. Boston, however, gave them the anonymity they needed to function as a couple. They could go out together, even hold hands in the street. On Saturday nights, they went to the movies or to a gay bar to dance. They especially loved the 1270 with its blaring music, flashing lights, and people of all genders and preferences, dancing and mating. They could let loose there, and flirt and dance with others, but they always arrived and left together.

After graduating from Wellesley, Robin had returned to her parents' home in San Francisco for the waitressing job she'd had every summer since high school. She and Stephanie promised to write and call as they had the two previous summers, and they planned to commute between Boston and New Haven when Robin began graduate school. Steph had told her more than once that she didn't believe in monogamy because no one could own anyone else; jealousy was an invention of the patriarchy, which saw women as property and baby makers. The philosophy of the day left Robin both committed and free to do anything she wanted, so once back in California, she went to straight bars, where she picked up guys and had casual adventures. She was a little out of control, but out of control didn't seem like a bad thing under the circumstances. Sleeping around enabled her to release the tension she experienced back home, and it also distracted her from memories of her uncle Gabe, who had molested her repeatedly when he visited. She'd been twelve and thirteen at the time, and her parents had been oblivious. These days, they were similarly unaware of when she was gone overnight because they constantly fought about money and property.

When her summer job ended, Robin returned to the East Coast via New Mexico, where she picked up Gloria to share the driving. Robin liked driving back and forth between the coasts. Her car was her power and freedom, and she wasn't about to leave it in San Francisco when she went east for school. She had time on the road to wonder whether Steph was sincere in allowing her to play around, but the wondering didn't lead anywhere, maybe because she and Gloria made a detour up to Boulder to visit friends and get stoned in the mountains, then stopped in Nashville to listen to music and do some serious drinking, and finally treated themselves to a poolside cabin and champagne at a Catskills resort. Gloria, like Robin, worked hard and played hard. She was good company, and the spaces in between being stoned and drunk were spent driving, yakking, and singing along to the radio. Gloria was a free spirit but also someone you could count on.

The summer had been one long stretch of fun. The best part had been her fling with a twenty-five-year-old rock musician, Theo. It had lasted two months and felt special, though they hadn't spoken about continuing long-distance. Robin had thought of herself as gay and monogamous, but maybe she was bi, or even hetero, or just needed multiple partners. The only way to find out was to have more experiences, and Stephanie was likely to stand in the way of that.

Around two or three in the morning, Robin put her anxiety and her conscience to rest with the comforting thought that if the week ended in a bust-up with Stephanie, her cousins and her best friend, Gloria, would be there to catch her when she got back to New Haven. She'd have plenty of shoulders to cry on.

When she woke up six hours later, the pillow next to hers was empty. She found Stephanie on the couch, drinking coffee and marking up a manuscript. Steph was in her fifth year of teaching women's studies at Wellesley. With two years left until her tenure review, she was prone to worry and overwork. If her book about women's poetry and her teaching evaluations weren't noteworthy, she'd be out of a job when her seventh-year evaluation came up.

Robin sat down next to her on the worn couch and kissed her lightly on the lips.

Steph stroked Robin's hair. "I'm so glad you're back. You're staying until school starts, right?" She gave her an odd look.

"I am," Robin said.

"Looking forward to it?"

"Yeah." Reflecting on their plan to commute between Boston and New Haven, Robin wondered how she could have agreed to such an arrangement. It had felt right then, given their intense involvement. But her summer had been eventful, and the future now seemed unclear.

"Thank you for the sweet reunion last night," Steph said. Her eyes shimmered.

"It's good to be home," Robin said, although she didn't know whether Steph's place still was home. "You revising your own work?"

"Yes." Steph gestured toward a Xerox copy of a manuscript on the coffee table. "I'm writing an article about Adrienne Rich."

"We read her poetry in your class," Robin said, nodding. She glanced at the title page bearing the words *Of Woman Born*.

"This book isn't poetry. It's about the social construction of motherhood. It's coming out in October."

"How did you get the manuscript?"

"I got a copy to get ahead of the game. She's a friend of mine. She's the voice of our generation of feminists, but what she writes is crucially important for everyone. *Everyone.* You need to read it when it comes out."

"Okay, I will." Robin was willing to receive enlightenment from her former teacher. "And what are you writing?"

"A talk for the winter conference," Steph said, making a face. It would be another paper to build up her already impressive CV.

"Why the frown? You're brilliant." Robin was being sincere: Steph's intellect had been part of the attraction.

"You know that sometimes brilliant isn't enough."

There had been a case the previous spring of an accomplished assistant professor and friend of Steph's who hadn't gotten tenure for reasons not explained by the institution. Wellesley was elitist, choosy, and harsh, and Steph's anxiety about her job and future had been high for over a year.

"All you can do is your best. And obviously you're on the cutting edge of things."

"I have to retype this goddamn thing," Steph complained.

"How about I start typing the pages you've already edited?"

"Would you really? I'd appreciate it so much. Can you make a carbon copy? Here, take her manuscript and check the passages I've quoted, will you? The last thing I want to do is misquote her."

"Sure, whatever you need." Given this was her first day back, Robin had hoped her girlfriend might have been willing to take some time off to have fun together. But she smiled, gave Stephanie a stroke on the knee, and gathered up the corrected pages. After pouring herself some coffee, she sat down at the typewriter and began to work.

She was glad to help Stephanie, and the hum of the electric Smith Corona had a soothing effect until a tension started inside her. Robin could hear Steph's teaching voice in her head as she typed her prose. Having a professor as a lover could be as oppressive as it was inspiring, and sometimes Robin didn't feel grown-up around her. But Rich's discussion of motherhood intrigued her. Robin had always thought of her own mother's parenting style as a product of her particular neuroses, frustrations, and disappointments; she'd never wondered how it had been conditioned by the patriarchy or previous generations of women. Her mind slipped sideways to her grandmother Iris, who'd been nine when her impoverished parents had fled the pogroms of Russia and come to New York in steerage. Iris had grown up in poverty, but her daughter, Sarah, had given her a step up by marrying a wealthy entrepreneur. By the time Iris followed that daughter to California, she had reinvented herself as a lady of aristocratic taste and nonconformist lifestyle. If Robin's mother was a snob, her grandmother was a genius at social climbing.

The thoughts about family broke Robin's concentration and took her back to her summer in California. Staring out the window, she thought about Theo and their two months together in San Francisco. He had a mass of pale curls, a charismatic smile, and a gift for songwriting. A tune he'd been working on that summer went through her head. He'd said she was its inspiration.

Why should I care what other people say
It's none of my business what they think of me
I have a lock on crazy, that comes easily
What I want above all else to be
Crazy free
Crazy free crazy
Like a dog on a beach
Crazy free

She'd loved listening to him sing and play and how he dressed in pink and purple and garish orange and took her to restaurants in neighborhoods she'd never have thought of exploring. And she'd loved the way he took instruction when he went down on her. She'd initiated him into the finer points of the oral arts so that by the end of the summer, if there had been an Olympic competition for male performers of cunnilingus, he would have been a gold medalist.

"You learn so quickly. Between your oral skills and your crazy shirts, you must have been a lesbian in a former lifetime," Robin had once joked during a postcoital cuddle.

"I'd be okay with that," he'd said with an impish smile.

Although their relationship had been casual, she missed him. Robin sighed.

Stephanie got up from the couch and came to stand next to her, putting an end to Robin's erotic memories. "You stuck on something? I know my handwriting can be illegible."

"No," Robin said. "Just needing a break." She gave in to her restlessness and stood up. "Or maybe another cup of coffee."

Stephanie followed her into the kitchen.

"You don't have to do the typing for me if you don't want to."

"I do want to. Because then maybe we can spend some time together and do something fun."

"Of course," Stephanie said. "I'm sorry. I should have offered to take the morning off. We haven't had a chance to catch up."

"It's all right."

"I'm so self-involved sometimes."

Robin said nothing.

"And we need to catch up," Stephanie continued, "because your letters were kind of brief." Placing her hands on the younger woman's waist, she gave her a reproachful look.

Robin hesitated, wondering whether Steph had read between the lines of those letters. "You know, between waitressing and dealing with my mother and . . . everything else . . . I was really busy."

"I gather you have things to tell me. About 'everything else.'"

Robin was startled. "You want me to tell you things?"

"We've always been open with each other."

"It's easy to be open when there's nothing to hide," Robin said.

"But now you have something to hide?"

Robin faced her. "No, not if you don't want me to." Her heart pounded and her mouth was dry.

"I don't want you hiding anything," Steph said.

Robin saw the beads of perspiration on Steph's forehead and knew the game was up. Might as well spit it out.

"I had . . . a few flings. There it is. Now you know."

"I'm not surprised." Steph stiffened a bit. "With guys?"

"How do you know?"

"Talk about being open, when I touched you last night, you were definitely more open."

Betrayed by her vagina, Robin blushed, then was vexed with herself for blushing. Why should she be ashamed? "You told me to be free," she said.

Steph didn't respond, just looked at the floor.

"You said you thought monogamy was ridiculous, an invention of the patriarchy," Robin continued, "and that you wanted for both of us not to be trapped by rules."

Steph's jaw hardened; a tear welled up in the corner of each eye. "Yes, I wanted us both to be free, but I also thought that your love for me was special, like mine is for you. Special enough that I'd be enough." She shook her head angrily, tossing her reddish-blonde hair. "But I'm not enough for you, clearly. I'm going out for a walk."

"Steph, listen—" Robin reached for her arm, but Steph yanked it away.

"You're young, you should fuck around! But now it's my turn to be honest, and I'm not going to pretend I'm happy about it." She grabbed her keys and ran out, slamming the door behind her.

Lightheaded, Robin sat down. It was a big life lesson: people can say and believe one thing but feel and do another. She wasn't about to label her lover a hypocrite for preaching non-possessiveness, then being jealous. It seemed normal, and the truth was that they'd talked a lot about relationships in general, yet had never spelled out the exact terms of theirs. How many people had the courage to do that, anyway? She poured herself a glass of water and dialed Gloria in New Haven. *Please be there, Gloria*, she repeated to herself as the phone rang and rang. And rang again.

"Hello," Gloria said.

"Thank God you're there."

"You sound terrible! Things okay with Mrs. Robinson?" Gloria saw Steph as an older, manipulative seductress.

"No, they're not. I told her about Theo, and she didn't take it well." Theo was the only fling Robin had mentioned to Gloria, who might have been shocked by the number of partners she'd had that summer.

"Hmm. So much for rebelling against the patriarchy."

"We had a fight and she walked out."

"She'll come round. She has to, after all the bull she spilled in class—"

"I didn't think it was bull," Robin said. "Steph meant it when she said jealousy is used by men to control women, and I agreed with her. I still do."

There was silence on the other end of the line.

"Maybe you need the freedom you'll get if she breaks up with you."

"That's not particularly comforting."

"I don't know what to say. Sorry."

"It's okay," Robin said.

"Okay, how about this? She believes her own ideology and she wants to promote it, so she'll have to calm down and take you on whatever terms you offer."

"You think so?"

"I'll bet you a round of drinks at the Duchess," Gloria said, referring to a lesbian club in New York they'd talked about visiting.

"Oh God, Gloria."

"What?"

"I got myself into a mess."

"It'll be okay."

Robin sighed. "I was happy driving back. We sure had a good time."

"Nashville especially! Jesus, we got wasted."

They laughed, then Robin turned serious again. "You know what I'm realizing? I want to always be that free. Free the way I felt on the road with you. Crazy free."

"Supposedly if you're really in love, you no longer want to be free. That must be what Steph is feeling."

"Maybe. But I don't get it. Why shouldn't I love more than one person at a time?"

"A lot of people don't want complication. And life is long. People change," Gloria said. "Maybe you'll want to be monogamous one day too."

"Anything is possible, I suppose."

They hung up, and Robin opened her diary. After recording what happened, she concluded with, *I honestly don't know who I am or what I want.* Then she hid the notebook in her bag. The heat was oppressive. Thinking it would be cooler by the water, she headed toward the Charles, stopping at Baskin-Robbins for a double-scoop cone. She chose banana and strawberry, the comforting flavors of childhood; the cold of the ice cream was refreshing in the August heat. The river came into sight, and a slight breeze riffled the water. As Robin walked west on the Esplanade, she crossed walkers, joggers, and a few bicycles; on the river were sailboats, a few canoes, and crew teams. Her eyes darted around looking for Stephanie; they both enjoyed walking here, and it was a natural place to come on a hot day.

And there she was, gazing at the river and braiding her reddish-blonde hair.

Robin walked over and sat down next to her.

Steph glanced sideways at her, then looked back out at the water as she continued braiding.

"Want a bite?" Robin extended the cone.

"Sure." Steph leaned over and took a lick of strawberry. "Hey, why don't you just hand it over for a sec?"

Steph reached for the cone, took a few more licks, and handed it back. There was a long silence.

"Are we going to talk?" Robin said.

"Sure." Stephanie paused. "I feel embarrassed. Like . . . caught not practicing what I preach."

"Your reaction was normal."

"But I want to change what's normal. That's why I teach women's studies." Steph stroked Robin's knee. "And I'm aware of the age difference between us. I'm thirty-two, I've had a bunch of relationships, so I'm ready to make a choice. But you're twenty-two. You gotta do what you gotta do."

"Meaning?" Robin looked out at the river. The movement of the sailboats, so graceful and unbound as they bent with the wind, reminded her of what freedom tasted like—cool water, fresh air . . . a dance of speed and light.

"Go ahead and have your adventures. Time will tell whether I can handle it."

"Wow. Thank you."

"Let's go to the 1270 tonight," Steph suggested. "That'll get us back to normal."

"Sure," Robin said.

As Robin took the hand Steph offered, relief mingled with a sense of disaster deferred. For she both loved Stephanie and wanted out.

The 1270 was as it always was, quiet at the bar by the entrance, loud at the disco upstairs. Robin loved to dance almost as much as she loved having sex. Sometimes she even loved it more because it put her back in her body in a way that felt pure, with a blank mind. She danced with Steph, then with a voluptuous redhead, then a tall, scrawny guy with a goatee. Steph danced with other partners too; they kept separating, then coming back together. It was the way they operated at the club, except that tonight Robin sensed her girlfriend's eyes on her when she danced with others.

Robin was gyrating to "You Should Be Dancing" when Steph disappeared from the dance floor. Robin found her downstairs drinking a Rum Collins at the bar and chatting with the gay Black bartender, their favorite because he poured generously, his extravagant pours being an act of general defiance. No one reproached him for his excesses, not even the bar owner, because revolution was in the air, although not seriously the way it had been in the 1960s. Ten years later, revolution was more of an ironic gesture, a jaded pose.

"Hey," the bartender said to Robin, "you'd better take care of your lady. She's killing me with that face."

Steph looked glum indeed.

"I'll take care of her." Robin took the barstool next to Steph. "You getting tired?" she asked.

"Yeah," Steph said. "I hate the Bee Gees. And an old gal like me—what am I doing at thirty-two going to discos? It's ridiculous."

"What's ridiculous about liking to dance?" Robin said, though the ten-year gap between them suddenly felt like twenty.

Steph shrugged. "Let's go home."

It was a beautiful summer night, and they walked down Boylston, holding hands until Steph let go to blow her nose. Then she put her hands in her pockets, and Robin waited for what was coming.

"You seemed pretty into that redhead," Steph said.

"Oh, fuck."

"Yeah, sorry. You're right! I shouldn't have said anything. God, I'm an idiot."

"If you're going to be jealous every time I look at someone else—" Robin started.

"No, I won't be. I'll adjust. Trust me."

Robin was skeptical but didn't have the energy to pursue it, and they continued walking in silence.

Later, they fell asleep lying back-to-back instead of spooning the way they usually did.

During the night Robin heard Steph get up and go to the bathroom. A door slammed. Maybe Steph had drunk too much and was throwing up. No, Steph was a grown-up who knew her limits. Too tired to investigate, Robin fell back asleep. Waking at dawn after only four hours' rest, she glanced sideways at her lover, who looked like she might sleep till noon. Robin was hungover and exhausted. Her night had been interrupted not only by Steph's getting up but also by ceaseless thought-dreams: imaginary conversations, analyses, and gut feelings, all leading to one conclusion—that from now on, she would feel oppressed in their relationship. If it was true, as the feminists said, that the male-female power imbalance permeated culture and society, it was also true that in a relationship, one partner could dominate without one being male and the other female. In this case, by virtue of her greater age and experience, Steph would always call the shots with her reactions, negotiations, and philosophies. And Robin, being rebellious, would fight back and cause her pain. Besides, she didn't want to be the guinea pig in Steph's experiment in non-possessive relationship. It would mean worrying about Steph's worrying about every new friend she made. What would be destroyed, in the end, was something precious to Robin—her sense of internal freedom. Emotional liberty—why hadn't that ever been written into the Constitution?

Robin made herself some strong coffee, then casually, as though just tidying up, started to pack while Steph slept. She didn't want to think or feel, for the idea of breaking up with Steph filled her with the same desolation she herself would have felt if Steph were the one leaving. She cringed before the cruelty of her own actions. Only when she snapped her luggage shut did she become fully conscious of what she was doing.

On her way out, she stopped in the living room, grabbed a pen and paper, and scrawled a note. *I'm sorry. I just can't continue this. If I do, I'll keep hurting you. Love, Robin*

She placed the note on the kitchen table, took the key off her key ring, and placed it on top. In saying goodbye to Stephanie, Robin was giving up her most important tie. Breakups were a miserable business, but she would find comfort and security in the reunion with her cousins.

Robin glanced at the windowsill. It upset her that Steph hadn't taken care of the plants she'd gifted her. She found a paper shopping bag and put them in it. Then, plants in one hand and suitcase in the other, she went down to her car. A brilliant patch of morning light bouncing off the windshield slapped her eyes. A piece of paper folded in four was stuck under one of the wipers. Robin unfolded it and read:

Please don't go. I love you. —S

Damn, they knew each other too well. It really was time to leave Boston. And Robin realized, as she threw her belongings in the trunk and slammed it shut, that she herself was the cataclysm she'd been waiting for. She was the only one who could set herself free . . . crazy free.

3

THE NIGHT
THEY MET

(Julia)

J ulia was the last to arrive in New Haven. Living in Manhattan, her father didn't own a car, so he rented a station wagon to drive her up there. They strapped the narrow mattress from the trundle bed to the roof—a twin would do for her—and set out without her mother, an actress who was preparing for a theatrical audition and couldn't join them. As they took the rapid curves on the Merritt Parkway, they heard the mattress shifting above them, and Sam would say, "Uh-oh." Then he'd go back to telling her stories about his youth at Yale, how he and her uncle Carl had been among the first Jews admitted, and how he'd supported himself in college as a jazz musician.

"I tried marijuana," he said, "but I didn't like the way it distorted sounds. I didn't know if what I was hearing was what I was playing."

Julia nodded and didn't say much. It was hard to imagine her father smoking pot in his youth. She herself had never enjoyed it. She enjoyed his stories and conversation and liked being alone with him, the way young women with supportive dads enjoy their special father-daughter times.

Robin and Anna were there when they arrived and helped them unload the car.

"We reserved the most private room for you," Robin said, leading Julia to the one in the back and to the right. "You're across the hall from me."

The room was bright and quiet. *Good for reading and writing poetry*, Julia thought. Robin went out, then came back with a couple of plants she set on her windowsill.

"You should have these since you face north," she said, stroking the fuzzy leaves of the African violet. "This one especially could be your friend. I've already got too many plants." Robin stepped closer. "I like your hair." She touched Julia's straight brown hair, cut shoulder-length.

"You think this length is good?"

"Yeah, the way it touches your collarbone—cute."

After they unloaded the car, Sam stayed just long enough to help her get the mattress and boxes up the stairs.

"Have a brilliant year," he said. "Get that A plus-plus."

"I don't know, Dad. I have a heavy schedule this semester. A's might be as far as I go."

"You're a senior. Time to give it your all."

"I'll try."

She accompanied him back down to the car.

"I hope you get along with those cousins of yours," he said. "Robin has always struck me as a bit crazy in a California kind of way."

"I don't think she's particularly crazy."

Sam looked back up toward the apartment anxiously. "Don't let her lure you into anything stupid."

"Dad! She's a graduate student."

"In psychology. Aren't they all doing psychedelics these days?"

"I don't think so," Julia said. "Not on a regular basis, anyway."

"You're still my little girl, and I worry about you."

"I love you, Daddy."

She watched him pull away from the curb. Although it was her fourth year in college, she still experienced separation pangs.

The three of them had their first dinner together that night. Robin made a tofu stir-fry, saying, "You guys do what you want, but when I cook, it'll be vegetarian." They opened a bottle of cheap wine, talked about the division of chores, and decided to post a rotating cleaning schedule on the fridge.

Julia asked Robin whether Stephanie would be coming to visit soon.

"We broke up," Robin said.

"Oh, I'm sorry."

Julia and Anna listened as Robin's story came out. It was a long one, starting with Robin's crazy summer in San Francisco, the bar pickups, the affair with Theo, then more about Theo. "I liked him so much, it was confusing." Then there was the return to Boston, the indecision about whether to tell Stephanie, the decision to tell, the conflict, and the explosions. It was a lot to absorb.

"So, if I understand correctly, she gave you permission to step out," Anna said, "but she wasn't happy when you actually did."

"That about sums it up, yeah," Robin said. "I can't blame her. And now I feel awful. Like screaming or crying, not sure which. Irritated and guilty. I want to sort it out, but I can't." A student in psychology, she used herself as her own laboratory, and the inner test tubes were boiling over. "I'm such a restless mix." She got up and moved around, came back, and poured herself another glass of wine. "What I feel is disappointed. In her and in myself." She sat down.

"You were brave," Anna insisted. "Breaking up is hard to do. But if you did it, you did it for a reason."

"I'm glad you can see it that way," Robin said.

Julia listened to the two of them. She'd been infatuated with a junior named Brian the previous year and almost had sex with him, but the night had turned into a fiasco when his drunken roommate came in and started throwing up. Brian had dropped her after that; she'd never understood why. In spite of feeling rejected and hurt, she'd been able to channel the first moments into an erotic sonnet, then had mentally disposed of the episode. She'd never been in a relationship, and horror came over her as she imagined Stephanie's suffering. In her years of dormitory life, she had often been shaken by the spectacle of women—strong, smart women—reduced to tears and incapacitated for days when men dumped them, betrayed them, or simply "forgot" to write, call, or show up for a date. How could you be in love with someone, whisper endearments, exchange kisses and bodily fluids, then turn around and stab her in the heart? She'd read a lot of novels but didn't have the experience to understand. The drama involved in love affairs terrified her, though she recognized it provided material for poetry.

When the cruelty of love appalled her, she thought back on the ending of *Nineteen Eighty-Four*, in which Winston betrays his lover to the totalitarian government by revealing her phobia of rodents. The authorities arrest her and set her face before an open cage of rats who attack and disfigure her. Maybe Julia had been traumatized by the scene because the lover's name was also Julia. What was disconcerting in Robin's story was that a woman had done the betraying. Robin had been as cruel as a man and cruel to another woman. There was no escape from the risks inherent in relationship.

Julia longed for a boyfriend. And for a suit of armor.

Julia might have been interested in protecting her heart, but when classes started, she fell in love with Ben, the graduate student instructor of her modern poetry class.

The moment he walked into the classroom, she was struck by his green eyes and Greek nose. His wiry upper body suggested the strength and agility of a fencer. When he spoke, she was transported by his perfectly balanced male voice, neither too deep nor too high, and the musical cadences of his British accent. Julia loved English spoken with any accent not American. She had a flash of the two of them visiting his parents in London—he had to be from London—then ferrying across the Channel for a romantic holiday in Paris. Her fantasy was interrupted by the sound of laughter. Ben must have said something funny because all the students were amused. His eyes landed on her, and she experienced a coup de foudre.

Julia wanted to draw his attention again after that but couldn't. She hated her own shyness, which she'd developed in reaction to her actress mother's narcissistic social style. Anna was taking the class with her, and Julia envied her ability to participate in group discussion.

"You always seem to have something to say," she said to Anna one time, as they left the classroom. "And I feel paralyzed."

"I don't know," Anna said. "I just say whatever pops into my head. Maybe you want too much to sound smart."

"No, it's not that. It's just that nothing 'pops into my head' when we're in class."

"Because you're infatuated with him."

"What makes you think I'm infatuated?"

"Come on, it's obvious."

"Now I feel ridiculous. Supposing he's noticed!"

"That might be a good thing, don't you think? It's called attraction and flirtation."

"I'm not good at that stuff," Julia said. "Besides, he's my teacher. It seems improper."

"Why don't you ask Robin what she thinks about it? Her relationship with Stephanie makes her an expert in these matters."

"I don't know. She can be pushy. I have to think about it."

At the end of the next class, Ben returned the first batch of essays by spreading them out on his desk. Julia held back in order to be the last one to step up and get hers. She turned to the last page and saw an A+ and the comment "Great job."

"That was a bloody good paper you wrote," he said.

She met his gaze. "Well, I'm bloody glad you liked it." Damn, she'd just made fun of her instructor!

He laughed. "I'm wondering why, when you've got so much to say on paper, you say so little in class."

Julia flushed. "My mind goes blank in class."

"Do you take notes when you do the reading assignment?"

"In the margins, sometimes."

"I'd like to hear your ideas, and you're on my radar now," Ben continued. "I'll find the right moment for you."

"I'm really more of a writer of poetry than a critic of it," she ventured.

"Are you sure that's true? One can write poetry and talk about it at the same time. The two activities aren't mutually exclusive. Think of W. H. Auden."

"I wonder . . . if you might be willing to read some of my poems."

"I'd love to. Feel free to bring some to class."

Julia walked home in a daze. How could she have asked him to read her poetry when, recently, all her poems had been about *him*? And if he ever found out what a lousy poet she was, he wouldn't give her the time of day. Of course, she could revise some older, not-about-Ben poems to give him. Kicking through the autumn leaves, she mentally sorted through ones she might share.

Back at the apartment, she went to the file folder with her creations in it. She had some interesting poems in a metaphysical vein, a couple based on dreams, and the one she'd written about her sexual tryst with Brian. She hesitated about that one. She preferred writing free verse and had written the sonnet as part of an assignment for a poetry class. Julia was proud of it, however, and including it might send a signal. She would copy the bunch. Feeling shy about handing them to him directly, she dropped them off in Ben's mailbox in the English department.

A few nights later, over more stir-fried tofu and vegetables at the round kitchen table, Julia told her cousins everything.

"I should have given them to him in class because he might have told me when he'd get around to reading them."

"I'm sure he'll read them straightaway," Anna said.

"Now is this an infatuation or an attraction?" Robin asked.

"I can't stop thinking about him. I think it's an obsession." Julia braced herself, expecting Robin to tease her.

But Robin didn't. "You could invite him to dinner," she said. "Or I could. I met him at the grad student welcome party."

"That's a crazy idea," Julia said.

"Why? Or do you enjoy moping about? You're so passive."

"He's my teacher! I mean, I know it worked with you and Steph, for a while anyway—"

"He's a grad student like me, not a professor," Robin interrupted. "Neither of you has restrictions. The only potential problem is a worse version of the one I had with Steph. When you get involved with someone older, they have more power. And if it's a man who's older—that could be double trouble."

"Thanks for the feminist perspective, pal."

"You're welcome."

"Anyway, I don't think I'm his type."

"How can you know what his type is?" Anna asked.

"He's European," Julia said. "He probably likes women with a lot of mascara." She wore no makeup.

"Oh, fuck that. I say you invite him to dinner on Saturday," Robin said. "If only to get him out of your system." She had developed a habit of giving direction in their household.

"It's a terrible idea. It'll be horribly awkward."

"I don't get you. Do you really like being a virgin? It's like you keep on putting off doing the deed."

Julia reflected that sex was a biological necessity for Robin, like food or water.

"It's not a question of liking or not liking it. I want to be with someone I feel comfortable with. And if I've put it off, it's because, believe it or not, I'd like to lose my virginity to a guy I'm in love with." Julia had reached that decision after the fiasco with Brian, which she'd never shared with them.

"How charmingly old-fashioned," Robin said dryly.

"Maybe it wouldn't be the best setup for a dinner party. One guy, three gals—that's not symmetrical," Anna pointed out.

"He can bring his roommate," Robin said. "He's a grad student in music, I think. That would bring us up to two guys and three gals. Which is perfect, Anna, since you've got Doug."

"It's not like I'm married to him," Anna said defiantly.

"As good as." Robin snorted.

"Fuck you."

"Stop it, you two. I thought this was supposed to be fun," Julia said.

"It will be. And I'll call him to make it easy for you," Robin said. "Like it's a graduate student thing."

That Saturday, while Robin and Anna shopped and cooked, Julia cleaned the house. Then she went to the gym to swim laps. Climbing the stairs back to their apartment, she smelled lasagna baking. But when she opened the door, there was a stench in the air. Robin and Anna were in a panic: the toilet was blocked, and sewage had backed up into the tub. Robin was working away with a plunger while Anna was on the phone, trying to find a plumber who could come out on a Saturday.

"I got someone to come Monday morning," Anna said. "In

the meantime, we can go downstairs." There was a toilet in the laundry area in the basement.

"What about Roto-Rooter?" Julia asked.

"They're expensive. He'd never reimburse us," Robin said, referring to their detestable landlord.

Julia fretted in the hallway outside the bathroom. In spite of her misgivings, she'd gotten her hopes up about the dinner.

"We're going to have to cancel," Robin said. "Julia, call him and move it to next weekend."

Julia dialed Ben's number. When he answered, she told him about their plumbing catastrophe and suggested they do the dinner the following Saturday.

"I was looking forward to tonight." Ben sounded disappointed.

"So was I. And Robin made this lasagna. It smells so good."

There was a pause. "Why don't you bring it over here?" he said.

"I don't want to put you to any trouble—"

"No trouble at all. Really." Ben insisted until she agreed.

A few hours later, Robin, then Anna, filed into Ben's apartment. When Julia's turn came, she met Ben's gaze and was struck by the kindness in his eyes. She glanced around the living room. The quantity of books and music suggested graduate, not undergraduate, work. She'd never visited a teacher's home before, and it felt both transgressive and pleasantly titillating. She embraced the novelty of the adventure.

"Michael will be out in a minute. He's busy not shaving," Ben said. The three women sat down on the living room couch, and Ben handed each of them a glass of Asti Spumante. He was freshly shaven and smelled pleasantly of aftershave. His crisp white shirt was tucked into a pair of ironed blue jeans. The overall look was European—slightly formal but relaxed.

Books and LPs filled bookcases, covered the coffee table, and crowded the space under the chairs and couch. Sheet music and notebooks lay on top of an old upright piano.

Ben saw Julia looking at it.

"The piano is Michael's," he said. "Now, don't be frightened. I took the liberty of preparing an antipasto." He went into the kitchen and returned with a tray of hors d'oeuvres: prosciutto-and-cheese rolls with toothpicks, olives, and marinated mushrooms. He presented it to Anna first. "*Signorina, prego,*" he said.

A tall man with large black eyeglasses emerged from the hallway. Michael.

He was a bit stooped and underweight—just what you'd expect of a pianist who spent long hours at the keyboard. He hadn't shaved, and a cigarette dangled out of his mouth like a bulb hanging out of a light socket in a cheap hotel. That aside, he was drop-dead handsome: his mouth had a promising sensuality, his nose was strong, and his expressive face conveyed a riot of need and desire.

Michael took the armchair next to Robin.

"So, these are the three Muses," Michael said. "Poetry,"—he gestured to Julia—"art,"—he gestured to Anna—"and . . . ?" He turned toward Robin.

"Not an artist," she said.

"That's right," Michael said. "You're the psychologist."

"That would make her Psyche, goddess of the soul," Ben said. Robin laughed. "As you like."

"And all you celestial beings are eligible, right?" asked Ben, who'd clearly started drinking before their arrival. "Or am I being crude? Rude? Maybe even lewd?"

"You're saying it like it is," Robin said. "Except Anna isn't."

"Oh?" He gave Anna an inquiring look as he added a drop of Spumante to her glass.

"Well, no, I'm not," Anna said.

"You've got somebody somewhere?" Michael asked.

"Yes, at Columbia. We met in high school."

"Someone from back home, then! How wonderful."

"You're making fun of me," Anna said. "You're a tease."

"Not in the least," Michael replied. "I'm curious about you guys, that's all."

"Oh, you're in for a treat then, because we're a fascinating bunch," Anna said.

Julia studied Anna's ease. Anna's childhood had been painful, but still, with her auburn hair in a loose bun at the nape of her neck and her artistic persona, her boyfriend and her dreams of adventure, she was like a large rosebud ready to burst open, and it was hard not to envy her.

"I'm curious," Michael went on, "about how three cousins ended up at Yale. And living together."

"Our dads—" Julia and Anna began, then stopped and laughed. Julia nodded toward Anna.

"Our dads went here," Anna said. "My dad was a student in biology, Julia's in English and music. They were friends from the same Brooklyn high school."

"They wanted us to come here," Julia said. "And we got in."

"What about you?" Michael asked, turning to Robin.

"My dad was at CUNY. I went to Wellesley, then decided to apply here for grad school."

"And the three of you are living together?" Michael asked.

"I persuaded them to live with me because I couldn't stand living in student housing at Wellesley," Robin said. "The lack of privacy and gossiping drove me nuts."

"How spectacular that you get along," Ben remarked.

"Robin bosses us around a bit," Anna said. "But we tolerate it."

"I can't help it," Robin said. "I always think I'm right."

"Basically, we're a mini-clan replicating our mothers," Julia explained. "They grew up together in Flatbush. My mom was an only child, but she had three female first cousins living next door, including Robin and Anna's moms."

"And your third aunt?"

"Doris. She exiled herself to Italy in the 1950s. Never married or had children, just dogs and the occasional stray cat. She was the black sheep of the family, a little crazy."

The three cousins laughed again. There were many humorous stories about their mothers and their mothers' mothers; the two families had lived in adjoining brownstones. Suddenly restless, Julia stood up and went to check out the music on the top of the upright. There were Bach partitas, Chopin preludes, a Gershwin songbook, and sheets of composition paper with scrawled musical notation.

Michael approached her. "You play?" he asked.

"On and off," she said.

"You look familiar. Have I seen you around the practice rooms?"

"I go there sometimes. Less and less now, actually."

"You should keep it up," he said. "People always regret it when they stop."

"I've had a lot of bad teachers," she said.

"You could try me. I give lessons."

"That's good to know," she replied politely, wondering whether he was coming on to her or trying to drum up new business.

Ben, who had stepped into the kitchen, was reheating the lasagna and tossing a salad.

"Dinner!" he shouted.

Ben took his place at the head of the table as the others gathered round. As Michael engaged with Robin and Anna, Ben focused on Julia. They talked about students in the poetry class; then the conversation turned more intimate.

"We have to talk about those poems you dropped off," Ben said, lowering his voice conspiratorially. "I read them, and they're good!"

Julia flushed. "Thank you."

"That sonnet you wrote—you should enter it in the campus sonnet contest."

"I didn't know there was a sonnet contest."

"There is, and yours would win it, I'm sure. 'It's dusk now, climb ahead, race the last stair,'" Ben said, quoting the first line. "I'd race into that contest if I were you."

No one except for Julia's parents and a poet friend of theirs had ever taken her poetry seriously. "You think it's that good?" she asked, flustered.

"Absolutely. There's a flyer about the contest outside the English department office. Promise me you'll enter it."

"Okay, I promise," she said.

"Do you hope to be a poet? Tell me your ambitions, your dreams."

"If it were possible, yes, and . . ." She hesitated, then yielded to his inquiry, which felt vaguely erotic. "To be honest, I'd also like to be a singer and write my own songs."

"You've written some already?"

"A few."

"So you sing?" he asked.

"After a fashion."

"Is there a singer who inspires you?"

"I love the Beatles, of course, and I'm very fond of Joni Mitchell."

"Joni is very sexy," Ben said, and launched into "A Case of You."

His falsetto drew everyone's attention, and a wave of laughter went around the table.

"I can't sing, but it seems Julia can," Ben said

"You sing jazz standards?" Michael asked her.

"I do."

"Come on, then." Standing up, Michael beckoned her toward the piano.

Julia held back for a moment, then followed him. "What

should we do?" she asked. Her love of music always won her battle with shyness.

"You choose something," Michael said chivalrously, settling in at the keyboard.

She thought for a moment. "A Garden in the Rain." It was a jazz standard dear to her. She'd learned it when she was twelve or thirteen, working on it with her father sitting next to her at the piano.

Michael opened the *Real Book*—the jazz musician's bible—to the song in question. He began to play, and Julia sang. The garden in her imagination was filled with spring flowers; the petals were damp from the rain, and the air was fragrant. It was a place where one could love and be loved perfectly. Julia wasn't afraid of sentimentality; as she closed her eyes, the words flowed from her heart. It was the kind of love where one could be entirely oneself, where nothing was measured or judged—a love that would reverberate through a lifetime. She finished the song and opened her eyes. Playing the last chords, Michael had his eyes fixed on her.

"Brava," he said.

"Well done," Ben added from the couch.

"That's it for tonight," she said. Singing the song in Ben's presence had left her a bit shaky. She sat down beside him while Michael continued to play. Robin and Anna were in the kitchen making coffee and looking for cups.

Ben took her hand in a caressing motion. "You have a beautiful voice."

"Thank you," she said, aroused by the warmth of his hand.

"Let's have some brandy."

Dropping her hand, he stepped into the kitchen and returned with a bottle. Julia accepted a glass. The liquor burned going down, enhancing the buzz from the wine at dinner. Anna and Robin appeared with coffee and cups.

Michael took a bag of weed out from its hiding place in the bookcase.

"Where are you from, Robin?" He sat down next to her and rolled a joint.

"Berkeley."

Michael smiled. "I thought you had that California vibe. Coming east is usually tough for you guys." He lit the joint and passed it to her. "Losing your tan in winter must be a real hardship."

"I guess you've never been to Northern California," Robin said with mock contempt as she took a toke. "We have a lot of fog in the Bay Area." She exhaled a stream of smoke.

"Probably gentle fog, though, huh? Warm fog?"

"No, cold fog. Damp fog," Robin said.

"Ah, then the lady might be a tramp," Michael said.

"Ah, trampitude—my highest aspiration," Robin joked.

"As Mark Twain said, 'The coldest winter I ever spent was a summer in San Francisco,'" Ben said.

"He has a literary quotation for everything," Michael said. "It's kind of irritating, but you get used to it."

"Just like the way you have a song for everything," Ben responded.

"Touché."

Robin got down on the carpet to examine the pile of records stacked under her chair.

"Let's see what treasures you got here," she said.

Michael sat next to her. "These are all destined for the garbage dump." Leaning against Robin's shoulder, he pulled an old Stan Getz album out of its jacket, exhibiting its scratches. "Isn't this pathetic?"

"And not a single pop album," Robin said. "How sad. Your taste is very square."

"Hey, I have *Fleetwood Mac*. I don't know where it is, but I have it."

"I have it too," Robin replied. "It's great."

"He'll never throw any of those out, even the most scratched ones," Ben said. "They've been sitting there for a year now. They're part of his—his—"

"Go ahead and say it. My junk collection." Michael gave his housemate an affectionate, tolerant look, then said to Robin, "Look under the couch." Robin lifted its skirt, revealing yet more records. "They're unlistenable, but I still can't get rid of them."

"And I believe," Ben said, "that you need to get rid of just *one* for the dam to break. Just one, Mikey, and the others will follow."

Michael shook his head despondently.

"It's a sad situation, old man," Ben continued, sounding very British. "Here, have another brandy."

"Maybe it's time to do something about this," Robin said. "Maybe destiny has brought us here tonight for a reason." She took a record out of its jacket and, with a pot-induced giggle, walked over to the window and opened it with a big yank.

"Jesus Christ!" Michael gasped.

Robin launched the record like a Frisbee, and a second later it clattered on the sidewalk. Julia groaned.

But Ben was excited. "Of course!" He grabbed another album and approached the window. *Whoosh! Crash!* they went as they shattered on the ground. "What fun!" he said. "Michael, I dare you to throw one."

Michael stood up and wavered.

"Let me make one thing perfectly clear," he said, walking over to the bookcase. "This stuff here is sacro-saint—sacro-sanct—sacro-sacro." He, too, was high and giggling now. "As for the rest—damn the torpedoes!"

They took batches of records over to the window, slipped the albums out of their jackets, and, with a flick of the wrist, tossed them out the window, while Michael screamed, "Goodbye, Ella! Ciao, Herbie! Fare thee well, Amadeus!"

A couple dozen albums had clattered below when they heard screaming from downstairs. "What the hell is going on up there?"

As Julia leaned out the window to throw another album, she sensed Ben leaning against her. Was it her imagination, or did she feel an erection through his pants? Was he usually this wild, throwing dinner parties at which people smashed and broke things?

A man stood by a car parked in front of the house. "What the fuck! If I find a single scratch on this car in the morning—"

"Bloody asshole!" Ben screamed in return. Shocked, Julia looked him in the eye and saw that he wasn't as drunk as he was making out to be. "I guess we'd better go and clean up," he said.

The frenzy subsided; equipped with paper bags, flashlights, a broom, and a dustpan, the group went down to reckon with the mess they'd made. There were few streetlights, and the front walk from the house to the sidewalk was dark.

"Here, let me help you," Ben said, and Julia was thrilled as he took her hand.

Back upstairs, post-cleanup, there was a sudden sense that the party was over, and it was time for the women to go home. They were gathering their things when Ben stopped them.

"But you don't have plumbing, do you?" he said. "Why don't you spend the night? You can have our rooms, and Michael and I will sleep out here." There was a moment of awkwardness, then a nodding of heads and bustling about as Michael and Ben changed the sheets and handed out pajamas and towels. Julia was assigned Ben's room; Anna and Robin took Michael's.

Julia closed the bedroom door and changed into the flannel sleep shirt and pants that Ben had given her. She sat on the bed and stared at Ben's pillow. She was about to spend the night in her beloved's bed. Getting under the covers, she heard the men talking softly down the hall in the living room. Nausea and a headache were beginning, but Ben's scent was in the air, and her euphoria and arousal promised a night of interesting dreams.

❖

After a long brunch the next morning, the five of them walked to the Grove Street Cemetery near campus. The yellow leaves drifting around the gray tombstones and the old trees muted any morbid associations, while the dates of the deceased, going back to the seventeenth century, gave the place an air of historical charm. Robin and Michael held hands and pulled ahead, leaving Ben to attend to both Julia and Anna.

Anna was talking about her junior year abroad.

"Makes me think of Paris and Père Lachaise," she said, waving her hand at the graves. She sighed. "The whole time I was there," she continued, "I felt like I was at the center of Europe."

Ben nodded. "And you were. If you look at the position of France on a map, you see that it's literally at a crossroads—between England and Italy on the one hand, and Germany and Spain on the other. There's a gigantic *X*"—he waved his hand in the air—"with France in the middle."

Robin and Michael were at the other end of the cemetery, leaning against a tree with their arms around each other.

"When Robin and I visited Anna in Paris," Julia said, "I felt like I was on the outside the whole time."

"You didn't get to know any French people?" Ben asked.

"Not really," Julia said, "but Robin did, even though we were only there for a couple of weeks. Everything's easy for her, somehow."

Michael cradled Robin's head with one hand in her short, curly hair as they began making out. Julia reflected bitterly that if Robin hadn't been flirting with Michael, Anna could have been with them, and Julia would have had Ben to herself. It was just like Robin to set a matchmaking plan in motion only to reap the benefits herself.

"I can see why. She's very outgoing, isn't she?" Ben said. "And as fast an operator as he is." He glanced sideways at Julia. "But that kind of temperament isn't always a recipe for happiness—you know that, right?"

"Yeah, I know. But it sure can help." Julia frowned. The dinner party wasn't supposed to have ended this way.

When Robin slid her hand down into Michael's pants, Anna groaned. "Jesus, in front of everybody! I think we ought to turn around, don't you?"

"Good idea," Ben said, and the three of them headed away from the embracing pair.

4

LOOSE ENDS

(Robin)

Robin felt from the beginning that Michael was keeping some part of himself in reserve, but each conjunction had its mysteries, and in this one, born of need and circumstance, the sexual momentum was strong, so she threw herself into it, hoping he would open up to her eventually.

He seemed curious about her. At least he asked all the right questions. In the first weeks of their relationship, they would lie in bed after sex and smoke pot and talk late into the night. The miseries of graduate school were a fertile subject for conversation.

"I honestly don't know what I'm doing here," he told her. Usually, they met at his place because of his symbiotic connection to his piano, but tonight they were in her bedroom decorated with hanging plants and big pillows covered in Indian fabrics dotted with tiny mirrors. "I love music and I love composing," he continued, "but what am I going to do with a degree in music composition? The only thing I can do is university teaching, but if I go for an academic career, I won't have time to be creative. That's what happened to my father."

"He teaches at Columbia, right?"

"Yeah. He's really talented, but he ended up writing about

music instead of making it." Michael shook his head. "I don't get it. He's been frustrated his whole career, but he's never stopped pushing me to follow in his footsteps."

"He probably wants you to be successful in some establishment way. And able to earn a living."

"Money! Who needs it? I'll figure it all out eventually." He passed her the joint. They were both floating, and life seemed full of possibility. "What about you?"

"I got fascinated by the statistical analysis of human behavior as an undergrad." Robin inhaled deeply. "But the more I get into it, the more it seems like bull. I mean, you can do a million studies, but if you're not asking the right questions, it's not going to get you anywhere. And nobody here is interested in asking the questions I'm interested in."

"Like?"

"Women's psychology from a feminist perspective." She sighed. "Going to a women's college got me interested in why women have such low self-esteem. We hate ourselves because our mothers taught us to. I want to look at how that's transmitted from generation to generation. Then there's the question of why God is a misogynist. He's gotta be, right? Otherwise, He would have given women a way to pee standing up." She giggled. "Jesus, I love getting high. It puts everything in perspective."

"All the faculty in psychology are men. You didn't expect them to be interested in women, did you?" When Michael smoked, he got mellow and philosophical.

"I never expect anything in life. I just wait and see what happens."

"Really? Is that the attitude of an experimental psychologist?" he asked.

"I guess that's it. You know, I could be happy living on a commune milking goats. Or I could go to India to be enlightened. Can't you see me in an ashram burning incense and meditating all day?" Not knowing herself whether she was joking or being serious, she pulled back to look him in the eye and get his reaction.

"Obviously. Everyone should go to India. Especially students of psychology."

"I mean, I'd love to be enlightened. I should put that on my list: get enlightened. By golly, someday I'll do it!" Robin said energetically, then sighed. "The fact is, I hate lab. I hate experiments, whether they're with people or rats."

"I'd ask what you do with the rats, but I don't think I want to know."

"No, you don't. You really don't." She paused. With smoke came clarity. "I need to get out of here. Drop out or change programs."

"Me too," Michael said.

After breakfast the next morning, Robin accompanied Michael down the stairs so she could get the mail. Standing next to her while she emptied the mailbox, he saw the letter from Stephanie at the top of the stack.

"She's not giving up, is she?" he said.

Robin met his gaze. She'd told him about Steph and had nothing to hide.

"She writes me every week."

"Wanting you back?"

"No. She just tells me what she's doing. She gives me detailed reports that are kind of boring."

Michael looked relieved. "See you tonight?"

"Yeah."

They kissed lightly, and he headed toward his car.

Back upstairs, she sat on her bed and opened the letter.

Dear Robin,

I get that you're young and not ready to be monogamous, and maybe being bisexual makes it difficult to make a choice,

*but I still can't understand your leaving the way you did after
I told you I'd give you the freedom you need to pursue relationships with guys. . . .*

Robin didn't mind getting weekly updates from her ex, but
she wasn't in the mood to be reprimanded. The words "give you
the freedom" made her angry. She had never thought of her
freedom as something that might be given away, and she had
certainly never made her lover a custodian of it. At twenty-two,
she wasn't about to put her future in a box with a ribbon on top,
then wait to see who might snatch up such a gift. And she didn't
think of herself as bi. She thought of herself as Robin. But of
course, if forced to make a preference choice, she wouldn't have
been able to, and that could only be a problem for Stephanie, who
described herself as a hundred percent gay. "Penises are just plain
weird," Steph had once said, recalling an encounter she'd aborted
when a potential partner had taken off his pants. "I said to the
guy, 'Please put that thing away.'"

Fuming, Robin continued to read.

*You've refused to talk to me on the phone or let me visit, and I
want to say that this is more than hurtful. It's just plain bad
manners. It's rude and messy to leave things unresolved like
this. It's cruel to wound your lover and not take the time to
put in a few stitches.*

It was true. Robin hadn't put in any stitches, and Steph's
words made her feel guilty. To be accused of rudeness was bad
enough, but the thought that she was a victimizer made her
squirm. For Robin wanted someday to be a healer. In order for
that to happen, she had to not only refrain from doing harm but
also clean up after herself when she messed up.

She put the letter back into its envelope and stuck it in a

drawer. Avoiding a final conversation had been cowardly, but if she agreed to Steph visiting, they could still have one. Of course, if her ex came, Robin would be busy for a couple of days, and she'd have to tell Michael about it. How would he take it? Would he be jealous or a good sport? Whatever the case, she had to call Steph.

"Hi. I was wondering when you'd write or call," Steph said.

Robin sensed Steph holding back tears.

"I just couldn't see how this could work without me hurting you," Robin said, "so I left."

"I really want to talk it through. Can I come down this weekend? You're still my sweetie pie."

A wave of yearning swept over Robin as she heard the love in Steph's voice. "Sure. Come down." The blue of Stephanie's eyes, the silkiness of her skin, and the delicacy of her touch came back, vivid and sweet.

"I miss you so much," Steph said.

"I've missed you too." It was half-true. When Robin wasn't hanging out with Michael or in bed with him, she did occasionally miss Stephanie. She might have missed her more if she hadn't felt so guilty.

The next day, Robin sat on Michael's couch, studying, while he tinkered with a melody at the piano. They were alone in the apartment.

"There, I got it. What do you think of this?" he asked.

She looked up as he played the tune over again, adding chords with his left hand. Because she blocked sounds out when she studied, she felt like she was hearing it for the first time.

"That's beautiful."

He leaned forward to make notations on the composition pad propped up over the keyboard. Robin went over to the piano.

"Michael, I'll be busy this weekend."

"You going somewhere?"

"No. I decided to call Stephanie."

"Ah. Her letter was convincing, I gather." He continued scribbling.

"Convincing enough that I called her last night. She really wants to visit, and I told her it's all right with me."

He finally looked up and met her eyes. "Are you wanting my permission after the fact?"

"I don't know."

Michael shrugged. "It's okay with me."

She felt both relieved and disappointed—relieved that she could do what she wanted but disappointed that he wasn't attached enough to be jealous.

"You sure?"

"As I understand it, you kind of left things dangling," he said. "You just walked out without officially ending it."

"Yeah, I guess that's what I did."

"You guess? If you didn't spell it out face-to-face, as in, 'We're through,' then you didn't officially end it. Especially if she's still in love with you. Because she'll be in denial."

"I just had to get out of there. So I left."

He shrugged again. "I'm no expert in these matters, but when I've done the breaking up without being explicit about it, I've regretted it and wished I had been."

Robin felt the disappointment again, but she also appreciated his generosity, which had to be the fruit of experience. Jealousy had perhaps been invented by the patriarchy to control women, but this male didn't have much of it as a gut reaction.

"Thank you for your understanding."

"Actually, I don't really understand. Do you prefer men or women? I mean," he went on with a stiff expression, "you really seem to like to fuck—unless you've been faking it. So how can you feel satisfied without it?"

"It's just a different experience, that's all. And I do like to fuck. I haven't been faking it."

Michael's expression relaxed. He smiled and put his pencil down on the ledge of the piano. "Well then, we'd better get some fucking in before she gets here."

Robin felt relieved. "Yes." And she wrapped her arms around his neck.

She couldn't concentrate on her homework while waiting for Steph to arrive. Robin had left Boston with the feeling of definitively, if impulsively, ending their relationship. But after their phone call, she realized how attached she still was. When she imagined disconnecting completely, grief came over her, as though Steph were about to die, and she longed to reconnect physically. And that was doable. Robin had her own room, and they would have the apartment to themselves over the weekend because Anna would be in New York with her boyfriend, and Julia would be at Ben's most of the time. She didn't have to tell Michael anything afterward.

Robin was in the kitchen cleaning up when Stephanie's red VW bug signaled her arrival with its distinctive sputtering noise. Looking out the window, she saw Steph get out of her car, grabbing her overnight bag and a bag of groceries. It was typical of Steph to arrive with food, even special pots to cook it in; she was generous, caring, maternal—all the things Robin's mother wasn't, and Robin, being a psychology student, wondered whether she had subconsciously chosen an older woman to re-mother herself.

Robin opened the front door and stood at the top of the wooden staircase waiting for Steph.

"Need a hand?" she shouted down.

"No, I got everything," Steph answered, trudging up the stairs with bags in hand. She reached the landing, kissed Robin lightly on the mouth, went inside, and put her stuff down.

"How was the drive?"

"Not too bad. A little traffic getting out of Boston, but the rest was smooth."

It felt normal having Steph there, and Robin let her in with the feeling—or was it the memory of a feeling?—that this was just another weekend together, like the weekends they used to spend in the Boston apartment, when Robin did homework and Steph prepared classes until they went out for dinner or drinking and dancing.

Steph put her hands on her lover's waist. "Thank you for agreeing to see me."

"I'm sorry," Robin said. "I mean, for leaving so abruptly."

"I was hurt, but then I understood. You didn't want the complication of—of—"

"Of worrying about hurting you more in the long run."

"I figured it was something like that."

"I just couldn't see how it could work, your letting me do what I want. I still can't."

"There's only one way to find out, and that's to try it."

"I—" Robin had an impulse to tell Steph about Michael, but Steph embraced her and they began to kiss.

"You going to show me where your bedroom is?" Steph asked.

Robin took her hand and led her toward the bedroom, thinking, *What the hell, why not?* It was November and a little drafty in the room, so when they slipped into bed and pulled the covers up, Robin felt a chill on her shoulders. Steph, in a passionate mood, took the lead. Even though Robin had always loved the way her partner went down on her, making tight little circles with her tongue, her mind got busy, and she couldn't have an orgasm. She looked out the window at the bare-branched elm thinking, *Shit, this was a stupid thing to do*, and finally she said, "I'm not going to come today, let's switch."

Under other circumstances, Steph would have understood

Robin wasn't in the mood and said, "Okay, let's do it another time," but tonight she willingly accepted Robin's attention. Robin had the feeling, as she went down on Steph, of performing a required duty, and was relieved when Steph climaxed quickly and they could stop. Enough with the charade.

"I love you so much," Steph murmured, as Robin settled in her arms. They were in the same bed yet in two different emotional places, having two entirely different experiences. Steph took Robin's face in her hands. "You didn't feel like coming?" she asked.

Robin almost squirmed. "No, it was nice, I was aroused, but I'm also . . . a little confused," she said, and with that, the whole mood shifted, and the joyfulness of their first moments evaporated.

"Then we need to talk some more." Stephanie's remedy for any relational issue was putting things in language, clearly and compassionately. "I don't think you believed me when I said I could tolerate your having other partners."

The words were spoken kindly, but one of them—"tolerate"—was not to Robin's liking. Still, she wanted to avoid the carnage of a melodramatic breakup.

"I believe you *want* to be able to tolerate it, but I think you'll suffer."

"I want to see whether I can do it. Give me a chance."

"All right," Robin said, though she wasn't sure she wanted to. Then there was the matter of Michael. But it was in her nature to postpone conflict. "You want to go for a walk or something?"

"Let's do some cooking. I bought veggies for a new casserole recipe."

They got dressed and went into the kitchen. Steph started grating the vegetables while Robin buttered a big dish.

"I brought eggs but forgot cottage cheese," Steph said, looking at the recipe. "Damn. Could you run out and get some while I continue grating?"

"Sure," Robin said.

It was a quick hop in the car to the nearest grocery store. When Robin returned with cottage cheese, she found the kitchen empty. The bathroom door in the hallway was open and the apartment quiet. Maybe Steph was napping.

She set the bag down. "Steph?" she whispered, and tiptoed softly down the hall to the bedroom.

Standing on the threshold, Robin saw Steph sitting on the edge of her bed, reading her diary with tears flowing down her face.

"You found someone else *already*? This Michael guy? Jesus, you're a fast operator."

"See," Robin said, "I knew you wouldn't be able to 'tolerate' it."

"I would have if you'd been honest and told me straight out—"

"You just got here and threw yourself at me! You think I should have told you about him the minute you walked in?"

"You're a real fuck, you know that?" Steph shut the diary and slammed it down on the bed beside her. "A real fuck who loves to fuck, obviously."

"Steph—"

Stephanie got up, walked quickly past her, banging into Robin's shoulder on the way, and proceeded down the hall to the living area, where she slipped her jacket on and started gathering her things.

"Steph, it's late, come on, stay over—"

"I'd rather sleep in my own bed tonight, thank you."

"You see, this is why I left Boston!"

"You were right. How about you just continue doing what you want to do and leave me out of it." With bags in hand, Stephanie walked toward the door. "I won't be calling you again."

And she was gone.

Robin went back into her bedroom and opened her diary, wanting to reread her own words and see what Steph had seen.

Damn, her entries were graphic. *I love it when he lifts my leg with his arm.* Ouch, it must have been hard for Steph to read this stuff. Robin was overcome with remorse—not about sleeping with Michael but for hurting Steph, who had always been so kind.

Emotionally exhausted, Robin lay down and stared at the ceiling. She closed her eyes and dozed. A couple of hours must have passed because when she opened them, night had fallen and she was hungry. She remembered the unfinished casserole and went into the kitchen where they'd left a buttered baking dish and grated vegetables in one bowl, beaten eggs in another. She turned on the oven and began mixing everything together.

She was about to pour the mix into the dish when, remembering she still needed to add the cottage cheese, it hit her like a punch—Steph had "forgotten" the cottage cheese on purpose so she could do some snooping while Robin was out.

"Boy, am I an idiot!" She shoved the casserole in the oven and banged the door closed.

Michael called Sunday night. "How did it go?"

"Awful. She read my diary and couldn't handle it."

"You left your diary out?"

"No, it was in the bottom drawer of my dresser. She went looking for it."

"You okay?"

"Yeah. I mean, I feel awful but sort of relieved."

"Well, then," he said, "do you feel like coming over?"

"Sure. Sure, I'll come over."

The break with Steph felt final now, leaving Robin to return peacefully to her graduate work and her relationship with Michael. But after the weekend of Stephanie's visit, she noticed a subtle shift in his behavior.

He'd never been very affectionate outside the bedroom, but

now there was something else: he always had a smoke before they had sex.

It began with a Sunday night she'd gone over to his apartment for dinner. At bedtime, he said he needed to unwind, and he reached for his stash and rolled a joint. Robin liked the occasional smoke with a friend or before sex, so she didn't think twice about it. But the pattern continued in the weeks that followed: he rolled a joint before each time they had sex.

"You can't have sex without a joint first?" she asked.

"It's not that," he said. "It helps me sleep afterward."

The semester became more intense as they moved toward Thanksgiving, and she decided to ride with whatever came up relationally in order to focus on her schoolwork. Michael satisfied her basic needs, and that would get her through the academic year. Occasionally she'd think back on her previous summer in San Francisco before she started graduate school. She hadn't expected the doctoral program at Yale to be so exhausting and intense, and the memory of her two-month fling with Theo refreshed her. Theo was devoid of Michael's seriousness about music; he was in it—and life, more generally—for the sheer fun of it and played rock guitar with manic, contagious joyfulness. She missed him sometimes because, as casual as their relationship had been, it had offered a lot of emotional connection.

One day she was singing the refrain of the last song he'd written—*I have a lock on crazy, that comes easily / What I want above all else to be / Crazy free / Crazy free crazy*—as she went down the external wooden staircase to the mailbox when, coincidentally, she saw a letter from him—a happy surprise, as they hadn't communicated since she'd left California. There was also a letter from Steph, which Robin stuffed in her pocket, as she wanted to read Theo's first. She sat on the bottom stair and opened it quickly, curious about what he had to say. He'd written to ask whether she would be coming home to San Francisco for winter break and wanted to get together with him.

This was a real head-scratcher. Of course, she wanted to see him—why wouldn't she?—but what about Michael? Robin assumed he'd tolerated her seeing Steph because she was a woman. She doubted he'd tolerate her reconnecting with a fling who was male. *Like a dog on a beach / Crazy free.* She didn't know whether she'd see Theo or sleep with him again or, if she did, whether she'd tell Michael about it, but the letter made her happy, and she climbed up the stairs with a feeling of joyful expectation.

Once back in the apartment, she remembered Steph's letter, took it out of her pocket, and opened it.

I'm gradually accepting the finality of our breakup and am doing okay. I just wanted you to know that I admire your adventurousness, which has inspired me to be more open and experimental. I've decided I should give men another shot, if only to make sure I'm not avoiding a potential avenue out of fear or inexperience. So I went to the gynecologist to talk about birth control. Who knows what lies ahead for me.

Best of luck to you,
Steph

Wow! Shaking her head in amazement, Robin shoved the letter back in her pocket. *Go for it, Steph*, she said to herself, laughing. Anything was possible, but she had a hunch Steph would continue to think penises were just plain weird.

5

THANKSGIVING SURPRISES

(Julia)

Six weeks had passed since Ben's crazy dinner party, weeks during which Julia expected him to ask her out. He'd flirted with her and taken her hand when they went to clean up the records thrown out the window—didn't that mean he was interested? And when she sat in his class on Wednesdays and Fridays, she often caught him looking her way, his eyes lingering on hers a second more than necessary. But he neither engaged her in conversation after class nor called to ask her out.

Maybe he didn't want to risk dating a student. She entered the sonnet contest as he had suggested, thinking that, if she won, he would hear about it and call. The winners would be announced in February, when she would no longer be in his class. In the meantime, every class meeting with him turned into a battle between hope and despair. By the Wednesday before Thanksgiving, when she boarded the Amtrak train from New Haven to New York, despair was winning. She had entered the spontaneous combustion stage of unrequited infatuation.

Her agitation was so intense that she was barely aware of

the passengers on the subway as she rode the East Side IRT from Grand Central Station up to her parents' apartment on Seventy-Sixth Street. She told herself that, in a year's time, her obsession with Ben would be history. She would graduate in six months, return to Manhattan, and find a job and an apartment. Exiting the subway at Seventy-Seventh, she passed a bar near her parents' building and wondered if that was the kind of place she'd have to frequent after college to meet guys, though she didn't drink much or like going to bars. After years on campus, all the men in Manhattan looked too old for her. When she got a job somewhere, the men there would be in their thirties and up. Maybe married. It was possible she'd still be a virgin at twenty-two or three or four. What a terrifying thought.

She nodded to the doorman as she stepped into her parents' building. The elevator arrived; the Puerto Rican man who ran it with his father was on duty. The two of them lived in an apartment on the ground floor and alternated shifts with one other employee.

"Hi, Rodrigo," she said.

"Good afternoon, miss," he replied.

"You can call me Julia."

Rodrigo had worked in the building for several years, but Julia had never offered her first name before. Registering the gesture, he nodded, and instead of facing the panel of floor buttons as was usual, he turned toward her while the elevator rode up.

"You look nice," he said. "Home for the holidays?"

"I've been traveling for three hours; I don't look nice," she said.

"To me you look very nice," he said.

"Thank you, Rodrigo."

The car reached her floor and stopped, but he didn't open the door.

"You've been working too hard at school," he said. "You need some fun this weekend." He gave her a steady look.

His directness was exciting, and she liked the amber color of his skin. His hands and neck, protruding from his brown double-breasted uniform, were smooth and hairless. He was probably that smooth and touchable all over.

"Do you have any suggestions?" she asked.

"I'm sure I could come up with something," he said.

"I'm sure you could." The attention felt good.

He pressed the button to open the door, they exchanged a last look, and she stepped out. The elevator made its whirring and cranking noise as it started up again.

When she stepped into her parents' apartment, she heard her mother mumbling to herself in the kitchen. It was Mariel's turn to host Thanksgiving dinner this year, and her competitiveness turned the holiday meal into an ordeal for everyone.

Julia put her things down in her bedroom and went into the kitchen.

"Where's Robin?" her mother asked. "I thought she was coming with you."

"She decided to spend the holiday with her new boyfriend."

"Ah," her mother said with raised eyebrows.

"'Ah'?"

"Choosing the new boyfriend over her family. Okay. She might have called to say she wasn't coming."

"Well, I'm telling you she isn't."

"She's always been unpredictable." Mariel sighed. "I went to the supermarket this afternoon, but of course I forgot half the ingredients."

Julia's mother was in one of her eclectic outfits: a tie-dyed top, a patterned sweater with fringe, and tight jeans. An actress, she took dance lessons several times a week and was, in her late fifties, fit and flashy. A normally self-confident woman, she became unhinged by preparations for any kind of dinner party and especially a family holiday meal, as though she were experiencing stage fright on the opening night of a Broadway show. The glass of wine she had on the counter wasn't helping.

"I can go shopping tomorrow while you start cooking," Julia offered. It would be a trying day, but when the guests arrived— Anna and her sister Evelyn with their parents and some friends of the family—everyone would get plastered, eat a lot, and have a good time.

Thursday morning, she was a little grumpy and disappointed to find Rodrigo's father in the elevator. But when she returned to the lobby forty minutes later with groceries and the elevator opened, there was Rodrigo.

"Let me hold those for you." As he leaned toward her to take her bag of groceries, she caught his pleasant scent.

"Thank you."

"And how's your day going, *Julia*?" Their eyes met.

"Oh, okay, I suppose." It was warm in the elevator, and she unwound the wool scarf around her neck.

"You're hosting the dinner this year?" He nodded toward the groceries in his arms.

"Yeah."

He laughed.

"What's so funny?"

"The way holidays make people suffer," he said.

"It's not suffering, exactly. It just makes me irritable."

The elevator reached her floor. Again, he stopped the car but didn't open the door.

"I think I could help you feel better," he said.

"Oh?" Her heart beat hard.

"At one o'clock I have an hour break for lunch. I'm in 1B. Come by for coffee."

She looked at her watch. "In an hour, then?"

"You want to?"

"I—maybe—I—" He was outrageous, but she felt tempted.

"Drop by if you feel like it. It can be just coffee if you want. No pressure."

When he gave back the shopping bag, their hands touched accidentally. Startled, she blushed and froze, wanting more. He leaned forward over the groceries and kissed her on the lips, then stepped back and opened the door. She almost tripped stepping out, then mixed up the keys for the three locks on her parents' door, fumbling as though she'd never opened them before. Finally, she let herself in, put the groceries down, and went to her bedroom.

She thought about Ben. She had been desiring him for almost three months, and suddenly she felt foolish for wanting her first time to be some big romantic experience with Mr. Right. She wore her virginity like handcuffs or a chastity belt; the sooner she got rid of it, the better. With shaky hands, she rummaged in her suitcase for the diaphragm she always had with her like a hopeful amulet. She found it and sneaked into the bathroom. Although she'd practiced inserting it at the gynecologist's office, she now grew hot and cold as she fiddled with the device, wondering if she'd positioned it correctly.

She went into the kitchen to help her mother. They chopped vegetables, mixed the stuffing, and set up the turkey in the roasting pan.

Mariel gossiped a little about Anna's mother. "I just hope Linda doesn't get plastered and make a fool of herself like she did last year." She took a sip of wine. It was her beverage of choice and generally didn't lead to any disgraceful acts, whereas Linda, when fueled with scotch, was an unpredictable weapon on the loose.

Julia glanced at the clock. "I have to go out."

Mariel looked surprised. "Everything's closing now."

"I need some exercise."

She put a coat on as though going outside, then took the

elevator (now being run by Rodrigo's father) to the first floor, where she walked bravely down the hall to 1B and knocked.

Rodrigo let her in. His just-shaved face was a little moist from aftershave or moisturizer. He was wearing jeans and a T-shirt. She'd never seen him out of his uniform before.

She glanced around at the simple hardwood furniture and the posters left over from the 1960s, with rock bands and psychedelic patterns. The blinds were drawn, not surprising since the apartment was on the ground floor, facing the street. Rodrigo placed a cup of coffee on the dining table.

"As promised," he said.

"So, Rodrigo," she said, wanting to defer the business at hand, "are you going to do this forever? I mean, operate an elevator?" Damn, she sounded like the little Ivy League Jewish princess that she was.

"I'm studying carpentry," he said.

"Really?" She was genuinely interested.

"I made this cabinet myself. Come look."

The cabinet held a stereo system with speakers behind sliding doors. She ran her fingers over the top surface. It was smooth and a dark tan color, like his skin.

"Very professional."

"I'm good with my hands."

She smiled flirtatiously. "Are you? Show me." Mentally, in that moment, she waved goodbye to Ben.

Rodrigo came up to her and put his hands on her face. "*Eres una mujer muy hermosa.*"

Julia didn't speak Spanish, but she got the gist. "Thank you."

"And I don't like to see a beautiful woman looking miserable."

"You going to put me out of my misery?" she asked.

"I'd like to. You'd feel better afterward."

He bent down, swept her up gracefully, and carried her into his bedroom. She could have been a child; he was that strong. He placed her on his bed. She cooperated as he undressed her, then he stood up and undressed himself. He lay down next to her.

"Beautiful, beautiful," he said, stroking her breasts. Naked, he was as she had imagined, smooth and dark all over, well-built without being overly muscular. His erection, when he uncovered it, seemed enormous. She was speechless as he caressed and kissed her. He kneaded her breasts and stroked her vulva before spreading her thighs forcefully with his knees and penetrating her. "*Delicioso* . . . nice and tight . . ." he murmured. It was both excruciatingly painful and exquisitely pleasurable. She wanted him to stop immediately. She wanted it to go on forever.

Afterward, they lay quietly for a moment.

"I hope that was okay for you. You didn't come." He put his hand between her legs. "You want me to help you?"

"I . . . I can't with someone new," she improvised, not wanting him to know she was a virgin. "But it was great. Thank you. I feel much better now," she said. Her head was empty. She was all sensation—dilation, burning pain, pleasure, and heart pounding.

"I'm glad. You want that cup of coffee now?"

"Sure."

When he left the room to get it, she stared at the psychedelic poster opposite the bed. Fluorescent greens and traffic yellows spiraled around a winged unicorn flying into a garish red sunset. It was so awful that it was fascinating.

He returned with the coffee, which he put down next to her side of the bed. She took a sip.

"Nice poster you got there," she said.

Rodrigo laughed. "I know you don't like it. I've been in some of the apartments upstairs—real paintings in fancy frames and stuff like that. Stuff I can't afford."

Julia grimaced. "You're right. I don't like it."

"And what about you?" he asked.

"What about me?"

"Are you going to be a college student forever?"

She liked his irony. "No. I'm going to come back to the city and get a job."

"The city is a nice place to be," he said, and she wondered whether he was holding out a possibility of repeated encounters.

They talked for a bit, then he looked at his watch. "My dad's shift is over. Time to get in my uniform."

They got dressed and went out into the lobby. Rodrigo pressed the elevator button, and when the car arrived, his dad looked at Julia, then his son.

"*Llegas tarde. Stupido,*" he whispered to him, getting off.

Rodrigo shrugged, he and Julia got in, and he took her up to her parents' floor.

The guests start arriving around four. Anna arrived with her family and Doug. Since high school, the two of them, like an established married couple, had alternated holidays between her family and his. Her sister Evelyn hadn't brought anyone because she had serial affairs with married men, which she always pulled off without a hitch. In another time and place, she might have been a French countess with a string of discreet lovers that her husband tolerated so he could tend to his own secret harem. Julia envied both of her cousins' amatory experiences, but at least now, after Rodrigo, she was "on the bus."

The men went into the living room while the women stayed in the kitchen. In her annual fit of conformity, Mariel worked to create a picture-perfect meal of turkey and stuffing with the usual condiments. But toward the end of the cooking, when the mothers and daughters gathered in the kitchen, there was always some drama around the gravy. Tonight Doug joined the women; he liked to make himself useful.

"As you all know," Mariel said, with the exaggerated, theatrical diction she took on when wanting to entertain or manipulate,

"I'm absolutely no good with sauces. Roasting—yes, okay. I can do that. Basting—yes, I can do that too. But the scraping and adding of this and that and separating out the fat—please, do not ask me to do that."

She made that speech every year. And Linda always gave the same reply. "I am the same. The same-same."

"Because . . ." Mariel said, making an invitational gesture toward Linda.

"Because . . ."

And then the two of them together shouted, "No sauces in Minsk!" They tapped their feet on the ground and hooted.

Absurd, Julia thought, remembering her great-aunt Iris's stuffed cabbage served in tomato sauce. Of course, they'd had sauces in Minsk. But, because of their mothers' laziness, Anna, Evelyn, and Julia had been making the turkey gravy since they were old enough to light a match.

"Clear out," Evelyn said to the mothers. As the oldest, she took charge.

"We'll take this handsome man with us." Passing her arm through Doug's, Mariel led him out, and Linda followed close behind them.

"They're crazy," Evelyn said as she put an apron on to protect her black sheath dress.

"'Ah, the Mothers,'" Anna said in her best baritone, tucking her chin and gesturing for them to repeat.

"The Mothers!" repeated Evelyn and Julia, dropping further to bass. The cry was followed by laughter. The routine had started in adolescence.

"What do you need?" Julia asked.

"Nothing. I've got everything under control."

"You can help me finish setting the table," Julia said to Anna.

From the dining room, Julia saw the parents laughing as they mingled with the handful of artistic guests her mother had rounded up for the evening. Doug talked animatedly with the poet who came every year. A striking middle-aged man with olive skin and bushy eyebrows, he might have been an actor if poetry had failed him.

"What can I do?" Anna asked.

"Here, help me with this." Julia fiddled with a cloth napkin. "My mother wants them to look decorative."

"We can make them into flowers." Anna turned a napkin into a giant rose. She was good with her hands. "You look really nice tonight."

"I have 'things' to relate," Julia said shyly.

"Oh? 'Things'?"

Julia gave a little nod. "You bet."

"Then there's a reason you look so nice. And how long do I have to wait to hear these 'things'?"

"Until after dinner."

"That's my dessert?"

"If you like a good story."

"What's the story on the poet guy?" Anna asked.

"Harold Lassen, poet laureate of Brooklyn. His wife is rumored to be a Polish princess whose family fled political upheaval."

"He's very handsome."

Julia glanced at him. She'd always had a bit of a crush on him because he'd praised her poetry when she was younger. "Yes, he is."

The older generation gathered at one end of the table, the younger at the other. Harold came over, patted Julia on the shoulder, and asked her to send him some poems. Dinner was delicious, with conversation spearheaded by the mothers. With Robin's mother, Sarah, in San Francisco and Doris expatriated to Italy, Mariel and Linda were the adults remaining to carry on the memories of growing up in Brooklyn.

They liked to tell stories about Iris, the family matriarch and wife of Isaac Lipski.

"Now here's a story for you," Linda said, pointing her knife at the poet laureate and his Polish wife. "My mother was the first woman to drive across the Brooklyn Bridge."

"You're giving me the kernel of a poem, I see," said Harold.

"Why, yes, it would make a great subject for a poem. Iris's epic journey across the Brooklyn Bridge!"

Conversation stopped; everyone was riveted by the vision of the first woman driving across the new structure.

"The bridge had just been opened," Linda began, "and people were afraid it wouldn't hold. But some brave ones wanted to be the first to cross. All the brave were men, of course, except for my mother. She got in her jalopy and set off after promising my father she would call when she reached the other side. And she did! As soon as she got to Manhattan, she found a phone and called. Then she went to buy her first lipstick. When she got home with bright red lips, my father saw it and said, 'You harlot!' and threw the lipstick out the window. She just harrumphed, marched outside, picked it up, and applied another coat."

Everyone chuckled. But the poet said, smiling, "There's just one small problem with your story. The bridge opened in 1883, and I'm guessing your mother was born after that."

Linda had only a second of embarrassment. "Okay, maybe it was my grandmother, not my mother. Who cares? Same idea." She waved her hand dismissively.

"Now, *my* favorite story," Mariel offered, "is about the time Doris went out to get the newspaper just wrapped in a towel after her morning shower and locked herself out of the house—"

"And went half naked knocking on the neighbors' door!" Linda added.

"No wonder she had to move to Italy!" Mariel said.

"To escape the shame!"

The two women could go on like this for quite a while. And they did.

Toward the end of dinner, Anna leaned into Julia and whispered, "Time for 'dessert'?"

Julia seemed embarrassed. "It's nothing, actually."

"You've changed your mind about telling me?"

"You won't think it's that interesting."

"How do you know? I'm already interested."

"Okay, follow me."

Julia led the way down the hall to the bedroom she'd grown up in. A few tattered stuffed animals were wedged in between old textbooks on the bookshelves. A cactus sat on the windowsill.

The cousins sat cross-legged on her bed.

"So . . . ?"

"I had an 'adventure' earlier today." Julia blushed.

"Something to do with Ben?"

Julia shook her head. "No, I've given up on Ben. You won't believe this—with the elevator man!"

"The elevator man? That gorgeous guy I saw on the way up?"

"Yeah. I went to his apartment."

"You went to his apartment? And you—you lost your virginity, didn't you?" Anna seemed both thrilled and appalled.

Julia nodded. "Yeah, just a few hours ago."

"God! How was it?"

"Exciting. Really exciting."

"You going to do it again?"

"Probably not."

They stared at each other.

"I've never done anything like that," Anna said. "I mean, had sex with someone I barely knew."

"You've only been with Doug, right?"

"That's right." Anna grew quiet.

"What? You think I'm crazy."

"No, it's not that. It's . . ."

"What?"

"I'm actually . . . jealous."

"Why?" Julia said. "When you have Doug?"

"Well, just because I've never been with anyone except him, that's why."

"I have no regrets, but honestly I'd prefer to be in your shoes. Doug's a good guy."

"I suppose. And good for you. I'm proud of you, Julia."

On Friday, Julia and her mother, as was their custom, took the subway and the crosstown bus to Macy's on West Thirty-Fourth Street. Mariel liked to try on winter coats, visit housewares—where she looked for more absorbent towels and better cereal bowls—then stop in the makeup department on the ground floor. Julia followed along as she had done since the age of six. It was all tolerable until Mariel paused in front of the Clinique counter.

"Want to have some fun?" she asked her daughter.

"Not really," Julia said.

"Why? Would it violate your principles?"

Whereas Julia avoided makeup to show she was liberated, Mariel considered it a womanly necessity and an actress's indispensable tool. She couldn't understand Julia's wanting to be plain.

"I just wouldn't use it," Julia said.

"Well, *I* want to have fun, so sit down." Mother pointed to one of the little padded stools. Daughter obeyed.

As Mariel hovered over her with brushes and colored pencils, Julia felt her lips getting too thick, her cheekbones too high, her eyebrows too dark, and her eyelids itchy and heavy. At that exact moment, she saw Ben and Michael coming out from the men's department and heading toward the exit, a path that would take them past the Clinique counter. Ben waved.

"Oh no," Julia gasped, "there's the English instructor I told you about and the grad student who's Robin's new boyfriend."

Mariel straightened up, an eye pencil in one hand. The men approached.

Flustered, Julia made introductions. Michael explained that Ben and Robin were spending Thanksgiving weekend with him and his parents, and they were holiday shopping for their parents.

"But where's Robin?" Mariel asked.

Michael shrugged. "She's off doing her thing with a friend."

"We were about to get lunch at that deli around the corner," Ben said. "Why don't you join us?"

"What a delightful idea!" Mariel put the makeup brush down.

As the four of them pushed their way through the crowd toward the revolving exit, Michael paired off with Mariel who took the lead, while Ben walked next to Julia.

"Did you have a successful morning shopping?" Ben asked.

"You call this successful?" Julia said, gesturing toward her caked face.

"Yes, I would," Ben said.

Making awkward conversation, they followed Mariel and Michael into the crowded deli where they were lucky enough to get a booth immediately. Excusing herself, Julia took refuge in the ladies' room. She pumped soap onto a paper towel and scrubbed her face. Unable to get the makeup off completely, she just made things worse. An older woman in a smart belted coat stood at the adjoining sink and watched.

"You were just at Macy's, weren't you?" she asked.

"It's that obvious?"

"I'm afraid so."

Julia threw the towel into the garbage and went back to their booth.

"Now you've made a fine mess of yourself," Mariel said.

The guys examined her.

"Hmm," Ben said.

"Hello!" Michael said.

"This is what happens when you go shopping with your mother the day after Thanksgiving," Julia remarked. The tension broke, and she let out a peal of laughter.

Her mirth proved contagious, and everyone relaxed. Ben poked fun at the enormity of the sandwiches, which he measured with his thumb, causing Mariel to pull out her ever-handy tape measure and take measurements. Then they got into a discussion about the effects of film on the modern novel.

"Cross-fertilization between the arts is always a good thing," Mariel said.

"You don't think audiences are being trained to want shorter and shallower stories?" Ben asked. "I predict that the effect of movies on the novel will ultimately prove to be deleterious."

Michael laughed. "Only you would drop the word 'deleterious' in casual conversation. Besides, that's a bunch of bull. You're the biggest fan of Fellini, Bergman, and—"

"That doesn't mean film is an art or has a positive influence on other arts," Ben countered.

"A bunch of bull," Michael repeated.

"It amuses me to provoke you."

Julia enjoyed the friendship between the two men.

Mariel picked up the bill, and they left the restaurant. Outside on the sidewalk, Mariel started talking to Michael about the performance scene in Manhattan, and Ben drew Julia aside.

"I've been meaning to call for weeks," he said.

"Why didn't you?" she asked, then flushed. Ben was her instructor and might want to avoid any semblance of impropriety.

"Because you're worthy of respect," he said.

Not sure of his meaning, she stared down at the pavement.

"But if you can forgive my delay," he continued, "we could get together tomorrow."

"I'd like that."

"We could meet for coffee in the Village," he suggested, "then take a walk."

Julia looked up at him. "Yes, let's."

"Café Dante at eleven?"

She nodded.

After a restless night in which she alternately pursued and was pursued by a man with Ben's face and Rodrigo's body, Julia took the subway down to Astor Place, then zigzagged toward the West Village, crossing Washington Square on the way. The winter sky was low and gray, the air crisp. Children ran about in the playground in the northeast corner of the park; in the opposite corner, drug pushers whispered their deals to passersby. Julia reached MacDougal Street and stepped inside the café to find Ben already there; with the deep red walls and dark oil paintings behind him, he appeared more polished and European than usual.

"Would you like a cappuccino?" he asked. She nodded, and he flagged down the waiter. "*Due cappuccini per favore.*"

The waiter asked him a question in Italian, and Ben answered in the same.

"You mentioned your mother was Italian, but I didn't know you spoke it," Julia said.

"I spoke Italian at home with my mum when I was growing up. Speaking of mothers, yours is quite a character. That was a jolly lunch yesterday."

"My mother's a treasure," Julia said. "Difficult sometimes, but a treasure."

"You grew up here, so maybe . . . you have an old boyfriend in the city?" he asked.

Julia blushed. "No, I don't. I don't have a boyfriend anywhere. What about you?"

"I don't have a boyfriend either—unless you count Michael," he joked. "Sorry. No, I don't have a girlfriend."

"Michael told Robin you had someone in Paris." Julia could be equally direct.

The waiter chose that moment to bring their coffee, giving Ben a moment to prepare his answer.

"I have a good friend in Paris," he said.

"A girlfriend?" Julia pressed. She wasn't usually so insistent, but she needed to know.

"She's an ex, but I still see her. It isn't a relationship that keeps me from entering other relationships, if that's what you're wondering. The fact is, she's far away, it's impossible, and I'm free." He waited for her reaction.

Confused by his answer, Julia said nothing, and he continued. "Almost everybody has some unfinished business somewhere, don't you think?"

Julia thought about Rodrigo. That wouldn't happen again. "Not necessarily," she said. "Take my parents. I don't think either of them has anyone anywhere."

"Parents! They belong to an inscrutable category."

Julia sighed, and the mysterious Parisienne evaporated. There was a pause, then the conversation went sideways to their poetry class, New Haven, and English department gossip. They fell into an easy silence. Outside snowflakes were beginning to fall. There was little foot or car traffic, and the soft, gray light turned the narrow street with its low brownstones and quaint shops into a dimly lit stage set for another century.

"Isn't New York magical sometimes?" Julia said.

Suddenly, Ben took her hand. It was a miracle. Every detail about the way their relationship started would seem miraculous for years. "I don't know you well," he said, "but I know you're wonderful, and I've been meaning to call you for weeks now."

"That's what you said yesterday."

"I was afraid you wouldn't want to go out with me."

"Why?"

"Me being older and your teacher. I mean, if this went somewhere, you might feel you were . . . sleeping with the enemy." He laughed uncomfortably.

She blushed. "I don't mind your being my teacher. The term is almost over anyway. I'm glad you asked me out today," she said.

"Let's walk," he said, and put a few dollars on the table.

Outside he took her hand, and they headed toward the middle of Washington Square, where they sat on a bench and let the snow fall on them. The square was emptying now; even the drug pushers were leaving.

"You need to cover your hair," he said. He took off his scarf and wrapped it around her head. Then, tentatively, he kissed her, she kissed him back, and they continued kissing for a long time.

"You must be getting cold," he finally said.

"My feet are freezing," she admitted.

"The way I see it, we have two choices. We can go get something for lunch or . . ."

"Or?"

He looked at his watch. "I was going to go back to New Haven tomorrow, but I—we—could go back this afternoon. Together. You could go home and get your stuff, and I'd go back to Michael's and get mine, and we could meet at Grand Central and take a late afternoon train back. We'd have the apartment to ourselves until Monday morning." Exhilarated, he spoke breathlessly.

"I like that idea. A lot," she said, and leaned in for another kiss.

A few hours later, after telling her parents she needed to go back early to work on a term paper, Julia met Ben under the big clock. They held hands on the train, sometimes talking, sometimes not. Knowing they would go to bed when they got to his place, Julia had heat in her sex and abdomen; the arousal made it hard to have a continuous thought. She castigated herself about Rodrigo. She had wanted an old-fashioned, wedding-night deflowering, updated for the 1970s, and now that was impossible. She should have had more faith and been more patient. *Oh well.* She leaned her head against Ben's shoulder, kissed it, and gazed out at the spots of ocean and quaint Connecticut towns passing by.

"Let me treat us to a taxi," he said when they arrived. She was happy for that speedier choice, as desire mixed with nervousness. They were soon at his place, going up the two flights to his apartment where they'd had the crazy dinner two months before. She wasn't an adventuress like her cousin Robin. She was hoping this would be the real thing, and although she'd done something casual in Apartment 1B, she hoped not to have to be casual again. She wanted special; she wanted magic.

They put their bags down in the living room and took turns using the bathroom. She went first and put her diaphragm in, more confidently this time. Then Ben went in. When he came out, he took her hand and led her down the hall to the bedroom she already knew from her night there. He lifted her sweater, then her shirt, until she had on only her bra. He removed his own sweater and shirt. They held hands.

"I wanted to ask you something," he said.

"What?"

"This isn't your first time, is it?"

"No. No, it isn't."

He moved his hands down to unzip her pants. "A woman of experience, then. Praise the Lord!" He sighed with relief.

She took it in. If only he knew how little experience she had! But what did it matter? Rodrigo had been a smart move after all.

"And praise the Lord for *you*," she said, and threw her arms around his neck.

6

LONG ISLAND

(Anna)

With Thanksgiving dinner concluded, Anna took a late train back to Long Island with Doug and her parents. Melancholy came over her as she gazed out the window at the city lights; happiness always lay elsewhere, out of reach. She envied her sister, who was staying in the city because she had an early morning flight to Bermuda for a romantic tryst. And she envied Julia for having the courage to throw herself into a stranger's bed.

Envy was followed by a nostalgic pang for her early years in Manhattan. Anna's family had moved out to Long Island when she was beginning high school because her father had gotten a position at Stony Brook University. The switch to a rural community had been a shock. When she was growing up in Manhattan in the 1960s, every outing offered amusement: hippies in colorful outfits, musicians on street corners, impromptu brawls, and the occasional, exciting-because-forbidden odor of the skunk plant. After so much urban excitement, Long Island was one long let-down. Doug and the beginning of sex had broken the monotony, but this, too, eventually became anticlimactic. The mental review of past disappointments had a numbing effect, and Anna barely felt Doug's hand as he intertwined his fingers with hers on the train.

He leaned his head on her shoulder to get her attention.

"Meet at the mansion tomorrow?"

Although they were adults now and both sets of parents knew they were sleeping together, they still went to an abandoned house on Crane Neck Road when they were home and wanted to have sex.

"Sure." She felt emotionally disconnected but didn't want to say no.

"Noonish? I'll bring a picnic."

Anna nodded. Planning their meeting around food took the emphasis off sex, and she liked that.

She got to bed around two in the morning and woke a little after ten. Her first thought was of Doug. Sometimes she saw herself as a painter married to a high-powered architect. When she felt focused and ambitious, she got into a rosy dream of a successful artistic career subsidized by an admiring husband. But this morning she had an uncomfortable visceral reaction to imagining their future together. The way her parents' marriage had turned out—her sculptor mother drinking herself to death while financially dependent on her alienated husband—was a cautionary tale. Even if she found work that she liked, maybe as a teacher, Doug would always be a towering presence. She lacked drive in comparison to him, and he had a willful, bossy streak that worried her. And then the sex—the sex was hit-or-miss. He always had his pleasure, but she didn't always get hers. If she had an orgasm, it was a happy accident, not the product of anything he did. After years of Anna's shy attempts to communicate her needs, he still didn't understand the way her body worked, and she'd given up trying to explain. Perhaps it was her fault; she was too inhibited to talk about sex.

She went downstairs and stuck her head into her father's office to say good morning. He was packing his briefcase because he went to the lab every day he could.

"Plans for today?" he asked.

"Going to hang out with Doug."

He nodded. "By the way, you may notice a difference here." He dropped his voice and nodded in the direction of her mother's backyard studio.

"What do you mean?"

"After I returned that letter to you, I decided to say something to her. Indirectly."

"Like what?"

"Very simply, I said she might want to watch herself when you were home."

"'Watch herself'? Is that how you put it?"

"She's actually able to control how much she drinks. She's not a typical alcoholic. Maybe she isn't an alcoholic at all."

"Uh, I don't know about that."

They heard the back door swing open and shut.

"I'm off," her father said.

As Carl slipped out without checking in with his wife, who entered the kitchen seconds later, Anna registered their dance of mutual avoidance. She wondered again, if she got that far with Doug, what they might be like together in twenty or thirty years. Fear grabbed her in the chest.

"I need a refill," her mother said, heading to the coffee machine. "Oh, this is sludge." As she moved closer, Anna caught her smell of garlic and tobacco but no alcohol. It was early yet. Or maybe, as her father had said, Linda was controlling herself.

"Let me make a new pot." Anna glanced at her sideways, trying to read her mood.

"And where was Robin yesterday? I don't understand why she didn't come if she wasn't going back to San Francisco for the holiday."

"She was with her new boyfriend and his family."

"Oh, the Michael guy?" Linda said. "Hmm. I was disappointed not to see her. And how am I going to report to Sarah?"

"Well, you'll have something to report because she and Michael are coming out for the day tomorrow—if that's okay with you."

"Of course it's okay. I love it when young people come to visit. They should stay over. They can have Evelyn's room."

"Thank you, Mom," Anna said.

"And you can smoke pot. You can do anything you want."

Anna raised her eyebrows at her mother. "You know I rarely use pot."

"But I'm sure Robin does."

"So we can smoke pot, and then you'll report it to Sarah?"

Linda ignored the question. "It's good for young people to have a day in the country," she said. She looked out the window toward her sculptor's studio. "Is there anything more beautiful than a bare tree against a winter sky?"

The air was cold and bracing, and Anna was happy to meet Doug on bicycle instead of by car. She loved the views from Crane Neck Road. Halfway along, she took her bike onto a wooded path that was a shortcut between one loop of the road and the next. The exercise was invigorating, and she arrived flushed and warm.

She and Doug had been meeting at the house for years. Who it belonged to and why it was abandoned were mysteries. It had probably been built in the 1920s or earlier, and everything about it was solid, so that even in its dilapidated condition, it felt sturdy and welcoming. Because it sat on several acres of secluded land, Anna could leave her bike unlocked by the entrance. As she put the kickstand down, a fantasy flashed through her head: she was about to have sex not with Doug but with a stranger, someone she'd met or known casually, the way Julia had done with the elevator man. Anna remembered the rugged, olive-skinned face

of the poet laureate at Thanksgiving dinner. The idea of having
sex with someone older, who might be sexually experienced and
know his way around a woman's body, turned her on.

Entering through the always unlocked front door, she found
Doug kneeling on the brick hearth in the living room, adding
kindling, and poking the fire. He had retrieved the two sleeping
bags they hid in a closet upstairs and unzipped them. Food and
wine could be seen in the open backpack by the worn love seat
facing the fireplace. The only piece of furniture in the room—
the couch—was large enough for preliminary petting but not for
the act itself.

"Hey," she said.

"Hello." He stood up to kiss her. Anna was tall, but Doug
was even taller. Their height and the way they'd towered over
their classmates had brought them together during their freshman year in high school. Only later did they discover they both
had artistic interests.

"How was your morning?" she asked.

"Good. I'm working on my applications."

"In the plural? I thought you were only applying to MIT."
She sat down on the couch.

"I'll probably, almost certainly get into MIT, but I'm applying to four other places as well, just to be safe." He sat down next
to her and went into the details, explaining the pros and cons of
each school. It was typical of him to begin a romantic interlude
with some practical life business, but he avoided talking about
the consequences for their relationship of the next academic step
he might make, and so did she.

"But enough of all that," he said. Doug grabbed the hem of
her sweater, which he pulled up over her head. They got down on
the blanket and began to make out. There were things about their
routine that had begun to wear on her. He seemed more interested
in being touched than in touching her, in being pleasured than

pleasuring her. There were times, and this was one of them, when he didn't seem to know where her clitoris was. Once again, it felt pointless to ask for what she needed. Anna tried to turn herself on by fantasizing about the poet laureate of Brooklyn, but the floor was hard and uncomfortable, so she went through the motions without satisfaction, hoping to satisfy at least some part of her need.

When Robin and Michael arrived on Saturday morning, they were greeted with a lunch spread of lox and bagels. In perpetual rebellion against duty and expectation, Linda wasn't about to do more. With Carl, Anna, and Doug, they were six around the big table. Linda had a little wine, but not too much. Anna was more embarrassed by how much her father ate. A big man with a big belly, he could easily consume three bagels at a sitting.

Toward the end of the meal, Linda made an announcement. "I'm taking my husband to dinner and the movies tonight, so you young people will have the house to yourselves and can have a party."

"Enough with the 'young people' thing, Mom."

"We're going to the movies?" Carl asked. "Is there a movie to go to?"

"In Port Jeff there's always something," Linda said.

The town had an art house movie theater with offerings that were offbeat or even risqué. It had dared to offer *M*A*S*H* and *Carnal Knowledge* when they came out.

"All right then," he said. "Under duress, I surrender to the idiocies of the day."

"We'll go out and come back quietly, like church mice, so you can drink and dance and smoke and have a ball." Linda stood up. "Just do the dishes. That would be nice."

The "young people" bundled up and took a walk out to Old Field Point, where a lighthouse sat on a promontory jutting out high above the water. Leaning against the metal fence that kept visitors from hurtling to their death, they gazed at the white-capped November sea. Then they went back to the house for the car and drove into downtown Setauket for groceries. They made pasta for dinner, drank wine, and told stories. When they settled by the fire in the living room afterward, Michael took out his pot pouch and rolled a joint. The four of them smoked, finishing off the wine.

"What? This house doesn't have a piano?" Michael said.

"I'm sure we can come up with something," Doug said. "Got an idea." He disappeared into the kitchen. A couple of minutes later, he was back with a tray, seven glasses filled with water to different heights, and a couple of spoons. "Go for it, maestro."

"Oh, thank God! Sound, music, self-expression!" Michael said. He began to fool around, creating a melody with the spoon and glasses.

Robin stood up. "Is there a radio? I need real music."

"You don't call this real music?" Michael asked.

"I want to dance. Anna!"

Anna tuned into the top hits station, and Robin extended a hand to Michael. "Dance with me."

"Men my height don't dance. Too august and majestic and all that."

"Oh, come on." Robin's hand continued to dangle out toward him.

"I make music. Music doesn't make me."

"What about you?" she asked Doug. "You're tall, but perhaps more daring?"

"Sure, but got to get my courage up," the cooperative fellow said. "One more toke." He took the joint from Anna. "You don't mind if I dance with your cousin, do you?" he asked her.

"Please, be my guest," Anna said.

"Don't Go Breaking My Heart" was on the radio as Doug

free-form danced with Robin. He was all elbows and spastic jerking while Robin moved like a ribbon, fluid and interconnected.

Anna and Michael watched from the couch. She felt his shoulder press against hers as he leaned in toward her. "God, he's an awful dancer," he said, "but a good sport, I have to say."

"That's the thing about Doug. He gets along with everyone," Anna said. His movements, progressively wilder, made her wince. "Jesus, I can't bear to watch this. Let's go do the dishes. Or make cocktails."

She got up, and Michael followed her into the kitchen.

"Where's the booze, and what are we going to make?" he asked.

"You're the cocktail man, I hear, so do what you like. Everything's in here." She opened the door to the walk-in pantry, and he stepped in.

"A Manhattan is usually a safe bet. Or what about—" He glanced back to the living room where Robin and Doug were whooping it up now as they danced, and he laughed. "A Hanky Panky? I bet your folks have the ingredients for that."

"A Hanky Panky?"

"Let's see, they've got gin, sweet vermouth . . . We just need some Fernet. Where might that be?" He ferreted through the bottles packed in tightly on the shelves. "Golly, your folks have a great collection."

Anna grabbed an ice tray and joined him in the pantry. "Once a week my mother calls her sister for a long-distance gossip session with cocktails."

"Gossiping about you and Robin, I assume."

"Yeah, and it's all lies and distortions, of course. One week they think we're brilliant and beautiful, and the next we're the ungrateful daughters in *King Lear*."

She handed him a cocktail shaker and watched him pour, mix, and shake.

"I don't think we've ever had a moment alone together for a real conversation, you and I," Michael said. "I want to know everything. I want the whole story."

"The whole story?"

"Everybody's got a story."

"I'm sure you've already heard mine from Robin."

"Yeah, I got her version, but not yours. I want it from the horse's mouth." He put the cocktail shaker down and, stepping toward her, took her face between his hands.

God, we're both stoned, she thought, and for a second she wondered whether he was going to kiss her then and there, in the seclusion of the pantry.

"But your mouth isn't at all horsey," he said. "On the contrary, it's quite human and very beautiful." He let her go. "Where are the glasses? Here, try this. And start talking."

Anna took a sip. "Yum. Okay, the story. My mother's an alcoholic. Maybe Robin told you that?"

"Yup, but not the details."

"You have to understand, I'm not talking about social drinking like we're doing now. It was all-the-time drinking, where she would get out of control and do and say terrible things."

"Physically violent?"

"Sometimes."

"I'm sorry."

"I threatened to end my relationship with her in a letter, but she never read it because my father intercepted it. But then he decided to speak to her and ask her to behave herself around me. And you saw, she was okay at dinner."

"As I understand it, your father basically lives at the lab," he said.

She nodded. "They don't have much of a marriage. He comforts himself with work—and food. She comforts herself with alcohol."

"A lot of women get crazy because they've ended up with men who aren't good enough for them."

"My father's a good guy. And a brilliant scientist. And I'm sure he's been a faithful husband."

"Men may be good guys, great breadwinners, smart, yada yada, but there's always a piece missing," Michael said. "And after a few decades of looking for that missing piece, the wives implode. Whence the necessity of cocktails—and the invention of Valium."

"A piece missing?"

"Yeah, because to turn a little boy into a man you have to cut out a piece of his heart."

"But I assume you're one of the rare men who doesn't have a piece missing?"

"On the contrary, I have plenty of pieces missing, but at least I try to show up."

"You didn't show up for a dance with Robin just now." Anna wanted to provoke him.

"I'll dance with you here if you like, to prove that I can." The radio was now playing "My Love," and, pulling her out of the pantry and into the kitchen, he wrapped his arms around her in an invitation to slow dance.

"Oh my!"

"The power of Paul."

"No, you're a flirt," she declared. "I suspected that about you."

"Nah. Not a flirt, just needy. And a lover of women."

Anna smiled at him. She knew now that he wouldn't kiss her, and she felt safe. He hugged her to him, and they swayed, and for a moment she was happy.

7

HARLEM
AFTERNOON

(Julia)

J ulia and Ben had their first extended separation at winter
break when he got on a plane to visit his parents in London, and she went home to Manhattan to spend the holiday with
hers. Being apart was painful for Julia and not only because they
had become symbiotic, seeing each other almost every day. Julia
wasn't happy about his plan to see his old girlfriend in Paris.

Ben had met Dominique years before when he'd gone to Paris
to study French. In an unguarded moment, he had described her
as "a free spirit and a real revolutionary," so that now Julia tortured
herself with thoughts about this mysterious Parisienne she imagined with silky hair and big silver earrings, miniskirts, and Italian
sandals. She consequently spent the first days of winter break
snacking on chocolate and making pathetic entries in her journal.
Fortunately, Michael called and suggested they get together.

"Come get me at my parents'. You can meet my brother, and
we'll go for a drink," he said.

Michael's father taught at Columbia University, which entitled him to one of its coveted prewar faculty apartments on West

End Avenue, between 116th and 117th Streets. Julia took the elevator up to the sixth floor and rang the bell.

Michael swung the door open. "Hello!"

He kissed Julia on the cheek as she stepped into the living room. The decor was casual and unpretentious: a couple of beat-up couches, a shiny grand piano, built-in bookcases, and a view of the Hudson and beyond. They were fortunate enough to have a view of the river, which had white peaks from the winter wind. Patches of snow glinted on both sides of the water, brightening the urban landscape.

"Nice apartment," Julia said. "And nice piano."

"My dad's."

"That's right. You mentioned he's a musicologist."

"A *distinguished* musicologist. Hey, Nick, come on out and meet someone."

Michael's brother came out of the kitchen and nodded at Julia. Younger than Michael, probably in his mid-twenties, Nick had the same height and big forehead but was slimmer through the body and fragile looking.

"This is Ben's girlfriend," Michael said to him.

Julia grimaced. "That's right, I'm 'Ben's girlfriend.'"

"Sorry!" Michael flushed. "Nick, this is Julia."

Nick stepped forward, then stopped just short of the doorjamb separating the dining alcove from the living room. "What are you guys up to today?"

"I thought I'd take her to the Peacock," Michael said.

"And visit Gladys?" Nick asked.

"Who's Gladys?" Julia asked.

"A very smart lady next door to the Peacock," Michael said. "You want to come?"

"Not really," Nick said.

Julia felt relieved he wasn't coming.

"Okay." Michael touched her arm. "Come on, let's go."

In the elevator Julia looked at him sideways, admiring his large, sculptural head and sensuous mouth. He was attractive although he hadn't shaved, and the collar of the shirt sticking out from his leather jacket was stained. *A complicated man and too old for me anyway*, she thought. He was five years older than Ben, who was five years older than she was. The math wasn't pretty, given that Michael was a graduate student.

"Where's the Peacock?"

"125th."

"Harlem?" She was surprised. In 1976, white people didn't go to Harlem to hang out.

"That make you nervous?"

"Of course not," she lied.

The walk away from the river and toward Broadway was uphill, a reminder that Manhattan was an island. Since Julia was sleeping with Michael's apartment mate, and Michael was sleeping with her cousin, conversation turned out not to be difficult despite their age difference. By the time they reached 120th, they were sharing stories about growing up in Manhattan and their favorite places, and school, of course.

"What did you do between college and graduate school?" Julia asked.

"I was a working musician. I gave lessons and played gigs. Honestly, I'm not sure what I'm doing back in school."

"Following in your father's footsteps?"

"Sort of. Maybe not the smartest thing. I like giving private lessons, but an academic career like my dad has . . . I'm not sure I'm cut out for it. But once I started composing, it seemed like the logical thing to try—now this bar we're going to, you'll like it."

"And who's this Gladys?" she asked as they approached 123rd, the dividing line between the white and Black sections of town.

"A kind of lay minister and therapist. You'll see. But first let's have a drink and decide what we want to ask her."

Julia had seen the eastern section of Harlem from the Long Island Railroad on her way to visit family. The train passed over the eastern and poorest areas, and she had always reacted to the broken windows, garbage-filled lots, and graffiti with a mixture of compassion and horror. She thought of Harlem as a sad and dangerous place, and so was surprised, when they reached Broadway and 125th, to find it bustling with commercial activity. It was Saturday, and people were milling in and out of grocery stores and lunch spots. Shops spilled out onto the sidewalks with cheap wares in boxes on folding tables: sunglasses, scarves, hats. The bazaar atmosphere was fun to behold. Drawn by the burgundy color of a beret, Julia stopped to look at it.

The Black shopkeeper gave her a big smile. "Three dollars," he said.

"Maybe on the way back," she replied, not being an impulsive buyer.

"Here's the Peacock," Michael said.

They went down five steps and stepped into a small, dimly lit bar. Julia and Michael were the only white people there. Two Black ladies in wide-brimmed Sunday hats, one a bright purple, the other bright red, sat at a little table by the wall. A couple of older guys were reading their respective newspapers at the far end of the bar. Two couples at a square table were having fancy-looking cocktails in coupe glasses.

"Beer?" Michael asked. Julia nodded. He sat down at the bar, and she took the stool next to him.

"You come to Harlem a lot?" she asked him.

"Not so much anymore, but I did when I was in high school and wanted a joint—or worse."

"You did a lot of drugs?"

"Mostly dope, but also some hard stuff. It was Gladys who helped me stop. At least the hard stuff. As you know, I still like my weed."

"How did she get you to stop?"

"This is the story. My kid brother started doing heroin at fifteen, and I was the first one to find out." The corners of his mouth turned down. "I realized it was largely my fault; I'd been setting a bad example for him. My parents weren't getting along at the time—in fact, they were talking about separating—so it was up to me to become my brother's keeper because no one else was going to do it. It was Gladys who made me see that." Michael pulled out a pack of cigarettes and lit one. "Maybe one day I'll ask her to help me give up cigarettes and weed too."

"And Nick?"

"I stayed with him whenever I could: moved into his bedroom, followed him everywhere." He laughed. "I'd frisk him before he went into the bathroom and check the size of his pupils after school."

Julia took a sip of her beer and began to relax. Nobody in the bar seemed to mind their white presence, so why should she be uptight about it?

"Are you still your brother's keeper?" she asked.

"Yes, but now he's mine too."

"I see."

"Now let's get down to the business at hand, Jul. What are we going to ask Gladys?"

She registered the "Jul." It was the first time he'd used a nickname for her, and she liked the intimacy it implied.

"I'm not sure."

"You know that last time you came over before Ben left, I couldn't help overhearing the two of you having a 'discussion.'"

"Did you know he has a girlfriend or an ex-girlfriend in Paris?"

"Yeah, Dominique."

"That 'discussion' happened when I found a picture of her in his wallet. I knew she existed, but I was surprised he was still carrying her photo around."

"You're a snoop then?" Michael chuckled.

"Not usually, but I felt something was up. He was being so quiet about his plans." Tears welled up in her eyes. "There I was feeling so in love and romantic about him—my first boyfriend, finally, yay!" Julia rolled her eyes in self-derision. "And there he was, planning a reunion with his ex."

"Maybe planning to see her, but not necessarily a 'reunion.' Hey, Jul, you may be working yourself up over nothing."

"What do you know about her?"

"Not much, really. But the fact that he's still in touch with her suggests he's a person capable of loyalty. That's a positive, don't you think?"

Julia sighed. "I guess. I hadn't thought of it that way. I was just wishing he wasn't going to meet her. He could have invited me to go home with him instead."

"Hey, you guys got together only a month ago!" he reminded her. "And as far as Dominique goes, whatever their tie is, it wasn't strong enough to keep him in Europe. He chose to do graduate school here."

"He could still go back. To London. Or Europe. And her."

"So you want to ask Gladys something about Dominique? Like whether she's a threat?"

"That sounds right." Julia looked at him. "And what about you? What's your question?"

"Your cousin . . ." Michael shook his head. "Robin is one complicated gal. I could ask a dozen questions about her. To start with, why can't she untangle herself from that Stephanie woman in Boston? Maybe she's really gay, not bi."

"Or maybe that relationship was an experiment. A women's college thing."

He shook his head. "I'm not sure about that. I think she likes sex with men, but she doesn't like men as a—as a 'species.' Like, the act is fun, but men are, emotionally, not to her taste."

"I don't know."

"I thought you guys were close?" he asked.

"Sort of, but not really. She was always like a big sister to me, telling me what to do, but a little remote."

"And there I was hoping for some inside information!" He grinned.

"And there I was thinking you just wanted to hang out and be friends!" She grinned back.

"Hey, Jul, of course I want to be friends."

The conversation went in another direction as they finished their beers. Michael put some dollars on the counter.

"Time to go see Gladys," he said.

In a gentlemanly gesture that surprised her, coming from such an informal, messy guy, he cupped her elbow as they went up the stairs. They walked down the street until he stopped in front of a pink neon sign that read "Psychic."

She balked. "Michael! This is ridiculous!"

"Trust me, she's a Harlem treasure and a fount of wisdom."

"I don't know."

"Jul!"

"Well, okay."

He rang the bell. A portly Black woman in African robes and headdress opened the door. Her face lit up. "Mike, baby doll! How ya doing? Home for Christmas? Tell me, tell me." They exchanged a big hug.

"Gladys, you look like a million bucks. This is Julia, my best friend's girl."

"Now, you watch your step with that one, boy," she laughed.

"It's not what you think," he said.

"I was kidding," she said. "This is Gladys, remember. I know what's going on. You both have love problems, you want advice, you're hoping for a two-for-the-price-of-one Christmas special, ain't you, boy?"

"You read my mind."

"That's my business, all right."

Julia took in the photo portraits on the wall, some of them signed, the shaggy gold carpet, and an Impressionistic painting of the African savanna. They sat down behind a little table with several tarot decks on it.

"You read cards?" Julia asked.

"The cards are to impress first-time customers. But with people who know and trust me, I don't do that racket. All I need is a hand. Give me your hand, girl."

Julia placed her slim, pale hand in Gladys's large, dark palm. There was silence for several moments.

"It's strange. You're twenty or twenty-one, but you seem like you're twenty-five, and your fella is twenty-five or so and seems like he's a kid of twenty."

Julia said nothing.

"I believe," Gladys continued, becoming more formal and oratorical as inspiration mounted, "you have not studied his character sufficiently. And the reason you have not done this is that he is a difficult one to understand, his character not yet being formed. He is a serious man and will have success in what he does, but this may be as much of a burden as a boon to you. You must be careful. This man you may decide to marry one day will not be the same as the one you met. He may be a less exciting man, too involved in his work, and not as interested in life as you think he is. And you"—she stopped, looking up from Julia's hand into her eyes—"you are a poet who needs to be out and about in the world, collecting feelings and impressions. And he may end up not liking your scribbling, because he is a competitive gentleman, and writing poetry is one thing he cannot do."

Julia glanced at Michael. "Did you tell her I write poetry? Did you tell her about Ben?"

Michael shook his head. "I haven't seen her since last summer."

Julia looked back at Gladys. "How do you know all this?"

Gladys sighed. "Your face, your fingers, your eyes . . ."

"You don't think Ben's the man for me, then?"

"I don't know 'cause I don't know what he's gonna turn into," Glady said, her speech and manner returning to earth. "It could go either way. But be careful—he's a fella who loves books more than anything. You could get awful tired competing with those books."

"Right now it's a woman in Paris I'm competing with, not books. I want to know whether I should worry about her."

Gladys shrugged. "Another woman is nothing compared to a pile of books."

Perplexed, Julia frowned.

"You gotta ride the river, honey. That's all I can tell you now."

"But you're saying I don't have to worry about the woman in Paris?"

"Nah, your fella's done with her. Or will be by the time he gets back. He hit the jackpot with you, and he's realizing it right now."

Gladys shifted her gaze to Michael. "Your turn, honey." She put her hand out, and he placed his in hers, palm up.

"The lady you're going with is a little wild. And wild isn't what you need. Wild isn't what you want. What you want is love. What you need is love. Don't waste your time on it if it ain't love."

"I hear ya," he said.

"And let me tell you why you shouldn't waste your time. You shouldn't waste your time because your heart gets broken either way, my friend, either way. Every time you take into your bed a lady who's not the right lady, a little bit more gets chipped away from that heart of yours. Because you're a man as deep as the ocean. Take my advice and find yourself a woman that deep, won't you, Mike? Stop wasting your time."

"I hear ya." Michael looked drawn and gray.

He withdrew his hand, but Gladys took it back and reached for Julia's. She joined them together. "You two will be great friends, and you must support each other through what is to come."

She released their hands, and Julia and Michael studied each other.

"Still twenty bucks?" Michael asked Gladys.

"Same price for you till the end of time."

He placed a twenty-dollar bill on the table, and they hugged. Gladys gave him a hard look. "You still clean, Mike?"

"As a whistle. Except for weed."

"You watch out for Mary Jane. Both a saint and a whore, that plant." She let go of him. "Tell your little brother to stop by."

"Will do."

"You come again soon," Gladys said. She walked them to the door where she stopped, put her hands on Julia's arms, and closed her eyes. "God bless you." Then she turned to Michael and did the same.

Julia and Michael went up the half flight of stairs back to the street. The workday was over, and the streets were crowded with people going home.

"Did you feel that? A blessing from Gladys is a powerful thing," Michael said.

"Yeah, I'm all tingly," Julia said, "but Jesus, I thought people paid fortune tellers to say nice things to them. That was really depressing."

"It was, wasn't it? But she speaks the truth every time. I've known her for fifteen years, and she's always right on target."

"Jesus," Julia repeated.

"Need another drink?"

"You bet I do," she said.

"Here," he said. "Take my arm."

She passed her arm through his, and they headed, a little dazed, back to the Peacock.

8

THE BLUE HOUR

(Ben)

I t was Friday evening in London, and the Shabbat candles were on the table ready to be lit.

Ben's mother carried in a fragrant casserole of lamb stewed with carrots and prunes.

"Call your father," she said. "He's in his study."

Solomon was a jeweler, a traditionally Jewish profession in London as elsewhere. Ben was grateful that his older brother was following in his father's footsteps, for it relieved him of any sense of pressure to do the same. Still, it hung there as an undesirable alternative: if Ben didn't get an academic job, or if he got one but didn't publish enough to get tenure and job security, he could always return home and enter the family business. The possibility of landing in such a safety net was terrifying; although he respected the handing down of a trade from one generation to the next, Ben couldn't imagine spending his life bent over jewelry with a monocle on his forehead.

Solomon had learned the jewelry business from his father, who had learned it from his father, and so forth, back several centuries. To fiddle with a chain or set a diamond was mindless work for him. But he loved watches, especially antique ones, and had his own collection, which he tended to in a little room in the back of the house. Not wanting to disturb him, Ben stood silently at the threshold.

"I'll be there in a minute," Solomon said, bent over a gold pocket watch.

It would just be the three of them at dinner. Normally Ben's older brother came for Shabbat with his wife, but she'd just had her first baby, and they were staying close to home.

When Ben's father came to the dinner table, his mother lit the candles, saying the prayers. Ben's faith had been challenged while reading Sartre and Camus, and he now had, around all things Jewish, a reaction of combined attraction and aversion. His affection for tradition alternated with a contempt for superstition in ever-changing proportions. He wondered whether Julia's family was observant. American Jews were a complicated lot, and New York ones another species altogether. It was within his power to shape his future, but a vagueness hung around his desires and direction. However, the time was coming for him to pick a mate for life, and whatever kind of Jew Julia was, she was a definite possibility.

When he had arrived the previous night, his parents had made small talk at the table about their new grandchild. Tonight Ben expected to be interrogated about his professional plans.

Sure enough, as Ben wiped his plate clean with a chunk of challah, his father asked, "Where do you see your future? You know we'd love it if you came back to London, but we will respect your decision, whatever it is."

Although Ben didn't feel bad about not going into his father's business, guilt came up around the idea of staying in the United States and not being there for his parents. "Being there" was a virtue, like honesty, fidelity, and generosity. But he was an ambitious young man, set on success.

"I'm going to try to get a job in the States. It's a better career path. And . . . I think the quality of education there is higher."

"That's something coming from an Oxford graduate!" his father said.

"The British tutorial system can't compete with the richness of the classroom experience in the States—"

"We sent you to Oxford for nothing, then?"

"That's not what I said. I loved Oxford, you know that."

Always the peacemaker, his mother changed the subject. "And how does Dominique fit into your plans?"

Ben's parents loved his Parisian ex-girlfriend. He had brought her home several times, and she had made a favorable impression. She and Ben were no longer officially together, but when he went to France, he still stayed with her and they had sex. Sometimes he still caught himself having a romantic fantasy about teaching English in Paris and living with her. But she had never participated in his fantasies. Besides, Julia was now in the picture. He couldn't explain all this to his parents.

"I'm trying to focus on my career these days," he said.

"But I thought you were going to Paris to visit her," his mother said.

"I am. But I'm not making life plans around her." Saying less was better than saying more.

"I don't understand your generation," his mother replied.

"I'm not asking you to understand it," Ben said, and cleared the table.

Doing the dishes, he remembered Mrs. X, the married woman who had initiated him when he was seventeen. The flashy wife of a friend of his father's, she was a rebellious older woman who wanted to take advantage of the sexual revolution before it was too late. At the time, he'd considered himself lucky to be seduced by such a gorgeous, sexually expert creature who explained women's mysteries to him. Now the episode seemed sordid, like something out of *The Graduate*, but without the saving irony you can milk out of California, swimming pools, and plastics. Doubling his shame was the suspicion that his parents had figured out he was having an affair with her. At Oxford a year later, he had taken up with Clara, whom they had disapproved of because she was Christian. It was understandable why they'd been so relieved and excited when he'd introduced them to Dominique. Paris wasn't that far away, and a Jewish Frenchwoman would be a lovely addition to the family. Julia, on the other hand, would distress them, for life with her would raise the possibility of expatriation.

His mother came into the kitchen and kissed him on the cheek. "We do want to be modern and support you in whatever you do," she said.

"I appreciate that," he said.

He read John Donne on the train to Paris, then some modern poetry. He stopped reading on the ferry across the Channel, then returned to it on the train on the French side. His PhD orals, coming up in the spring, were on his mind. If he passed them successfully, he could move on to writing his doctoral dissertation. With a degree from Yale, he was confident about getting a good job.

His anxiety about his exams and hopes for the future receded as the train pulled into the Gare du Nord. He got off and headed toward the metro that would take him to Dominique's street in the Latin Quarter. He loved Europe, the easy moving from one country to the next, the mixing of cultures and languages, the cross-fertilizations. Arriving in Paris, he was relieved to leave the ugliness of London behind. Everything here filled him with ecstasy—the slightly burnt smell of the rubber tires in the metro, the high sound of the horn as the cars approached the platform, and the exit into the winding streets of Dominique's neighborhood. In the 1970s, the prewar coats of paint on the building fronts were cracking and flaking off; for Ben, the shards of peeling paint that flapped and fluttered in the breeze were ruffles, an additional, charming ornament.

He hoped to share all of it with Julia someday. Of course, if he made his life in the States, he wouldn't be able to go to Paris as easily or often. The thought of such a geographical divorce distressed him as he reached Dominique's building.

The narrow spiral staircase hugged him gently as he climbed to her apartment on the top floor. When Dominique opened the door, he was struck yet again by her soft, sensual mouth. Her hair was brown like Julia's but had some Jewish frizz and wayward bangs that hung a bit below the eyebrows. She wore a long wool skirt and a brown-and-white scarf with a key pattern. He noted a wool bag with the same color scheme and pattern hanging from the back of a chair. The bag and the scarf looked Greek; maybe she had picked them up in Greece on a trip with a lover. The curtains were drawn and the little electric heater was going, so he knew she was in the mood. She grabbed him and they started to kiss. As he unwound the scarf from her neck, he reminded himself that their lives were separate now. There was no reason why she shouldn't go to Greece with another guy. Maybe the guy was Greek. How would he feel about that? Or maybe she'd gone there for research. Because she was a student in classics, Rome had long been a second home to her, and Athens might now be a third. Thankfully, once they were in bed, he forgot about the scarf and the bag and the hypothetical Greek lover.

A Parisian garret was not always the most comfortable place for lovers. The head of the bed was right under the window, and when a December draft came in through the casement, stirring the curtains, they pulled the covers up over their shoulders. Their sex was lovely, weaving together, as it always had, different acts and positions, some playful conversation, and sweet epithets.

"*Raconte-moi tout*," she said afterward. ("Tell me everything.") They spoke mostly in French. Ben's French wasn't bad;

he'd learned it from her, years ago. "I bet you have a new girl-friend. You must have an American girlfriend by now."

"And you, you must have a Greek lover," he said. "Where else would you have gotten that scarf and bag?"

She let out a high peal of laughter. "I got them on the Boul' Mich," she said, referring to the main drag through the Latin Quarter where people, mostly from Africa, sold cheap goods from sidewalk stands. Her laugh and her voice, like that of many Frenchwomen, had a slightly higher pitch than that of the average British or American woman. It wasn't a linguistic inflection, Ben had concluded after years of reflection on the topic, but rather a gendered one, a sign of enhanced, practiced femininity.

"I don't believe you," he said.

They fenced around it for a moment until she confessed she did have a new boyfriend, and he was Spanish, not Greek, and they were going back and forth between Madrid and Paris. Once she had delivered the whole story, it was his turn, and he told her about Julia.

"It just started a few weeks ago," he began, and she listened as a friend would.

They could share things like that and not be jealous. It was wonderful, if a bit unsettling.

Later, after dinner in a little bistro, they made love again, and Ben got into a sleeping position with his arm around Domi-nique's waist. She was slender, as slender as Julia was, but more relaxed sexually. In time, he imagined, Julia would be as easy. He was patient and enjoyed the fantasy of being Julia's teacher in as well as out of bed. He could even teach her to do that thing Dominique did with her hips when she was on top—and there he stopped himself. He didn't like himself when he compared his lovers. There was something crass about it, internally dishonor-able. Each relationship should have its own "I" and "Thou," as in

Martin Buber's relationship with God. In this moment, he was with Dominique. At least he wanted to be. He struggled as he tried to put Julia away in a mental glass cabinet until he finally fell asleep.

When he woke up in the morning, he caressed Dominique's sleeping face and then got up to go to the bathroom. Wanting to take in the view of the city's pearl and gray rooftops, he opened the curtain a little, revealing on the windowsill over the bed a display that hadn't been there the previous summer: a dozen perfume bottles, some empty, some not. The ones with crystal cuts reflected the rays of sun coming in through the window, casting dots of colored light on the walls. Third from the right was a bottle of L'Heure Bleue that he'd given her in the spring of 1970, at the end of his year in Paris. He remembered going into Guerlain and buying it for her. He'd been nineteen and had never been in a *parfumerie* before, and his heart had beat fast on entering the fancy shop. The elegant saleswoman had initially been (as most were in those days) arrogant and cold. But once she understood that he was motivated to drain his student bank account by a *passion véritable*, she mellowed and gave him the tour of labels and scents. He bought the bottle and presented it to Dominique like a vassal bringing the flag of a conquered country to his queen. To see the bottle now, so many years later, empty and surrounded by others, was a blow to more than his ego. He'd felt that his relationship with Dominique was, unlike his experience with Mrs. X, "special." Now he realized it was simply one in a series. A melancholy mood came over him as he sat down on the bed, transfixed by the glass bottles glinting in the morning light. He shivered and got back under the covers with her.

He spent a couple of days in Paris with Dominique. They took walks, went to a museum, and visited old friends. Paris around Christmas was festive, even if you were Jewish and the damp cold sank into your bones. The boulangeries had beautiful displays of tiny holiday pastries, and strings of lights twinkled through the windows of neighboring apartments. When they stepped into bookstores, Ben browsed modern French poetry, Dominique feminist literature. He had always loved the opposites in her: how she reached back in time studying ancient languages yet was so progressive in her social and political views, heading toward a better future. She'd been on the barricades in the student protests of 1968 and was still on them now, at least intellectually. All this was stimulating and enjoyable, and Ben acted like his usual self, but inside something had shifted. When he was in Dominique's apartment, his eye kept going back to the perfume bottles. He wondered whether she'd put them out on purpose for his visit, as a message or signal. Perhaps she sensed that he'd never completely given up his romantic fantasies about her, and this was her way of putting a stop to them. It was, as rejections go, as subtle as you could get.

On his last day she accompanied him, as she had many times before, to the Gare du Nord to say goodbye. As they stood on the *quai* talking, their breath made clouds in the bitingly cold air.

"Do you think you'll come next summer?" she asked.

They had left the question of when they'd see each other again until the very last moment.

"I don't know," he said. "It depends . . . on what happens with school and . . . with Julia."

Dominique nodded. His saying Julia's name in the context of trips and calendars made her real

"Of course, if you bring her to Paris, I'd love to meet her." She had switched to English, which was a signal of distancing. "But who knows, I might be in Madrid for the summer, or in Grèce."

"Greece," he corrected, and took hold of the Greek scarf wound around her neck to pull her closer for one last kiss.

"Goodbye, Dominique."

"*Au revoir, mon ami.*"

The trip back to London was one long processing of their goodbye. As the train pulled across northern France, Ben felt miserable, then a little better crossing the Channel, with some guilt toward Julia. He praised her to himself—how straightforward she was and unafraid of being in love, how she saw the poetry in little things and made him see it too. By the time the train approached London in the violet-blue winter dusk, he was missing her eyes, voice, and flesh with desperate yearning; he needed to talk to her as soon as possible. He took out John Donne and read one of the love poems, mentally dedicating it to her.

He went to the back room of his parents' apartment for privacy. In 1976, a transatlantic call, with its disembodied voices, static, and muffling whooshes, was a poetic act. A longing heart reaching across an ocean comes into self-knowledge. Ben's feelings for Julia were clearer, more intense. He now knew.

"I miss you," he said.

"I miss you too," Julia said. "How was Paris?"

"Paris was amazing, as it always is. I want to take you there and enjoy it with you."

"I'd love to visit Paris with you."

"You'll come to London," he said, "and meet my family, then we'll go over together."

"That sounds like a great plan."

There was more static, a click, and a bleep.

"You're the real thing," he said. "And I can't wait to see you again." Now he was on a roll. "I made a mistake. I should have invited you home with me for the holidays. I'm so sorry I didn't. You have to forgive me. I'm kind of slow sometimes."

"It's okay," she said. "We haven't been together long. I wasn't expecting it."

"You're the real thing," he repeated. "You're the one."

"I know," she said. "I feel that way too."

His heart was beating with joy and a bit of fear after he hung up. Decisiveness granted him strength. Ben went into the dining room, where his father was reading the paper and his mother was setting the table for dinner.

"I need to tell you something," he said. They stopped what they were doing and gave him their full attention. "I have an American girlfriend, and her name is Julia. I'm going to stay in the States and make my life with her."

9

DOG
ON A BEACH

(Robin)

In the 1970s, California was crazier than the rest of the country—or ahead of it, depending on how you look at things—but still clean and uncrowded compared to the East Coast. Robin's family lived on the edge of Nob Hill in San Francisco, where they'd bought a three-story Victorian after leaving Los Angeles ten years before. Robin's dad had fallen out with his brother Gabe there—the uncle who had molested her in her childhood—and her mom had shocked and alienated their Reform synagogue (and her husband) by going to services braless, with her nipples visible through her chiffon blouse. Sarah had been a hippie back then, but after moving north, she'd reinvented herself as a proper lady to save her marriage. Despite her family's difficult history, Robin enjoyed coming home, mostly because of her grandmother Iris, who had the ground-floor apartment opening onto a small backyard garden. Her parents resided above, with the living area and master bedroom on the second floor, and a couple of extra bedrooms, including Robin's, on the third.

When Robin was home, she had breakfast with Iris. Her

grandmother was used to a modest meal—strong black coffee, stewed prunes, and oatmeal—but she put out coffee cake when Robin came. A fine-looking woman of almost eighty, she liked to wear dresses and heavy gold jewelry that she'd either received from a lover or bought with the money her husband had left her. Men were generous with her, and she with them. In exchange for their gifts of flowers, jewelry, and meals out, she made stuffed cabbage, gave massages, and did a little ironing. Sometimes, if Robin went downstairs early, she would be treated to the sight of Iris in a stretchy white corset and girdle, doing her morning neck and shoulder rolls. This morning, however, she was already at the breakfast table, wearing a tweed dress and a wool jacket with short sleeves that revealed the big gold bangles on her arms.

"I want to know everything," Iris said, cutting Robin a piece of cake. "First, how's school?"

"School is so-so," Robin said. "Actually, I don't like it, and I'm applying to a more progressive school here." She'd started filling out the forms on the little desk in her bedroom upstairs. "It's called CIIS—California Institute of Integral Studies. They have a doctoral program in consciousness studies." She always wanted to share things with her grandmother, even things an older woman might not understand.

"Consciousness studies. Okay." Iris made a point of being open-minded. "That sounds more like philosophy than psychology."

"It's a blend of both and more, including spirituality. I don't like the approach at Yale, studying rats and running experiments on students. And there's this thinking now called behaviorism that drives me nuts."

"So you're going to pass up an Ivy League doctorate to try something different. You are a California girl, after all." Iris chuckled. When Robin didn't respond, she continued, more serious, "Are you sure about this? After only a few months at Yale, you're ready to leave?"

"I don't know. I want to keep my options open."

"Your mother was so proud when you got in there. A daughter with a PhD from Yale—now *that* would be a dream come true for her."

"You're not telling me anything I don't know," Robin said, dropping her voice. "Let's face it, she's a snob." Her mother had become a social climber who always wanted more distinction and prestige. In high school, Robin had responded to the constant push to achieve by working hard, then playing hard with pot, parties, and a couple of LSD trips for perspective. In college, she'd settled down a bit, but made a point of getting to all her classes fifteen minutes late.

"That can be a good thing, you know," Iris said. "Wanting your family to shine, what's wrong with that? But tell me more. Have you made any ties there yet? Met anyone special?"

"I'm seeing a graduate student named Michael. But I don't know yet if he'll be 'special.'" Robin had never told her grandmother about her affairs with women, but she could tell her about men, knowing that nothing would be reported upstairs. "There's something a little remote about him."

"Then you shouldn't get too attached."

"I'm trying not to, but I don't know that I'm succeeding."

"Is he also in psychology?" Iris asked.

"No, music."

"Like the guy you were seeing last summer?"

"Theo? Not exactly. Theo's a rock musician. He wouldn't be caught dead *studying* it academically. Michael is more intellectual. Into jazz and classical composition."

"You like musicians."

Robin shrugged. "I don't know. In any case, I doubt either of these guys is going to be around for long."

"You never know, and you have to keep trying," Iris said. "If you're not completely happy with someone, you try till you can't anymore, then you move on." Her face, though lined, had the animation of someone with a young soul. "I've moved on."

"No more Bert?" Robin asked, referring to her grandmother's last boyfriend. She wondered whether Iris had sex with her elderly lovers or whether her relationships were more platonic.

"No more Bert. He didn't treat me right. He wasn't . . ." She paused. "Courtly."

"Courtly? You mean courteous?"

"I mean, I want a man to worship me. Otherwise, why bother? I can go play canasta with the girls." Iris laughed. "But this new one I met in September, he worships me. His name is Andy."

"I'm glad, Iry," Robin said, using the nickname she and her cousins had invented when they were little.

"He's a banker or something and plays golf, which I don't understand, but otherwise we're a match. He likes historical novels, and we read the same books at the same time." She glowed.

"You get clear so quickly."

"That comes with age and experience."

"I guess I'll have to make a decision about Michael at some point," Robin said.

"But what about Theo? Are you going to see him while you're home?"

"He's supposed to call this morning."

"Who might call?" Her mother's voice floated down the stairs.

"Someone," Robin said, vexed and irritable.

Sarah, wearing a sleeveless sheath dress, came in and sat down at the breakfast table. "I don't know why the fuck you can tell your grandmother things and not me."

"Why don't you relax?" Iris said. "She'll tell you in due time."

Robin set her jaw. "I don't tell you things because if I do, it becomes cocktail gossip. 'Robin this, Robin that.' Like high school."

"First of all, that's not true. Well, maybe a little bit, with Linda. She's my sister. But my friends aren't like that. Secondly, I can't believe it—you've only been home twenty-four hours and you're already picking a fight with me." Sarah stood up, smoothing her dress. "I don't need this." She headed back upstairs.

Robin took a sip of coffee. "I'm going to heat this up." She went to the stove and added a dash from the aluminum percolator while Iris ate her prunes and stared at the newspaper.

"You need to go upstairs and fix this," Iris said calmly.

"I guess."

"Come, give me a kiss."

Robin did as she was told.

"About your love life—nothing wrong with seeing two guys at once," Iris said. "Do some sampling, then choose."

"I just don't want things to get too complicated. Theo has a girlfriend, and I have Michael."

"Sometimes things have to get complicated before they get simple again."

"Maybe you're right."

Robin had a knot in her stomach as she went upstairs to apologize. She found her mother on the living room couch, smoking a cigarette and doing the crossword puzzle, her slim legs in nude stockings crossed daintily at the ankle. It was hard to believe that ten years earlier, she had been a scandalous object of gossip, but perhaps the women in her family had some gene for dissimulation and self-reinvention. If her grandmother had evolved from a shtetl peasant to a Nob Hill grand dame, why shouldn't her mother go from rebel to conformist? Sarah, who had once had the same curly Jewish hair as her daughter, now even went so far as to straighten it and lighten the color a shade. *All she needs is a perfume called Eau de WASP*, Robin thought. Sometimes she loathed her mother, but apology was the path of least resistance.

"Sorry, Mom," Robin said.

"All right," came the dry answer. *Scratch, scratch* went the pencil on the newspaper.

Robin stood, waiting for more.

Her mother finally looked up. "Just so you know, regarding your grandmother's most recent pick—I don't approve."

Taking in this gesture toward normal conversation, Robin sat down on the opposite couch. "You mean Andy?"

Sarah nodded. "When he comes over, it's like he's casing the joint to see if we're good enough for him. As though we might not be." She waved her hand at the living room decorated with antiques and mid-century furniture in an eclectic mix ahead of the times. On the walls, large modern canvases hung in expensive-looking frames. Their house and its art collection were her life's work. "He's a banker or something and thinks he's better than us."

"Iry didn't make him sound that way."

"Your grandmother is truly blind when she's in love. Like she's learned nothing in eighty years."

The phone rang, and Sarah answered it. "Yes, she's right here." She handed the receiver to Robin.

It was Theo. Because the receiver was corded, Robin couldn't take it to a private place.

"Hey," he said. "You with your mom?"

"Yeah."

"You want to meet?"

"Yeah." She said "yeah" repeatedly to tease her mother, who would wonder what she was saying yes to.

"Meet on the beach at the end of Judah Street?"

"That would work. I can be there in a half hour."

"Can't wait," Theo said. "We won't be far from my new place."

"Great."

Robin hung up. Her mother stared at her.

"You think you're so smart?" Sarah said. "You and Iris both

think you're so smart." She threw her chin upward in a gesture that felt like an insult, then picked up her crossword puzzle again.

Robin went upstairs to get an extra sweater and a hat. It was cold and damp out, and she wanted to be warmly dressed for the beach. Looking out the window, she had a partial view of San Francisco, houses and small buildings that went up and down the hills along streets most often set at right angles, but not always; the city had a layout with the lines of plaid and occasional forays into paisley. It would take her twenty minutes to get to the beach. She was curious to see Theo's new place, though not sure about going to bed with him. She wanted to but was confused by her involvement with Michael. She was heading toward the front door when she heard Iris calling from downstairs.

"Robin, come back down, please."

"Yeah?" Robin asked when she reached the lower floor.

"Where does he live?"

"Sunset," Robin said.

"Would you mind swinging by the Russian grocery and bringing back some rye bread and piroshki?"

"Of course not."

"Come here."

Iris kissed her on the lips, Russian style. "Have fun," she said with a twinkle in her eye. Robin shrugged. "You come from a long line of wild women," Iris continued. "Do what you want, without guilt or afterthought."

"It makes for agitation," Robin said.

"Oh, you can lead a tidy little life if you like and die with a suitcase full of regrets."

"I could have regrets either way."

"Honey, there's nothing wrong with having secrets. You don't have to tell Michael a thing. All this openness stuff that started in the sixties, it's a fad."

Robin hugged her again. She knew that Iris usually saw only

one man at a time, but sometimes there had been two. Iris had, since her husband's death, conducted her love life with appetite and no shame, offering Robin a precedent that might be followed. And Robin was grateful for her grandmother's support as she struggled with an unresolvable contradiction. Deep down she had the conventional desire for a stable committed relationship, but being both restless and bisexual, she couldn't imagine committing to a single partner for life.

She sighed as she stepped out into the street and into the car. It was best to stay in the moment and not think about the future too much. She was excited about seeing Theo, and the song he'd written for her went through her head again.

Crazy free crazy
Like a dog on a beach
Crazy free

She drove west, humming to herself and thinking about his curly blond hair.

Robin parked by the beach and went down the stairs. A low blanket of fog over the water had spots of blue sky. A few people were out, some jogging, others walking dogs. Her senses were sharp with anticipation. When she'd been with Theo the previous summer, she'd enjoyed his rock musician vibe, crazy outfits, and sense of humor. He was also affectionate; there was something juicy and nourishing about his hugs. As her eye scanned the beach looking for him, she realized how Michael's minimal expressions of affection had left her wanting more.

She saw a man down the beach in a light-blue puffer jacket and bright-orange sneakers. It was Theo, and he had a big husky with him. They started running toward her.

Theo came up to her and took her in his arms. They kissed, and he tasted good. She nestled her nose in his neck, finding a spot of warm skin inside the collar of his parka. He put his hand on her face, and the cold wind made the warm touch of his hand doubly delicious. The dog barked and wagged its tail as it leapt wildly around them.

"Who's this?" she asked.

"Lobo," Theo said. "I found him. Or he found me." He got on his knees and scratched Lobo's neck, and Robin kneeled next to him. "After writing that damn song for you, I got obsessed with the idea of getting a dog, and then this fella showed up, homeless, in my neighborhood, and I couldn't find the owner and he was in pretty bad shape, so what was I supposed to do?" The dog licked his face gratefully.

"It looks like you both lucked out," Robin said.

"I sure did," Theo said. He let go of the dog and grabbed Robin and wrestled her down onto the sand, where they kissed and rolled around as the dog went back to jumping and barking joyfully around them.

When they got back to his apartment, Theo settled Lobo on a dog bed outside the bedroom.

"What a wonderful dog you are. Yeah, you really are."

What a loving guy. One day he'll make a great father, Robin thought as he took her hand and led her into his room.

"I like your new place," she said. Two guitars, one electric and the other acoustic, stood propped up in their stands between an amplifier and a dresser, and a poster of the Rolling Stones and a Matisse reproduction hung on the walls.

"You cold? You want some tea? Or something stronger? I got tequila." He bent over to fiddle with the baseboard heater.

"Nothing now. Tequila later."

They were, she thought as they came together, a perfect fit, equally sexual and affectionate, fully in the present without demand or expectation.

He was very oral and loved to tease and please her, building and pacing her arousal until she would come in a rhythmic explosion that spread out from her center to her legs and arms, which beat the bed as she rocked with waves of pleasure. And his enjoyment in her pleasure made her extra giving in return. The main course was as wonderful as the appetizers.

When they were resting afterward, Robin picked up the photograph of a young woman in a silver frame on the bedside table.

"Is this Lizzie?" she asked.

"Yup, that's her."

There was a bark outside the door. Theo laughed. "He knows we're done or . . . taking a break?" He raised his eyebrows suggestively.

"Yeah, probably just a break, but you can let him in for a bit. And I'd go for that tequila now."

Theo opened the door, and Lobo bounded in and onto the foot of the bed where he settled down. Theo stepped into the kitchen, then returned with two shots of tequila he set down on the bedside table.

"So, about Lizzie . . ." Robin prompted.

"She's in Mexico with her parents for the Christmas holidays. I was going to go join them, but then I got some gigs." He got back into bed and gathered Robin in his arms. "I think I'm going to marry her."

"Really? And then will you continue to do . . . this?" She waved at the space between them. "I mean, not just with me, but with other women too."

Theo hugged her tighter. "In an ideal world, I wouldn't continue to do . . . this," he said, making a similar gesture with an ironic smile. "I wouldn't want to or need to. But realistically, I don't know. I've looked around. People rarely keep their vows."

"Then why get married at all?"

"I need a center, a piece of emotional ground I can call my own."

"A refuge?"

"Yeah. I mean, I know there's no such thing as absolute security, blah blah, but Lizzie's a great gal; we have fun together. And her family's great too. When you choose a mate, you have to consider the in-laws."

"What happened to wanting to be 'crazy free'?"

"Hey, I wrote that song for you. A gal who likes both gals and guys is going to need to be free."

"You understand me so well."

This was another thing Robin loved about him: he was so intuitive, that, without her saying much, he saw her dilemma and could even project it forward in time. She stroked Theo's arm, then his face.

"Speaking of which, whatever happened with Stephanie?"

"That's over."

"Sorry. Maybe I shouldn't have asked."

"It was for the best. And you can ask anything," she said. "After all, we're friends too, aren't we?"

"Of course we are." He shifted to his side and looked into her eyes. "God, you're beautiful and interesting and special," he said.

Seeing them kiss, Lobo jumped off the bed and left the room in disgust.

They parted a few hours later, after agreeing to meet again in a couple of days. Robin took a detour through the Russian neighborhood, where she stopped at Iris's favorite grocery store. It was stocked with provisions flown in from the old country: dry goods in square tins, glass jars filled with tired-looking vegetables conserved in water, and slabs of frozen fish. Robin went there for the piroshki, blini, and fragrant rye bread made on the premises. She wandered up and down the aisles slowly, wondering if she loved Theo, if it was possible to love more than one person at a time, and whether Michael would understand what she'd done if he found out. She wanted to see Theo again but was also uncomfortable about it in a way that felt familiar and old. Shame was as much a part of her psyche as desire and joy.

She came home with a big bag of groceries. As soon as she opened the door, she sensed something was wrong. Normally in the late afternoon, there were kitchen sounds as her mother prepared the evening meal, and downstairs she would hear Iris on the phone or the sound of her television. Robin's grandmother was addicted to *Dark Shadows*, which came on at four o'clock, and after that she watched one of the soap operas that came on at four thirty. She rotated between them, following several concurrently.

But there were no cooking or phone or TV sounds.

Robin put the groceries down on the table in the foyer, then went to her parents' room. Sarah was lying propped up on the bed, smoking a cigarette and staring off into space.

"Mom?"

"You were gone a long time," Sarah said. "Probably out fucking that musician character."

"You should talk!" Robin suspected her mother had affairs because her father, who was never around, certainly did. "Can't I have a private life? Anyway, what's going on?"

Sarah sat up, swung her legs over to the side of the bed, and looked at her daughter.

"You won't believe it." She was furious.

Robin sat down next to her. "What?"

"That guy, that shmuck dickhead your grandmother has been fornicating with, he invested her money, and now it's gone!"

"I don't understand—"

"She can do stuff like that because she knows your father will support her in the event of a disaster."

"What exactly happened?" Robin asked.

"Go talk to her. Get it from the lady herself."

Robin headed down to her grandmother's apartment.

Iris was on the couch, weeping.

"Iry, Iry," Robin said, sitting next to her and taking her in her arms.

The old woman was convulsed with sobbing; tears had streaked her wrinkled face with mascara. "I'm so stupid."

"Iry, tell me, please."

"Andy, he offered to invest my money for me; he said he could double my nest egg—" She sobbed some more. "That was money I hoped to pass down to you. And now it's gone. I'll never forgive myself."

"But how—"

"He said he thought it was a good investment. I thought he knew what he was doing, but he didn't—"

Appalled but sympathetic, Robin listened, wondering whether she would ever know the whole truth. "He cheated you?" she asked.

"No, it was some kind of mix-up—"

Sarah appeared at the bottom of the stairs, went to the liquor cabinet, and poured three whiskeys, which she placed on the coffee table. She sat down across from Iris and Robin and pulled out a cigarette. Somewhere between hope and dread, Iris and Robin watched her expectantly. Sarah lit up, inhaled, and exhaled slowly.

"I hope you learn something from your idiot grandmother," she said, looking at Robin.

Iris sobbed.

"And what, pray tell, would you like me to learn?" Robin asked, angry.

"You don't see a lesson here?"

"Okay, she made a mistake—"

"Once again taking your grandmother's side! Look at the two of you, always in alliance against me and against common sense!"

"Mom, stop it—"

"No one ever listens to me. I don't know why I even bother coming down here."

With her whiskey in one hand and a cigarette in the other, Sarah stood and drew herself up to her full height. When she threw her shoulders back, her breasts landed exactly where they were supposed to, in the darted bustline of her formfitting dress.

"Learn this, young lady," Sarah said to her daughter. "You can fuck around with as many guys as you want, but hold on to your wallet." She considered the weeping Iris and shook her head in disbelief. "Thanks for the drink, Mom," she said, and, giving the old woman one last look of contempt, she went back upstairs, whiskey in hand.

10

PAINTING
FACE DOWN

(Anna)

Anna spent the week between Christmas and New Year's at her parents' home on Long Island. It was business as usual: her mother drank all day, her father went to the lab, and her sister acted smug and important. The difficulties were broken up by a daily visit with Doug, long walks in the snow, and runs to the grocery store. On the second of January, as soon as the festivities were over, she and Doug decamped and took the train into Manhattan, where they stayed in the apartment on the Upper West Side, a few blocks south of the Columbia campus, that he shared with another senior.

Anna was used to spending weekends at Doug's place in New York, but a miserable restlessness had descended upon her after two weeks of vacation. She wanted to return to her art projects in New Haven, but the crush she had developed on Michael made her dread going back. That moment the day after Thanksgiving, when they'd made cocktails and then danced in the kitchen, kept coming back to her. The way desire had sprung up so spontaneously when he'd touched her was an experience she'd never had with Doug. And now, in her imagination, she kept on rewriting the scene and ending it with a kiss in the pantry. His obliviousness to her existence made her fantasies ridiculous, and her infatuation was a betrayal not only of Doug but also of Robin.

Her internal agitation contrasted with Doug's bright and focused mood: he had just submitted his applications for architecture school and expected good news in the spring. He rattled on about his prospects as he made them dinner while Anna, sitting at a tiny table next to the kitchen window—protected by bars from intruders who might climb in from the fire escape—listened distractedly and sketched nervously in a small notebook. In her drawing practice, she searched for the sweet spot between representational and abstract, and it kept escaping her. She didn't yet know who or what she was as an artist. Meanwhile, she didn't have the money for Europe, and the approach of graduation weighed on her.

"If I get into MIT," he said, dropping the pasta into boiling water, "and I *will* get into MIT, I'm sure of it, we could live either in Cambridge or Boston, wherever you'd prefer. You could get a job and save up for your Europe trip." He liked to think she wanted to go away for a month or two, whereas she wanted to live abroad for a year or more. "We could drive up at spring break and check out different neighborhoods."

"Yeah, sure." She kept drawing the forks and soup spoons he'd set on the table for twirling pasta. She disliked the way he brought up serious topics while doing something else.

"You don't sound enthusiastic," Doug said. "You never sound enthusiastic about us living together."

Anna looked up from her drawing. He seemed even taller and stronger than usual, standing over the low counter in his little New York kitchen. His large frame, which had once felt protective, now oppressed her. He was making angel hair, which only required a minute or two of boiling. "Shouldn't you be paying attention to what you're doing?" she asked.

He grumbled, strained the pasta, and put the warmed sauce over it. He brought it to the little table with a scowl on his face. She hated seeing him like that and wanted to soothe him.

"I just wish I knew what I was going to do with my life," she said.

"You're going to make art. You're going to do marvelous things. You're really talented and you have a vision."

She felt mollified by his praise. "Thank you, but how am I going to make money?"

"I don't know. You'll fall into something, and in the meantime I'm happy to pay the rent." He didn't explain how he would support her while in graduate school, but one thing was obvious: he was confident about his future and cut out for the breadwinner role. But Anna was suspicious of the obligation that her economic dependence might create. She changed the subject.

"I'm having coffee with Leila tomorrow," she said, referring to her advisor in the art department.

"She'll have some ideas for you."

"Probably graduate school or a teaching certificate. Nothing I haven't heard before."

"You're so negative about everything," Doug said. "Why don't you give it a break?"

She studied him, wondering what she was doing with someone who made her feel great about herself one minute and awful the next.

Anna had arranged to meet her teacher at the Amsterdam Café, an old European-style coffee house with wallpaper, landscape paintings, and dark wood furniture. When she arrived, her advisor was already seated at one of the little tables. A tenured professor in her early forties, Leila had a pageboy haircut with bangs that lined up perfectly with the top of her big tortoiseshell glasses. She dressed in button-down shirts and tailored pants in neutral colors; today a camel hair coat and plaid scarf topped her outfit. Perhaps she cultivated a conventional persona because she had a female romantic partner in Manhattan and wanted to protect her professional ass.

Anna ordered a coffee and sat down.

"How was your holiday?" Leila asked. They talked a bit about New York, then gossiped about faculty and students in the art department. Leila treated Anna as an equal and a friend, which Anna found flattering, for she revered her as the only older woman in her life who was professionally successful. Today Anna sensed Leila had something particular to discuss.

"Are you making progress with your thinking about your future?" the older woman asked.

Of course, her mentor would want to know.

"No. My boyfriend is hoping to get into an architecture program, and he wants me to move in with him, wherever he goes."

"Ah, yes. Of course. The woman should follow the man."

"Maybe he has that assumption. I don't like it, but part of me thinks, 'Why shouldn't I follow him if I don't have a better idea?'"

"And if I had a better idea?"

"You mean graduate school?" They'd talked about it before, and Anna had resisted.

"Something else. I just got offered the directorship of a study abroad center in Paris, and I'm going to accept it."

"Wow, and congratulations!" Anna said. "But what does that have to do with me?"

"It'll give me an opportunity to work on a book I've been wanting to put together for years, compiling images of women in French popular culture in the nineteenth century—in newspapers, magazines, that sort of thing. It's a huge archival project that will require some note-taking, photography, and record-keeping, and I need an assistant." Leila leaned forward. "I'd like to offer you the job."

Anna was speechless. "Wow," she said again.

"You're interested then? In spite of the boyfriend?"

"Of course I'm interested! I would love to be your assistant!"

"I don't know whether your salary would come from Yale or the center in Paris, but I'll figure it out, and either way I can help you get a visa."

As they discussed the details of the job and the practical steps involved with moving abroad, Anna grew more excited. Then, since Leila had asked about Doug, Anna dared to return the question. "And what about your girlfriend? Is she coming too?"

"She can't come for the year, but she'll visit at some point."

"I'll have to find a place to live."

"We could think about sharing an apartment," Leila said. "I promise not to be too maternal." She laughed. "No curfew. You can spend the night out or bring someone back."

Anna laughed too. "Thank you. Thank you so much," she said, sincere in her gratitude. She had no connections from her junior year abroad and didn't want to land in Paris without a friend or a place to live.

"It's a big decision," Leila said. "I know you've said yes, but it'll affect your relationship. I'll give you a couple of days to really think about it."

Doug seemed an abstraction, farther away than the five blocks separating them at that moment in time. "I appreciate that," she said.

A dream job that would take her to Paris for a year or more—what a gift! And it dovetailed with the secret plan she'd always had for her life: to paint, travel, and have lots of lovers. Heading back to Doug's apartment, she mentally sorted through her clothes; she was packing for France in her head by the time she reached the front door to his building. Then the reality of Doug hit her. When she told him about Leila's offer, he would be sad, disappointed, maybe angry. She suddenly wished he would just disappear so she wouldn't have to deal with him. Anna had an impulse to stay out and walk around for a while, but the cold was biting. She climbed the steps to the front door, turned the key, and went upstairs.

Doug was studying in the bedroom.

"What did Leila want?" he asked.

There was anxiety in his voice. Or was she imagining it? "Let me take my coat off." She removed her parka, scarf, and boots and went to the bathroom. When she returned, he spun around in his chair and faced her. She sat down on the bed.

"She got a position in Paris and offered me a job as her assistant."

"That's interesting. What kind of job? And what's the salary?" He asked a series of practical questions in a dry, analytical tone of voice, but she knew the wheels were spinning in his head. It was Doug's way to be "rational" before the emotions broke through. And the more questions he asked, the worse the storm afterward, so that as the interrogation proceeded, a constriction came into her chest and throat. There was the dread of an argument and the fear of losing the man who had been her rock during years of being battered emotionally and at times physically by her mother. The tension was nauseating. Finally, he concluded with, "And did you accept her offer?"

"I told her I would think about it."

"So you'd just pick up and go away for a year?"

"I did it junior year and we were okay. And you could visit," she said. "That would be pretty great, wouldn't it? A girlfriend and a free place to stay in Paris—you could visit more than once."

"Or you could come to Cambridge and move in with me and we could go to Europe together later, when we have money."

"I don't want to wait till 'later,' and I don't want to go for a vacation; I want to go for a year. I want to help Leila with her project and work on my French and—"

"And scope out other guys, right? That's it, isn't it? You want to get away from me and 'sow your wild oats'!" He was shouting now.

"If I wanted to scope out other guys, I could do it anywhere! I don't need to be in Paris!" she screamed back. Michael flashed through her head yet again.

The argument escalated from there. A few minutes later, Anna was packing her bag to head back to New Haven.

"Don't you dare . . . don't you dare leave before we've resolved this!" He grabbed her arm, and for the first time in their many years together, she was afraid of him. But that lasted only a second. Her anger made her fierce.

"Let go of me!" She quickly put her winter coat, hat, scarf, and boots back on—the whole damn armor needed for winter on the East Coast. A moment later she was going down the building staircase, even as Doug, on the landing, continued to yell at her.

Her thinking went in circles as she took the subway to Grand Central, then the train up to New Haven. She had been ecstatic when Leila made the job offer, but now she thought she'd never been so unhappy. Would going to Paris be a mistake? Doug's fury had frightened her, but he'd saved her emotionally so many times that it was hard to imagine life without him. Maybe he was a "good thing" she shouldn't let go of. On the other hand, if she removed herself from her mother, she wouldn't need to be saved again and again. And if she and Doug were meant to be, they would survive the separation.

When Anna got back to the Orange Street apartment, it was late afternoon and already getting dark. The lights were on in the living area, yet it was quiet. She put her things down, then peeked into Julia's bedroom. Her cousin was curled up in bed with her clothes on under the covers, her fine brown hair falling across her wet cheek.

"Is that you?" Julia said.

Anna stepped in. "You okay?"

"I feel like shit. I have my period."

"You want some warm wine for the cramps?"

"Sure."

Anna went into the kitchen and poured some red wine into a small saucepan. She added a stick of cinnamon and turned the radio on low. When the wine began to steam, she added a dash of brandy, poured a glass, and went to set it down on her cousin's night table.

"Doctor's orders," she said.

Julia propped herself up and took a sip. "Thanks. You mind keeping me company for a moment?"

Anna slid in next to her, under the blankets. It was the way they liked to hang out together: clothes on, under the covers.

"What's going on?" she asked.

"I'm worrying about Ben."

"About him and that woman in Paris?"

Julia nodded. "He's there now."

"But he's head over heels about you."

"You think so?"

"It's obvious."

Julia sipped her wine. "I waited so long for a relationship, and now I'm frightened. I mean, he's wonderful, and I love finally having sex, but I don't like this . . . insecurity."

"He went through a long mental process before choosing you. It wasn't a random pickup."

"You're right. He was very affectionate on the phone." She took a big gulp of wine.

"He called you from London?"

"Yeah."

"Come on, that's a sign he's serious."

"Supposing it doesn't work out? I'll be devastated."

"Well, if it doesn't work out, why would you want to stay in it?" Anna asked.

"Gee, I hadn't thought of it that way . . ."

"Yeah, people don't always crash and burn after a breakup. Anyway, you guys will be together forever, I know it."

"Maybe we will be, like you and Doug."

"I don't know about me and Doug. We had a terrible fight." Anna told her about his reaction to Leila's job offer.

Julia thought it over. "You can't really be in love with him if you can imagine being separated for a year."

"We were separated when I took my junior year abroad, and it was okay."

"'Okay'?"

"I'm confused."

"Obviously . . . Hey, the wine is helping," Julia said. "I might try to nap."

Closing the door behind her, Anna went back to the canvas she'd been working on before winter break. Two dancing figures, their shapes abstracted, faced each other with their arms extended, touching hands. She dreamt of a relationship that would be just like that—a joyful dance in which connection didn't impede individual freedom or movement. Working on a painting was the only thing that calmed her, as though she had under her fingers the means to order, pacify, and contain all the contradictions in her life. She took off her sweater and put on an old, paint-splattered sweatshirt. Everything—Doug, Leila, the future—could wait until later.

She studied the work she'd done so far. The range of colors felt dull, narrow. She began to add some deep reds and oranges to make the dancing figures pop out. She didn't have the kind of relationship she wanted in her own life, but playing with a symbolic image of it made her hopeful. Anna was lost in the flow of painting when the sound of a key in the front door lock startled her. Robin wasn't due back from California yet, and her heart jumped as though it might be an intruder.

The door opened, and it was Michael in his leather jacket with the fur collar and a messenger bag over his shoulder. Robin must have given him a key.

"Jesus," Anna said to him. "Didn't you see the lights were on? Haven't you heard of knocking?"

"And how was your Christmas holiday?" he asked.

"You scared me!"

"I'm sorry! I thought you guys had left the lights on to ward off burglars."

Her heartbeat slowed.

"Well, as you can see, I'm back, and so is Julia. Robin's still in California."

"I know. I came to get a notebook I left in her room."

"Go ahead."

He went to Robin's room and returned with a composition book in his hand.

"You want some mulled wine?" she asked. It irritated her beyond measure that he was so handsome and interesting—and her cousin's boyfriend. Yet she wanted to detain him.

Sticking the notebook into his big bag, Michael followed her into the kitchen and looked at the wine in the saucepan. "Wine with a cinnamon stick?" He laughed. "You call that mulled wine?"

Anna laughed too. "Go ahead and make fun. It's good." She poured him a glass.

"Not as good as our Hanky Panky," he said, sipping, "but not bad either. Any news from Robin?" he asked.

"You're more likely to hear from her than I am."

"She called when she got to San Francisco, then silence. I called a couple of times but got her mother, and Robin never called back."

They stepped back into the living room.

"My aunt Sarah is crazy. She probably didn't give Robin your messages."

Michael laughed again. She liked that he laughed easily. "Are all the women in your family crazy?" he asked.

"No, Julia and her mother aren't. And I'm not, at least not yet, though my mother has for years been doing her best to make me that way."

"And what makes Robin's mom crazy?"

"Maybe she's not really crazy, just a hypocrite. She's always disapproving of how everyone else conducts their personal life, while she has lovers on the sly. Robin thinks her mother has been betraying her father for years."

"She's probably got a reason for it," Michael said. "People generally do."

"It's true. My uncle Herbert, there's something slimy about him. Nobody knows where he got his money."

Michael walked over to her easel, put his shoulder bag down, and crossed his arms as he studied her painting. "You think Sarah is why Robin is so complicated? Or her dad, or both?"

"I have no idea. I probably don't know anything about her that you don't."

"Know anything about who?" Julia asked, emerging from her room.

"Robin," Michael said. "Hey, Julia." He planted a kiss on her cheek.

"Oh, Robin," Julia said, and headed to the kitchen for more wine.

"It's not just her being bi that's confusing," Michael went on, "if she really is bi, and I don't know if she is. It's this mix of neediness and restlessness." He continued staring at the painting. "It looks like an angry dance."

Anna was surprised. "No, it's supposed to be the opposite.

It's a love dance, a picture of connection and equilibrium—"

"Then why all the hot and angry colors? That orange—yikes! You know I once read something in *Psychology Today* about how orange is universally a 'least favorite' color. But it's so attention-grabbing that they use it a lot in advertising."

"You don't like this orange? Or you don't like orange in general?"

"This particular orange, or maybe the way you've used it. It throws the whole painting off-balance."

"Maybe I want it to be off-balance." She was used to being critiqued in studio art classes, but she was on edge after the fight with Doug, and she wanted to work without getting feedback.

"You just said it was supposed to be a picture of equilibrium—"

"I'm in the middle of a process, goddammit, how am I supposed to know what it is or what it's going to be?"

"Hey, you guys, stop—" Julia began.

"You don't have to get defensive," Michael said. He and Anna had squared off now in front of the painting. "I thought you'd appreciate an honest reaction."

"I don't need an honest reaction right now. I need to paint."

"All right," Michael said. "Sorry to disturb you." He set his glass down on a side table. Then as he swung around toward the front door, the messenger bag hanging from his shoulder hit the painting, sending it flying off the easel, past the drop cloth. *Crash!* It landed face down on the carpet.

"Oh, shit, and sorry!" he said.

Anna crouched down beside him, so close she could smell his soap or aftershave, and they turned the painting back over together. Lint from the carpet had stuck to the canvas, and paint had stuck to the carpet. A double disaster.

"I can't believe it!" she screamed. "It's ruined!"

"What can I do to help you?" Michael asked. "There must be a way to fix it—"

"Just leave, would you? Just leave."

"Hey, Anna, come on—"

"Get the hell out of here!"

As Michael slunk out, muttering apologies, Julia came in with a couple of wet rags, and she and Anna worked on the carpet. Acrylic paint was water-soluble but fast drying, and they had to work fast to avoid a bill from their landlord. By the time they were done attending to the rug, the little carpet fibers were firmly attached to the dried surface of her painting.

"My own fucking fault for not securing the canvas properly," Anna said. "And now, look, it's ruined. The fibers are stuck in it."

"You can't scrape them off?" Julia offered.

Anna tried doing so with a palette knife but without success.

"Maybe you could just leave them and use them as texture," Julia said. "Don't painters do that sort of thing these days?"

"That's an idea. Okay, let me work with it."

Julia watched as Anna worked on incorporating the carpet fibers into the painting.

"This is hopeless," Anna said.

"I've never seen you so angry," Julia said.

"Michael can be so annoying sometimes. He knows nothing about painting or the painting process, so he should keep his mouth shut." Anna was furious with him, but his wanting to critique her—and the fact that he was open and brave enough to do so—only made him more interesting. He was creative and a risk-taker, and why wasn't she with someone like that instead of Doug, who played everything safe? The comparison triggered frustration and fury. She'd had a job offer and two arguments since that morning; it was time to conclude the art project, have dinner, and go to bed.

She went to the kitchen, found a sharp knife, and returned to the living room.

"Anna, stop!" Julia cried out. "What are you doing?"

In her first act of violence against another being, Anna hit the painting hard with the blade. The canvas resisted the first blow, so she hit it again harder, then harder, until she pierced the surface. With that first opening made, the rest was easy. Fierce and powerful like a Hindu goddess with many arms flailing, Anna slashed her painting to bits.

UNSTABLE
EQUILIBRIUM

(Julia)

Julia was in the habit of making the trip from New Haven to Manhattan once a month to spend time with her parents, and her reunion with Ben after winter break had been so joyful that it seemed natural to take the next step and invite him home with her for the weekend. That cold Friday evening in early February, he had gone into the city ahead of her in order to meet up with a friend, and the plan was for him to come meet her at her parents' apartment in time for dinner.

On leaving the Orange Street apartment for the train station, she stuck her hand in the mailbox and found an envelope addressed to her from the English department.

Julia opened it and read the letter. She had won the sonnet contest!

"Oh, wow, wow." All lit up, she headed out propelled by joy. She could celebrate the good news with Ben and her parents that night. Pride and satisfaction canceled out the unpleasantness of the grimy train rides home, then uptown. She was filled with the sense of setting out on a path that would realize her dream of becoming a real poet. She could become someone who published books, gave readings, and was invited to teach places. She might even turn into a songwriter, like Leonard Cohen. Anything seemed possible now that her talent had been validated.

Once at her parents' house, she decided to wait for Ben's arrival to share her news. When he walked in, Mariel greeted him with a big hug, and Sam gave him a warm handshake, placing a kind hand on his shoulder. As they grinned at Ben with delight, it occurred to Julia that they were relieved she'd emerged from her arrested development and found a boyfriend.

Not that she had ever considered herself arrested. She'd thought of herself as romantic and selective. But her mother, who had sampled a variety of men before her late marriage, had never understood her hesitations. And her father, endlessly preoccupied with her security, just wanted to see her "settle down."

Now Julia, if not quite settled, had satisfied them, and their happiness was palpably in the air.

"We'll have a homestyle family dinner in the kitchen; I hope that's all right," Mariel said.

"Perfect! Superb!" As Ben sat down at the little round table, there was a pouring of wine and exchanges of meaningful glances and compliments.

"I've always loved British accents and especially men with British accents," Mariel said, bringing a chicken stew to the table. She wore one of her outfits from the '60s—wide pantaloon pants made of Indian fabric, a mock turtleneck top with short sleeves, and big turquoise earrings. She leaned a little too close to Ben as she served him, and Julia flushed at her mother's flirtatious behavior.

But Ben took it as it was meant—harmless play. He leaned back toward the older woman. "And I've always loved American English, especially when spoken by a beautiful actress."

"You're too kind," Mariel said with a southern accent. "Much too kind."

"I'm always kind to strangers," Ben returned, trying to do southern and failing miserably.

"But a stranger no more," she responded.

"You better watch out for my wife, she's one hot potato." Sam chuckled, then perhaps remembered his daughter and said, "And now, why did you decide to come to the United States?"

Ben spoke of his regard for American higher education, which led to a compare and contrast discussion of US and British universities.

"And where are you in your studies?"

"Right now, I'm preparing for my qualifying exams, so I'm studying all of English literature. If and when I pass my exams, I'll move on to writing a dissertation, probably on twentieth-century American poetry."

Sam raised his eyebrows. He was an avid reader with a special fondness for poetry. "Any candidates? Wallace Stevens? William Carlos Williams?"

"Not sure yet. But isn't it fascinating, these American poets who had nine-to-five jobs and wrote 'on the side'?"

The two men were off to the races, and Julia reflected that, when required, Ben delivered not only answers but also charm and erudition. She felt proud of him and of herself for choosing him.

"Yes, light years from, let's say, Wordsworth—" Sam said.

"Or from Rimbaud, who worked, but not exactly nine to five."

"That's right—arms dealing! What a great profession for a poet, don't you think?"

The conversation went on in this vein for some time until Julia cleared her throat. "Speaking of poetry, I have some good news to share."

Everyone fell silent.

"I got a letter from the English department, and I—I won the sonnet prize!"

"Mazel tov!" Mariel cried, rising to hug her daughter.

"This calls for champagne!" Sam said, getting up from the table. "I think we have a bottle left over from the holidays."

"Congratulations," Ben said, a bit flatly Julia thought. "I didn't know you'd entered that contest."

"You're the one who told me to."

"That was a while back. You never told me you'd actually entered it."

"Well, I did. And I won."

"It's not cold," Sam said, fussing over a bottle he had pulled out of the pantry.

"We'll chill it in a bucket and have some with dessert," Mariel said.

As the parents tended to the champagne, Julia and Ben looked at each other quietly.

"I'm very proud of you," Ben finally said, and squeezed her hand.

"Thank you."

"We are turning into a literary family—a poet and a professor of literature," Sam said, and Julia noted the assumption that her boyfriend was or would become a relation. "Now, Ben," he continued, "I have a first edition of *Ulysses* you might like to see. Come with me."

He stood up, and Ben followed him into the living room. Julia was disappointed at their departure. She wouldn't have minded another dose of praise.

"The men of letters have found each other! A match made in heaven," Mariel whispered—to which Julia objected internally, *But aren't I a woman of letters and now part of the club too?* "That day we were at Macy's and I met Ben," her mother went on, "I knew it would happen." She looked self-satisfied as she sat, with her elbows on the table and one hand in the air with a glass of wine.

"Why? It wasn't obvious to me."

"I sensed it. Not immediately, but during lunch at the deli.

He's obviously crazy about you. And there you were, over Christmas, worried about him and that ex-girlfriend of his, what's her name?"

"Dominique."

"Worrying when there was nothing to worry about, right?"

"Yeah, it seems he saw her briefly in Paris, as just friends. At least that's what he says."

"And why not believe him? The important thing for you to remember," Mariel went on, lowering her voice again as she leaned toward her daughter, "is that there are plenty of others out there. If he doesn't work out, someone else will." She was willing to share her wisdom anytime and especially after a couple of glasses of wine. "Remember . . . 'other fish in the sea.'"

"Mom!"

"The thing about first love is that it's so magical you consider yourself lucky, as though you've found the best man on earth. But you haven't."

"I thought you liked him."

"I do! I do! I adore him! He's smart and delightful, and he has wonderful posture." Mariel, who did dance classes three times a week to stay fit for auditions, considered good posture a necessary virtue. It drove her mad that her husband, who'd been a musician before becoming an accountant, had a slump from his years bent over the piano, then a desk.

"So why are you going on about 'other fish in the sea'?"

"I'm not 'going on' about it," Mariel replied. "I think you've done a splendid job. And you have nothing to worry about, I'm sure. Why wouldn't a professor of English want to be with a poetess . . ." —she fumbled for the right word—". . . indefinitely?"

The sound of piano playing drifted in from the living room. Her father was putting on a show for Ben.

"Why don't we clean up?" Julia said. "Ben and I are going out tonight."

"But what about the champagne?"

"We can drink it tomorrow. His roommate is playing in a club in the Village."

"That tall handsome man he was with that day at Macy's?"

"Michael."

"That's right, Michael. There, you see."

"I see what?" Julia asked, exasperated.

Mariel leaned forward again and whispered, "Another fish."

"Mom, Michael is seeing Robin!"

"Well, Robin's a real case, so we know that won't last!" Mariel rolled her eyes.

It was hopeless. Julia got up with a sharp gesture and cleared off the table.

"Oh, don't pout," her mother said.

"Why shouldn't I?" Julia replied, washing the dishes.

"Because I made up the trundle bed so the two of you can sleep in the same room."

Julia felt mollified. Not all parents were so open-minded. "Thanks, Mom."

Mariel came up to the sink and added more dishes. "Gimme one here," she said, pointing to a spot at the center of her cheek to Julia, who kissed it.

"You're the best," Julia said, and she meant it.

When Julia and Ben arrived at the club, they found Robin already there, seated at one of the little round tables. She wore a fur hat in the round Russian style that she must have picked up at a vintage store, a long wool skirt, and a rhinestone brooch pinned to a jean jacket. She was drinking a margarita, probably her second Julia guessed from the animated way she greeted them.

"Hey! Isn't this exciting? Getting to see Michael perform for the first time!" Robin said.

As an amateur pianist, Julia was curious to hear Michael

perform with his band. Her father had passed on to her an appre-ciation of jazz and a knowledge of its theoretical rudiments. She had once thought of following in his early footsteps and pursuing music more seriously, but she was as practical as he was, and the prospect of always living on the edge economically was enough to rule that out as a possibility. She didn't want to have to worry about money.

Robin grasped her wrist. "What do you think? Isn't this exciting?"

Julia nodded. Ben ordered them a couple of glasses of wine.

The club was smoky, and the ambient noise made it impossi-ble to have a real conversation. Julia decided not to share her news just yet. After what seemed like a long time, Michael came out. Unshaven, in jeans and an old, navy crewneck sweater, he looked relaxed, almost indifferent. Accompanying him were three other male musicians. Michael took the microphone and introduced the bassist and guitarist first. Then he saluted the third man, a saxophonist with a thin, flat nose and a cherub mouth, as though his lips had been pursed from years of playing a wind instrument.

"And last, but not least, Frank Bruno—saxophonist, wood-wind wizard, and bandmaster! Big round of applause, please!"

Frank bowed and took the microphone from Michael.

"Don't let him fool you, folks! Michael Chambers is the real genius behind this operation, and on his road toward fame and fortune as a composer too!"

The band settled in and began to play. Julia felt the notes Michael played inside her, as though he were inscribing his improvisations directly on her brain. But her concentration was broken by Robin's restless shifting. Nervous and distracted, her cousin ordered another drink, then another. Occasionally, between numbers, she would lean toward Julia and Ben and say, "Wow, wasn't that amazing?" or, "Great, huh?" Julia, knowing that her cousin didn't care for jazz, thought her enthusiasm a sham. As for Ben, he was attentive and quiet, not letting on to his true opinion. He could be cryptic in that way—one of the few traits that Julia, three months into their relationship, found annoying.

Like Julia's father, Michael was proficient at more than one instrument. The set culminated with him exchanging the piano for his clarinet. He and Frank did back-to-back solos culminating in a riveting duet in which they improvised off of each other's phrases with so much humor that the audience laughed wildly. Julia was mesmerized.

The break came and, putting his clarinet down on the piano, Michael was heading to join his friends at their table when two young women, one in jeans, the other in a miniskirt, intercepted, engaging him in conversation.

"Jazz groupies," Ben said. "I didn't know there was such a thing."

Robin looked cross. "Look at how they're flirting with him. Women probably throw themselves at him all the time."

"You're not jealous, are you?" Julia asked.

"Of course not. But I didn't come just to hear him. I was expecting to spend time together."

The woman in the miniskirt was now touching Michael's arm and shaking her head to get her bangs out of her eyes.

"Jesus!" Robin said.

"I don't think it means anything to him," Julia said, for Michael was neither pulling back nor leaning forward. He stood firm, calm, and polite. Finally, smiling and nodding, he stepped away, came over, and sat down at his friends' table

"Hey, the whole gang. What a treat!" he said, grinning.

"And it's a celebratory evening of sorts," Ben added. "Julia won the sonnet prize."

"I didn't know there was a sonnet prize," Michael said, giving her a big hug. "Good for you!"

When Robin offered effusive congratulations next, Julia realized there was a limit to how much praise she could take.

"She'll be a big woman on campus now," Ben said. Julia thought he sounded sarcastic.

The saxophonist approached, and Michael motioned for him to sit down on half of his chair. "Frank and I have been playing together for years," Michael explained.

"Music buddies forever," Frank said as the two men passed an arm around each other's shoulders and exchanged a brief sideways hug. "Hope you guys are enjoying the show."

Michael took a sip of Robin's margarita and grimaced. "Odd choice for a winter night."

"My favorite drink," Robin said.

Michael looked at Julia. "What do you think of the band?"

He wanted her opinion because she also played jazz and shared his love of music. Yet the way he locked eyes with her in front of her cousin made her uncomfortable.

"They're wonderful," Julia said. "Not sure about the guy on bass, though."

"I know. I thought you'd catch that. Our regular guy couldn't come, so Dan—the manager—found us this guy at the last minute."

"He seemed kind of lost or distracted."

"He's headed to the guillotine," Frank said.

Michael shrugged. "The great thing is that Frank and I can carry anything." He looked at his friend and glowed. "Can't we, friend? And we're really in the groove tonight, don't you think?"

Frank glowed back. "We're unbelievably great tonight."

As the two men laughed at their own lack of modesty, Julia took in their synergy. She'd always thought of Michael as depressive. Maybe the graduate program at Yale was making him that way by sucking the life out of him. In this club, with his band, he seemed naturally happy.

The two musicians were talking about the bassist's solo when the manager came up and tapped the two of them on the shoulder. "Hey, back to work."

As Michael stood up, he met Julia's glance and rolled his eyes.

When the show was over, Robin stayed behind, and Julia and Ben bundled back up and walked to the Astor Place subway station, barely speaking. They got down to the platform and waited in the bitter cold for a late-night train.

"What did you think of the show, really?" Ben asked.

"It was great, except—"

"Except for the guy on bass, right?" Ben laughed. "You musicians! I thought that guy was fine. I couldn't even hear the problem you were talking about."

"Well, what about you? Did you enjoy it?" Julia asked.

Ben nodded energetically. "Yes. Great." His expression changed. "But somehow I couldn't help thinking that Michael could be using his time better."

"What do you mean?"

"He's at Yale doing a master's in composition, which might turn into a PhD if he gets his act together. So why the hell is he playing gigs on the weekend?"

"You expect him to compose night and day?"

"Not necessarily. But gigs require setting up and practicing, and then the next day he's always hungover. Did you notice he was nursing a drink the whole time?"

"It's normal for performers to drink in a club. Better that than doing drugs."

"He smokes beforehand too."

Julia was taken aback. Ben didn't reveal his judgmental side often, and she didn't like it.

"The world of composition is incredibly competitive," Ben went on. "If he's going to rise to the top, he needs to devote himself to it entirely."

"I'm not sure I agree." Julia's father had once been a performing musician, and her mother was an actress, so the cross-fertilizations of the performance world were familiar to her, and she had an instinct to come to Michael's defense. "I'm guessing his compositions feed his gigs, and vice versa."

Ben shrugged. "He's supposed to produce a major piece as a master's thesis project by the end of the semester, and I know he's not on track. It's not going to be fun living with him when he fucks up. For one thing, they won't let him into the doctoral program."

Julia had known from the beginning that Ben was focused on his work, and she had found his ambitiousness attractive. But he seemed unaware that other people might not be as dedicated, or that Michael, under pressure from his famous musicologist father, might be confused. "Has he shown signs of being about to fuck up?" she asked. "Maybe he'll surprise you."

"You don't see what I see?" Ben studied her for a moment. "I get it. Like most women, you're charmed by his self-destructive side."

"'Like most women'? Thank you very much." Angry now, she shifted from one foot to the other in the cold.

"But it's true. Women find the whole down-and-out artist thing 'romantic.' And he does it so well."

"What are you implying?" Julia asked.

"I'm suggesting you don't see him for what he is."

"How about instead of talking to me about him, you just talk to him about him?"

"I will." He hesitated. "Not sure how to broach the subject, but I should try, and soon. Because time is running out."

"You don't really like artists, do you?"

"Now where did that come from?"

"You didn't seem very excited about my prize."

"Of course I'm excited!"

"No, I don't think you are," she insisted.

"Okay, you picked up on something . . . It's just that, well, I feel a little embarrassed. That sonnet is so erotic—and I'm your boyfriend—so people may assume it's about me, which makes me feel exposed, though I know it was about my predecessor, since you wrote it last year. In which case I'm a cuckold."

"How can you be a cuckold when it was before you? And I told you, I never had sex with the guy!"

"You asked me to explain my . . . mixed response, and I did."

"Maybe you should stop worrying so much about what people think," Julia said.

"I don't live in a vacuum, and neither do you."

The train's white light approached in the dark tunnel. They stood back from the platform as it pulled in, and the subject of the artist's way was dropped into the icy wind of the subway.

The tension of that night quickly dissolved in the warmth of spooning on a twin mattress. Julia forgave Ben his lack of enthusiasm about her prize, which she decided might have more to do with something other than a concern about appearances. Like most professors of literature, he probably would have preferred to make poetry than teach it, and his envy had come out sideways. She could forgive him for that.

As for the argument about Michael, Julia didn't know whether he was truly behind schedule or not, but the harshness of Ben's work ethic reminded her of the Harlem fortune teller. The anguish that Gladys's predictions had triggered came back in February as she watched him sink deeper into his studies. She ruminated on her words: *He's a fella who loves books more than anything. You could get awful tired of competing with those books.* She didn't know how seriously she should take them. She'd felt good about being a smart girl who liked smart guys, but maybe that would get her in trouble. Would he not give her the attention she needed? Or maybe he'd be competitive and put her down at every opportunity?

The following Saturday night, she and Ben were studying after a light dinner at his place. When she suggested going to a movie, he refused.

"We went out last night," he said.

"But that was just for dinner."

"It cut up the evening, and I really have to get serious now. My exam is in two months. I'm happy you've started sleeping over, but I have to stay with my study schedule."

"Okay. I brought my books." She had reading to do for English and problem sets for her math class.

He sat at his desk in the bedroom, and she was on the big bed behind him with *Middlemarch* open on her lap. It wasn't so bad to stay in on a cold winter night and get lost in a big novel while Michael played the piano softly down the hall. She'd studied like this as a kid in her bedroom while her father "fooled around" on the baby grand in the living room. She was immersed in Dorothea's world when Ben turned around in his chair.

"Julia," he said.

"Yeah?"

He looked uncomfortable.

"What is it?" she prodded.

"This is awkward, but—"

"But what?"

"I have difficulty concentrating with you sitting behind me."

"Oh." She looked around the room. There was no other place to sit. Then she got it. "You want me to go home?"

"No, no. I really do like your staying over. But would you mind reading in the living room?"

"Okay."

Rebuffed and confused, she picked up her book and tea, then left the room. She didn't make any noise while reading, and she was staying over so that they might enjoy each other's company, but now he'd kicked her out of his room. She sat down on the couch a little heavily. Michael stopped playing and scrawled something on the composition paper in front of him. He swiveled around and faced her with a sardonic expression.

"You been exiled?" he asked.

"Yeah. You mind?"

"Of course not."

He wore a cardigan over the two men's collared shirts he'd put on, one over the other. A comfortable, if eccentric, outfit.

"Where's Gladys when you need her . . ." he said.

"What about you? Where's Robin?"

"Robin is studying for an exam with Gloria."

"Everybody wants to work tonight except me."

"I wouldn't mind a break," he said. "We could go out for a beer and a bite. That wasn't much of a dinner we had."

"Sure."

Standing up from the couch, she made an instinctive motion to go tell Ben they were leaving, then stopped herself. He might resent the interruption. She redirected herself toward the coat hooks by the front door and grabbed her puffer.

It was quiet in the pizzeria, maybe because of the bitter cold outside. They took a booth in the back and ordered a pie with the works. Julia didn't want a drink, but Michael asked for a beer and a whiskey sour.

"Can you mix those two?" Julia asked.

"What do you mean?"

"And not get sick?"

"I never get sick from drinking." He gave her a polite smile, then added, "You can have a sip of either."

"Thanks," she said, and reached for the whiskey sour.

"You okay with being kicked out?" he asked.

"Yeah. I mean, he really does have to concentrate on preparing for his exam."

"Honestly, he's been a pain to live with recently," Michael said. "He takes everything too seriously. I'm also trying to wind up my master's, but I allow myself a couple of nights off a week."

"Maybe you know how to manage your time better."

"No, it's not that. I'm just not as invested."

"Meaning?"

"I enjoyed my life before graduate school. Frank and I had this group going, we had gigs all the time, I gave private lessons, and it was fine. A full life and a reasonable income, so I can't help asking myself what I'm doing here."

"I thought you wanted to follow in your father's footsteps."

"That's right. We had this conversation already."

"I don't mind having the same conversation more than once," Julia said, smiling.

"I'm glad to hear you say that because repetition is at the heart of every friendship."

"You're quite the philosopher," she teased.

"Thank you, but no applause."

The pizza came, and the conversation drifted sideways to New York, events on campus, and Jimmy Carter, while Julia took an occasional sip of his whiskey sour.

"Just take it," he said, pushing the drink toward her. He flagged the waiter down and ordered another.

After a momentary silence, she returned to the subject of Ben. "When he asked me to leave the room, I thought about Gladys too." The uplift at the end of her statement suggested an investigation that might be pursued.

Michael met her gaze. "You mean, about it being harder to compete with a pile of books than another woman?"

"You remembered her words exactly."

"Hard not to. And I can see you're frustrated. You're not getting the companionship you were hoping for."

"Yeah. But am I—am I overreacting? To being kicked out, I mean."

"You said before that you were fine with it."

"I am and I'm not."

"Okay, Jul, listen up. You did the right thing tonight. You gave him the space he needed, and you didn't make a fuss about it. You're letting Ben be Ben, and that's the best you can do. There may be problems ahead, like in any relationship, but you guys are fantastic together. And if he doesn't give you the time together you want, well, you can fill in the gaps with friendships. I think the two of you might actually have a 'future.'" He laughed. "Unlike me and Robin."

"Thanks. And I hope you're right. I hope we have a future together. And I'm sorry if Robin's making you suffer."

"It's weird having this little graduate student affair at my age when I can see clearly that it's a dead end. Superficial is getting old. Or I'm getting old. You know, I'm old for a graduate student—thirty-two."

Julia considered him for a moment. His wild hair neared shoulder-length, and he needed a shave. She preferred groomed men, and she loved that Ben always shaved out of consideration for her. But there was the sensuality of Michael's mouth, the strength of his nose, and the steadiness of his gaze. His features were hugely expressive, as though he had more spirit, creativity, and aliveness than one person could possibly contain—intensity to share and generate—and that made him appealing, if not in a conventional way. She felt angry at Robin for toying with him.

"You're a great guy," she said, "and it's too bad Robin doesn't appreciate you. But someday you'll find someone who does."

"Thanks," he said. He reached across the table, took her slim hand in his large warm one, and squeezed it.

"You're welcome," she said, and squeezed his in return.

They held hands for a moment in the fullness of suspended time. She felt the smallness of her hand in his larger one, and for a split second she wondered what such large hands would feel like against her naked skin.

Then they let go, and hands returned to drinks.

TRYING
FRIENDSHIP

(Michael)

The elation Michael felt after the gig soon wore off under the pressures of graduate school, and he was happy when, a couple of weeks afterward, Frank made a special trip up to New Haven from the city so that they could play together and make plans for the future.

When Frank walked in with his saxophone, Robin waved hello, then took refuge in Michael's messy bedroom to study. With Ben already locked up reading in his bedroom and Julia in Manhattan for the weekend, the two musicians were able to take over the living room and practice.

Frank, who was the more business minded of the two, usually took care of making phone calls to clubs and lining up gigs. Michael chose tunes for the shows and made creative suggestions for new arrangements. They had been a good team from the beginning, and their synergy had improved over the years regardless of who else joined or left them.

After playing for an hour, they took a break and sat across the coffee table from each other, with Michael on the couch and

Frank in one of the armchairs. They were both sailing on a mellow high from the excellent weed Frank had in his pocket.

"And now that you're in a properly elevated frame of mind," Frank said, "I brought you a gift that'll send you to the moon." He pulled a copy of *The Village Voice* out of his backpack, opened it to the music review section, and handed it to his friend.

"Oh my!" Michael's eyebrows shot up and he read out loud: "'The Contraries gave a stellar show, with Michael Chambers and Frank Bruno demonstrating a sense of humor and easy repartee rarely seen in the jazz world.'" He stopped talking and continued to read silently, a smile spreading over his face. "Wow! By golly, we've done it! 'A group to be followed and appreciated. See them now before ticket prices shoot up.'" Michael shook his head in amazement. "This is a milestone for us." Putting the paper down, he leaned forward and extended a hand that Frank shook vigorously.

"You happy?"

"I'm manic," Michael said. "I was depressed this morning, but I'm high as a kite now."

"That's the life of a musician."

"Much better than the life of a graduate student," Michael said. "God, I hate producing under pressure. I'm struggling with a composition that has to be done *soon*, and my advisor isn't happy with my progress." He reached for *The Village Voice* again and reread it. "But this, *this* is a real shot in the arm."

"With your permission," Frank said, "I want to put my manager hat back on and get us out there more."

"You bet."

Ben emerged from his room, an empty coffee cup in hand. He gave Frank a friendly handshake.

"You guys were great at the club," Ben said.

"Read this." Michael passed him *The Village Voice.*

Ben took it from him and scanned it. "Wow." He met

Michael's eyes. "Seems like you're on two roads at once. One foot in the ivory tower, another in the street."

"As behooves an all-around musician," Frank said.

"I guess. Though if Michael is hooved," Ben punned, "he'd have two legs in the ivory tower and two in the street." He spoke slowly as he looked back down at the paper.

Michael sensed something was going on in Ben's head about the review. *Is he jealous?* That didn't make sense. Ben wanted to teach; why would he envy a musician's success? Michael reached for the joint, took another toke, and decided to let it go. Ben was entitled to his reactions, and Michael didn't have to pay attention to every one of them.

Ben got his coffee and went back to his bedroom, while Frank shared some of his ideas about promotion.

"That recording we made of the show," he said, "I'm going to circulate it."

"Cool," Michael said.

"What would you think about me looking into Philadelphia?"

"Why not?"

They grinned at each other.

"Time to get back to work?"

"You bet."

Michael took his place at the piano, Frank picked up his saxophone, and they started playing again. Michael's elation was almost too much of a bounce from his earlier negativity about graduate school. He had never shied away from competition, but the ferocity of it in his department did nothing for his creative process. At Yale, he'd found an undercurrent of arrogance and mean-spiritedness that was in his mind antithetical to the musician's creed of endless work inspired by endless joy. The academic creed, in contrast, seemed to be endless work and no joy. When he played with Frank, however, he forgot about school. It was fun to daydream about more gigs in New York and elsewhere.

When they paused between tunes, Frank took a bathroom break, and Michael fiddled with a chord sequence. Robin was still in his bedroom; to his disappointment, she had no appreciation or curiosity about music or his career. If Julia hadn't been at her parents' in the city, she would have been in the living room, reading a novel and listening to them play at the same time, and in her Julia-fashion, she'd have said something that made it clear *she* understood. When he was at the keyboard and she was on the couch, he sensed her supportive presence with the skin on his back, and her smile and hazel eyes danced inside him.

But how much of that "support" was projection? He was aware he needed a muse to do his best work, and since Robin didn't fulfill that role, he gravitated toward Julia as a source of inspiration. When she listened to music, she would tilt her head to the right; her straight hair would drape off the left side of her neck and offer a spot to be kissed. He knew the workings of his own creativity well enough to see what was happening, and he didn't like it. Julia was his buddy's girl; he couldn't use her as a muse.

Frank returned, and they played and talked for another couple of hours until it was time for Michael to drive him back to the scummy train station. If New Haven was the armpit of the East Coast, the station, with its grime and homeless population, was the collection spot for its sweat and stench.

When he pulled up to the drop-off curb, Frank said, "You think you can handle it?"

"Handle what?"

"More gigs this spring while you're finishing your thesis project."

"Sure." Michael wasn't completely sure, but he'd let Frank down once before, when he'd canceled a series of engagements at the beginning of graduate school, and he hated the idea of doing so again. And it would be crazy not to follow up on the opportunity presented by *The Village Voice* review.

"I'm asking for real. I don't want to go to the trouble of setting things up and then have you pull out because you have to do a song and dance for some professors with bow ties and funny hats."

Michael reflected. "I'm sorry about before. And I do want the gigs. I want us to continue as a team." His energy surged as he spoke the words. Suddenly, he knew who he was, he coincided with himself, as though he had dispelled his father and professors with a magic wand.

"We could also wait till after you finish graduate school."

"Why don't you lay the groundwork now for summer? I'll be finished with my master's project by then."

"And the doctorate?"

"I'm not going to stay for the doctorate. I don't want to spend my life in libraries and classrooms. I want to play and teach privately, the way I did before. High school would be okay."

Frank nodded. They shook hands, and Frank got out and headed into the station.

Driving back, Michael reflected on the fact that Frank was going back into Manhattan, one of the jazz capitals of the world, while he was going back to his apartment in New Haven to work in solitude on a piece that would probably never have an audience. He'd started graduate school to appease his father, but the recent gig and Frank's visit reminded him that playing with a band had always worked as an antidote to the loneliness of composing. Being by himself inside his head while he made music was both soothing and painful, the solution and the problem. If he left school, he could have the best of all worlds.

Michael believed in the guidance of his intuition and gut feelings. In impulsively shaking Frank's hand, he'd recommitted to their working together at a deeper level.

When he got back to the apartment, he found that Robin and Ben had made dinner and set the table. There was salad and a big bowl of pasta with a lumpy-looking vegetable sauce made of chunks of carrot, celery, and broccoli in a tomato base. Michael, who had a good appetite, found Robin's vegetarian meals unsatisfying, but he appreciated having others do the cooking he didn't enjoy himself.

Robin had read the review while he was out and gushed about it as they sat down.

"It's really amazing! You should be proud." She squeezed his forearm.

Michael smiled, leaned forward, and kissed her on the lips. The gesture came to him as both natural and perfunctory. Pot made him a little ragged and fuzzy about everything. "Thank you," he said. He leaned back and looked at Ben, who was making a face. "What's up with you?"

"You want to know?"

"Of course I want to know. You're my guiding light." Michael was being only partly sarcastic. In fact, he appreciated Ben's opinions because, at least in the domain of work and maybe even relationships too, his friend had that elusive thing—good judgment.

"I think you're sabotaging yourself by committing to more gigs with Frank right at the moment your master's project is coming due."

"That's not my intention. I just want to spend more time performing. And we're talking about the summer."

"But you'd have to start rehearsing beforehand. Fact is, you were seduced by that review." Ben shook his head.

"'Seduced' is a little strong. I'd say I was flattered. And maybe you didn't hear what I just said. I love to perform. I love making music with other people."

"I think you're making a really stupid choice."

"You're always a crab when Julia isn't here. Why don't you just go into the city with her?" Irritated, Michael put his fork down.

"Because, unlike you, I take my exams seriously. And that means staying put and working hard. It's like you want to be a loser—"

"Oh, come on, Ben," Robin said. "Enough."

But Ben was on a roll. "Life isn't a river where you get on a boat and let the current take you to some magical land. It's a crazy ocean subject to storms and wild waves. You have to grab the rudder and take control of the course."

Michael got up.

"Where are you going?" Ben said.

"I'm thirsty."

Ben followed him to the kitchen and squared off with him. "You're the most talented man I've ever had the privilege to know, and you could have a brilliant career as a composer, yet you've decided to sacrifice it for some two-bit gigs in the Village."

"Or Philadelphia. Frank and I talked about Philadelphia. City of lights. Streetlights, that is." Michael hoped to pacify him with a bit of banter.

"Since you don't want to look at what you're doing, I'll tell you. You're wasting your genius." Hot and flushed, Ben poked his friend in the chest with his index finger.

Assaulted by his friend's rage, Michael stepped back quickly and returned to the dining table. He knew the power of his own anger and had the wisdom to take a moment to regroup.

Ben didn't stop. "Is anything I'm saying sinking in?"

"Now listen to me, buster," Michael said. "You know nothing about the music world, and you talk about genius and fame like a six-year-old. There's no connection between talent and success. Ninety percent of it is about who you know or just luck—"

"If it's about who you know, isn't Yale the right place to be?"

"Yeah, if I want to spend my life in a bow tie being a pompous ass. But not if I want to perform or get my compositions produced."

"You're the most self-destructive person I've ever met," Ben said, standing up.

Michael shrugged, then looked at Robin. "What do you think? Do you think I'm sabotaging myself?"

"I don't know." She glanced at Ben marching off. "Maybe he's right. If you give the program your all, you could come out on top."

Michael frowned. "People are so focused on this idea of artistic success," he said, "that they destroy themselves going after it when it's a dangerous myth and for almost everyone, unattainable."

He knew that many graduates of the music program had gone on to fame because they came from wealthy families with connections in the concert world, but he wasn't in the mood to give Ben or Robin an explanatory discourse on the "scene," its backstage maneuvers, and its manipulations. One thing he was sure of, however: no matter how much he dreamed of glory as a composer, he wasn't socially or emotionally equipped to attain it.

"Sorry," she said.

He looked at her. "You haven't been happy here either."

Robin pushed her food around on her plate. "It's different." She shrugged. "I landed at Yale almost by accident, and my destiny as a psychologist is going to be modest. I'll have a little career as a researcher or a therapist. But you—Ben is right. You could do something big. You could have your music played by the Philharmonic or write scores for Hollywood movies."

He felt a weight inside him as he listened. Her words would have been true if he'd had the necessary ego to believe in himself more, but he didn't.

"I know you're not happy with me," she continued, "because I don't know enough about music to appreciate it like—" She paused. He guessed she was about to say, "Julia," but she didn't. "Like other people. But I appreciate it enough to agree with Ben

that you're really a genius and getting through the Yale music program could position you to be a winner. Like . . . to be famous."

"Since when have you become so conventional?" Having lost
his appetite, Michael got up and took his plate into the kitchen,
where he scraped the remains of his meal into the garbage. He
stood over the sink, filled a glass with water, and drank it looking
out the window at the winter sky. A juicy steak would have been
nice, or some roast chicken. He had boxed himself in—in the
music program at Yale, the apartment with Ben, and the relationship with Robin. He wanted his old life back, the freedom
he'd had before graduate school, the ups and downs of gigs in the
city and on the road, the endless encounters, personal and professional, some serious, others casual—the big crazy adventure of
being a working musician. He flashed back to one summer when
he'd worked at a resort in the Catskills, the euphoria of playing
in a big band late into the warm night, guests dancing, the hooting and applause, one time a girlfriend there, going back to their
cabin afterward and having sex for hours. In the morning, the
trees and grass were covered with sparkling drops of dew, and
the next night he had picked up his saxophone and done it all
over again.

Yale drove him crazy. He'd never been surrounded by so
many people who took themselves so seriously. He couldn't stand
it anymore.

But he wanted to be kind. To extricate himself slowly, when
the time was right, from academe, apartment, and relationship.
He took a deep breath and went back to the table.

"I'm sorry," Robin said "I don't know anything about your
world."

"It's okay. I'm sorry too."

"I feel stupid."

"No, in fact, you were probably right. But there's more to this
whole thing than talent or 'genius.' It's about having a certain kind

of ego that gives you a certain kind of drive." Michael poured himself more wine. Robin was sexy and smart and sensitive, but maybe he was wasting his time with her. Or maybe it was all about just getting through this chapter of life, and she was the right one for that. Here, too, he felt confused. "Let's make up."

They stood up and hugged. She felt good in his arms, and he loved her in a way, even though she was the wrong one.

"You want to get in bed and have a smoke?" he asked softly.

"I'd love to."

Once he and Robin were in bed, he took another toke, gathered her up in his arms, and began to stroke her. It never ceased to surprise him how good sex with the wrong person could be, and how it left him feeling that maybe she wasn't the wrong person after all.

ACCIDENTAL COMMITMENT

(Robin)

Robin had enjoyed sex with Michael so much from the beginning that she still didn't know what the relationship was exactly, even after several months. Whether they had a quickie or went at it till late at night, whether they were sober or used pot, she felt high before, during, and after. They did normal boyfriend-girlfriend things, like going to movies and taking walks, and even had big talks about their crazy parents and their ambitions—his about composing, hers about a career in psychology. But the sex was the main course, and as winter moved into the spring of 1977, Robin became uneasy. She was becoming more attached to him but couldn't read his feelings for her. He was sexually passionate but not one to whisper endearments or caress her face, and not very affectionate outside the bedroom. Sometimes she wondered whether he was capable of love for a woman or whether he reserved all his love for his music, and it pained her that she couldn't join him there.

One Saturday night in April, they were in his bed after a

first round. It was almost midnight. "I think that's about it for me tonight," he said. He patted her on the shoulder as though to apologize in case she wanted more, but she didn't. She still had a restless energy in her body, but it wasn't more sex she wanted— she wanted cuddles and a bit of pillow talk.

"You're staying over?" he asked.

She usually did on Saturday nights, but she hesitated. She didn't want to risk not being home when Gloria came by for the study date they'd made for Sunday morning.

"I should go back," she said.

"Why?"

Robin shifted uncomfortably, aware of the emotional mess she'd gotten herself into. Her confusion about Michael was amplified by the growing ambiguity in her friendship with Gloria. Thinking about her attraction to her, Robin wondered why they'd never fallen into bed together while driving cross-country the previous summer. She remembered the first time she'd seen Gloria naked, stepping like some goddess out of the shower in their motel room in Decatur, Illinois. Then there was that night in Nashville when they drank and danced, then went back to the motel, their arms intertwined. Robin might have taken the first step if she hadn't felt restrained by a fear of rejection. After all, she was on her way "home" to Stephanie in Boston, and Gloria might have been shocked by her infidelity.

"I have a lot to do tomorrow," Robin said.

Michael sat up in bed. "Okay, then I'll get out of this comfy bed and drive you back." He put on her navy beret, which she'd set on the bedside table, and looked at her coyly.

He was cute in her hat, which, too small for him, threatened to slide off. He had this ability to put her in knots of a desire that went beyond sex but wasn't exactly love either.

"I'll make you a deal," she said. "Tell me about your marriage, and I'll stay over." She knew he wanted her to stay, if only because it was late and he was tired. She could get up early to get home before Gloria arrived.

"All right." He grimaced. "It's funny to hear you say, 'your marriage.' It was so short and painful that now it feels more like a natural catastrophe. A tornado or a flood."

She propped herself up against a couple of pillows and gave him her full attention.

"You know, first love and all that," he began, "there's very little thinking that happens in it. You just do stuff, you're emotionally hyped up all the time, darting right then left like a scared mouse."

"What happened to end it?"

"She slept with my best friend."

"Oh." Robin was disappointed by such an ordinary plot twist.

"Yeah. An old story, I know."

They fell silent. She thought about brushing her teeth and going to sleep.

"But the way I found out was traumatic," he continued. "My 'wife' and I were camping in Canada on my parents' property. My best friend showed up for a few days—before I got married, he was the one I'd go camping with. Anyway, the fourth or fifth day he was there, I told them I was going downstream to the supply post to get some stuff. I set out in the canoe and halfway there, I realize I forgot my wallet. I go back to camp, but they're gone. Oh, no, wait, they're not gone. I hear them . . . Where's that noise coming from? Hey, dumbo, it's coming from the camper!" Agitated, he seemed to be reliving the whole damn thing. "And I go up to it and stand on my tiptoes and I look through the window, and inside . . ."

"How awful," Robin said.

"It was good in a way because it clarified my future in one respect. I'm unlikely to ever get married again." The hardness in his eyes made her feel an insurmountable distance between them. "And since I'm likely to be an impoverished musician, it's just as well."

"She obviously did a number on you," Robin said, "but that doesn't mean you won't eventually recover." She spoke with the healing intentions of an aspiring therapist, but now that the words were out, she regretted them. He might think she was making a pitch for a long-term relationship.

Michael looked away. "Anything is possible, but *recovery*, as you call it, is light years away."

She didn't sleep well after that, while he dropped off with an almost audible thud. *Everyone*, she reflected, *has some primal trauma that impacts the course of their lives. Most often, you don't realize the extent of the impact until years later.* She herself hadn't. She'd been molested several times between the ages of ten and thirteen by her father's brother. When her uncle appeared in her dreams, she would wake up with a sensation of her body vibrating in a low, continuous shiver. Robin had never spoken of it to anyone, not her cousins, not even Stephanie. She knew that if she was going to be a therapist, she'd have to unpack the abuse someday, but the time hadn't yet come; she didn't yet have the time, space, and resilience she needed to tackle her toxic past. So for the time being, she buried what had happened under as many new experiences as possible.

During the night there was wind, then the sound of rain and occasionally, in the early morning, the muffled sound of a car passing down the damp street. Anxious to get home, she woke when light broke and dragged herself out of bed. She thought she heard cooing noises. Ben was at the dining table, and Julia, who'd slept over, was sitting on his lap. Pretending to be baby birds asking for food, they were taking turns feeding each other bits of toast with strawberry jam. They were obviously crazy about each other. It was revolting.

"Good morning, lovebirds," Robin said.

"Good morning!" Julia kicked her heels joyfully, then cackled as Ben crept a hand up to her armpit. "Stop that!" She giggled like a four-year-old.

"Why should I when it's so much fun?" Ben asked.

"Don't mind me," Robin said.

"Wait up, ma'am!" Ben reached out and grabbed her arm. "We need your opinion about something."

"No, we don't," Julia said.

"What?" Robin asked.

"I'm trying to persuade this gorgeous lady, this woman of my dreams, this sex go—"

Giggling some more, Julia put a hand over his mouth, but Ben shook his head free. "Sex goddess, to stay in New Haven and live with me with after graduation." Ben looked at Robin. "Don't you think that two people who are completely in love with each other should live together?"

"Sure, why not?"

"Because New Haven is a pit, that's why not," Julia said. The giggling had died down. "And there aren't a lot of job opportunities."

"It's true," Robin said. "New Haven is a pit. So Ben, how about you get off your ass and live with Julia in New York? You could commute back here for your dissertation work."

"It's too far from the library," he said.

"Ah. So much for the idea of compromise," Robin said. She shrugged, stepped into the kitchen, and put the kettle on. The rain had started again. Julia and Ben were whispering in tones that were sometimes affectionate, sometimes tense. At times, Robin didn't like Ben very much or think him good enough for Julia. And their being so in love made her envious, though mostly she was happy for her cousin who had languished so long in virginity.

Her mind went back to the story Michael had told her the night before. She was anxious now, for they were clearly on uneven terrain. Putting her psychologist hat on, she analyzed it as a case of unequal cathexis, meaning she was more focused emotionally and sexually on him than he was on her. When she reflected on the inequality of their affections, she went to a place of cringing pain and self-hatred. *Jesus, what a stupid idea to get involved with this jerk.* Maybe she should ditch him before he ditched her. Or maybe her attachment would spontaneously dissolve, and a break would be mutual and not as painful as she imagined. Or she could wait it out because people's feelings evolve over time; sometimes they intensify in ways that can heal previous, bruising experiences, and she might help him forget his disastrous early marriage.

She heard Julia screech again in the dining area.

"Oh, stop it, would you?" Robin yelled.

"Yes, ma'am!" Julia answered. There was silence. They were probably making out or fingering each other.

Robin took her coffee and headed back to the bedroom. "Coming through," she announced, in case they were doing something indecent. She sailed past them back into Michael's room. He was awake now, with some music composition paper in front of him on a clipboard. He glanced up, then refocused as he made some notations. He didn't need a piano in front of him to compose; he transcribed what he heard in his head.

"Want some?" she offered.

Michael took a few sips and handed the cup back to her. She set it down and started to dress.

"The problem is, I'm too much under the influence of Bach," he said.

He spoke as though she could respond constructively when she was neither a musician nor a creative sort. All she could say was, "You'll figure things out."

As Robin pulled on her jeans, he looked up. "You seem to be in a rush," he said.

"I've got to get some studying done today. I have a midterm exam this week." She slipped her turtleneck sweater over her head.

"Do you want me to drive you?" he asked, still looking down at his composition paper, scribbling.

"No, I like walking in the rain."

Once outside, Robin made her way through the drizzle back to her apartment. The sense of being headed for an emotional train wreck made her want to cry in anticipation of it, the way Alice cried before pricking her finger with a needle in *Through the Looking Glass*. Then she thought about Gloria, about how smart she was and modest about being smart, about her long blonde hair, so straight and shiny, and how good it smelled.

Gloria was part California girl, having grown up in the hills east of San Diego before her parents moved the family to Albuquerque. A feminist witch with a wild side, she had been catapulted into the Ivy League by her stellar SAT scores. Robin also talked revolution, but she had an urban veneer that left Gloria spellbound. Because a sense of erotic possibility was opening between them, Robin had avoided mentioning her involvement with Michael so as to keep the field clear. This had required some subterfuge. Of course, it was possible Gloria might at some point see her hanging out with Michael on or off campus. Robin preferred not to think about it.

They had met at Wellesley while working on the campus feminist magazine together, then got to know each other driving across the country on vacation breaks. They'd applied to graduate school at the same time. At Yale, their friendship became more intimate when they both enrolled in a class in neuroscience— the area of overlap between Gloria's work in biology and Robin's in psychology. They studied sitting close together on the bed;

sometimes, when she needed a break from absorbing so many facts, Robin would lean her head on Gloria's shoulder. Once Gloria had passed her arm through Robin's, and they had intertwined their fingers and breathed quietly for a moment; then a noise down the hall startled them, and the opportunity was lost.

No one was home this Sunday morning. Julia was still at Ben's, and Anna was visiting Doug in New York. Chilled from walking in the rain, Robin turned up the heat, took a hot shower, and put some coffee on to brew. The night with Michael, the reckoning with the inequality of affection between them, and the anticipation of the smell of Gloria's hair—a generic herbal scent from some shampoo that had for Robin become a part of Gloria's essence—all put her in an uneasy state.

There was a knock at the door.

Robin opened it, and Gloria came in with her backpack, a paper bag, and a slicker covered with raindrops.

They greeted each other with awkward nods.

"I brought bagels for study break." Gloria put them on the small table in the dining area.

"Thanks. Let's go to my room."

Robin's heart pounded as she watched Gloria take off her boots and jacket. When they stepped into her bedroom, she had an impulse to close the door but left it slightly ajar. Then she changed her mind and closed it. She wondered whether Gloria had caught her little dance, but her friend's eyes darted away when Robin looked at her.

"You all fired up about studying synapses today?" Gloria asked as she sat on Robin's bed and tucked her heels under her buttocks, like a cat folding in on itself.

Nervous, Robin rummaged around. "I don't know what I did with my goddamn book."

"If we're going to quiz each other, we only need mine."

"Okay."

Robin sat on the bed next to her, and Gloria opened the book, positioning it on both their laps. The rain had stopped, and the sunlight brought welcome brightness. The soft pressure of Gloria's shoulder against hers calmed her anxiety. Time slowed as Robin's arousal mounted.

"You want to start with the questions?" Gloria asked. She absorbed information easily, and if she gave answers first, Robin would have extra time for review.

"Sure." Robin quizzed her friend about the neurotransmitters, chemicals, and structures of the brain and nervous system. Gloria answered everything perfectly.

Robin sighed. "I don't know how you do it."

Gloria shrugged. "I have a great memory and I'm good at analysis, but my brain isn't so good at other things."

That piqued Robin's interest. "Like what?"

"Like knowing what other people think and feel. Knowing how to act in certain situations, what to say."

Robin's heartbeat accelerated. This had to be a come-on. "You mean, in general or in specific?"

"Both."

Robin put her head on Gloria's shoulder, taking in the smell of her hair.

"This is nice," Robin said. "Cozy."

"Yes. And sweet."

They were quiet for a second.

And then Gloria said, "I didn't sleep much last night."

"Why?"

"Thinking about seeing you today." Gloria looked away as she stroked the back of her hand. Robin found her timidity adorable.

"I'm happy you're here," Robin said.

Their eyes met and they started kissing.

Robin hadn't realized how much she'd missed being with a woman, the softness of breasts meeting breasts, the fragrance that came to her as she lowered her lips between Gloria's thighs. Robin had thought her friend shy, but now, as they intertwined, their eyes met, and Gloria's blue irises shone like portals to the sky. The receiving of so much tenderness made Robin want to give it in return. She hadn't thought she was in love with Gloria, but as they made love, she became so.

By late afternoon, Robin was lying on her side, resting her head on Gloria's shoulder. The two women cuddled and caressed until they heard the front door open and slam. Then again a few minutes later. Robin's cousins were home.

"I should get dressed and go back to my apartment," Gloria said, sitting up.

"Hey." Robin reached for her arm. "We're going to do this again, right? I mean, you want to be . . . lovers now, right?"

"Obviously. Why don't you come over later and spend the night? I'll make you dinner."

"Sure."

They got dressed and Robin walked Gloria to the door. Anna and Julia waved to her from the kitchen where they were doing an inventory of the fridge.

"Your hair!" Anna exclaimed, laughing, after the door slammed shut, and Robin realized that her curls must have gotten wilder than usual in the afternoon's play. "Something going on we should know about?"

Robin was not prone to blushing, but she did now. "Yeah. We just . . . Yeah. I like her." She grinned. "A lot."

"Congratulations," Anna said.

"But you're still seeing Michael," Julia said. "What are you going to do? Are you going to tell him?"

Robin didn't enjoy her cousin's judgment. "Of course I will. When the moment is right." The truth was she didn't know when the moment would be right, but things were happening fast. "In the meantime, do me a favor and don't tell him, okay? Or anyone else."

Anna nodded. "Sure."

Julia stood quietly.

"Julia?" Robin pressed. "I know you and Michael are close, but you just can't tell him."

"I'm not a good liar," Julia said.

"Well, try, for my sake. Try to keep it to yourself for a bit."

"Okay." Julia looked distressed.

"Oh God, you want everything so neat and simple, it's unbelievable."

"I just don't see how you're going to do this. You're going to continue to see him? And sleep with him?" Julia asked.

"I'm going to figure it out in my own sweet time, thank you very much. And I'll tell him when I'm ready." Irritated and anxious, Robin stomped back into her room and gathered her things for her night out.

And so it happened that after spending Saturday night with Michael, Robin spent Sunday night at Gloria's. Robin had been to her attic apartment only once before, when she'd needed a place to land after breaking up with Stephanie. Returning there now, as Gloria's lover, she noticed everything afresh. It was cozy but a bit dark, with light coming in only from skylights. Robin wondered how one could be happy without being able to look out a window. One wall was devoted to scientific posters: a chemical periodic table, a map of the human brain, and another of the human body. On the opposite wall, two reproductions of Impressionist paintings featured a woman having tea in a flowering garden and a nude. Bookcases flanked the double bed. A built-in kitchen had open shelving with dishes and serving ware organized in a way that struck Robin as very grown-up.

Gloria said, "Why don't you relax while I make dinner?"

"Can I help?"

"No, it's easier if I do it myself. And you need the time to study."

Robin opened her textbook at the little dining table. She had to study more than Gloria for exams. Memory was her weak point, and she had a hard time remembering the names of brain chemicals. She was used to making the extra effort to assimilate material, but it tired her. Glancing up at Gloria, who was standing at the kitchen sink, Robin admired her form. When she looked at Gloria from the front, she tended to fixate on her large breasts; now, seeing her from the back, Robin appreciated her small waist and the way her ass looked in jeans.

Robin watched Gloria work on a stir-fry with tofu and peanut sauce. Gloria was a natural cook who loved the ritual of dinner, from the cooking to setting the table and lighting candles. Interested in the presentation of a dish, she minced some chives and scattered them on top of the food before serving it. Robin was impressed.

After dinner, Robin washed the dishes while Gloria puttered around the bed, moving the candles to the nightstands. When Robin was done, they got into bed and lay on their sides, gazing at each other.

"I'm so happy," Gloria said. "So, so happy."

"When did you start . . . wanting to?" Robin asked.

"Last summer when we drove east together. But you were still with Stephanie, so I didn't dare. What about you?"

Robin's hand traced the contours of Gloria's face, then moved down to hold her breast.

"I'm not sure." Her mind slipped sideways and back remembering Stephanie, then Theo in San Francisco, and Michael. Michael here, in New Haven, a few blocks away, whom she'd slept with the previous night. If things worked out with Gloria—whatever that meant—she would have to dismiss him. She would want to, and she had to do it soon. Julia was right to be disconcerted.

"The attraction was there all along, but there was Stephanie, and I wasn't sure whether you were interested in women or just a feminist. I never saw you with anyone."

"There were a couple of short things, but Wellesley was such a fishbowl, I couldn't stand all the gossiping, so I tried to keep my private life to myself. But if you're happy with me and we . . . we continue"—Gloria looked away shyly—"then I want everyone to know. I mean, if you do too." Her eyes came back up to meet Robin's, and Robin was filled with love and desire.

"My thoughts exactly. Everyone except parents, obviously," she said, though she didn't know who "everyone" might be if they both left graduate school and ended up in different places. *Aren't we moving kind of fast here?*

Gloria must have had a moment of wondering the same because she said, "Sorry if I brought that up too soon."

"No, no, it's okay. We'll work it out."

Between one set of kisses and the next, Robin saw again in the brilliant blue of Gloria's eyes the relationship she'd been looking for, one in which she might feel love while making it.

Gloria was glorious, but Robin kept on seeing Michael despite her nagging conscience. For two weeks, she juggled two lovers. Every time she went out with one, she was afraid of being seen by the other. She could have told each of them the truth, but she was paralyzed by anxiety about the consequences of such a move. She knew she had to break up with Michael. But she didn't want to because she enjoyed his company and having sex with him, and she didn't know where things with Gloria would go; moreover, his apartment—what with Julia staying over with Ben so often— had begun to feel like a second home, and she didn't want to give up one of her communities.

Robin usually had a high tolerance for uncertainty because she thought of life as one long experiment, but the waiting to hear back from the graduate school in San Francisco put her in a turmoil. If accepted, she would probably leave the program at Yale and move back to the West Coast for its progressive approach to psychology. Every morning, full of hope and dread, she checked the mail at 9:30 a.m. There was nothing until finally one day the letter came.

She had been accepted. Her mood swung back and forth as she processed the news. Excitement arose at the prospect of studying exactly what she wanted to, and once back in California, there would be more opportunities for adventures in consciousness. She was struck by the prospect of leaving both Michael and Gloria; she couldn't begin to sort that one out. Maybe one of them would convince her to stay. If neither did, she had to inform her advisor that she was leaving, and she dreaded it. He would tell her she was crazy to pass up a Yale degree in statistically based psychology for a newly established school that had classes on esoteric subjects such as archetypal mythology and Eastern thought. She doubted herself as she imagined their conversation because she wasn't immune to the lure of the Ivy League and what it represented. Then she remembered the out-of-body experience she'd had the summer before her junior year, when she and Gloria had driven across the country together for the first time. After taking LSD in the desert of New Mexico, Robin had experienced her soul floating up into the ethers, and looking down at the top of her curly-haired head from the clouds, she'd wondered, *How did I get in there and why? How can my body be down there and my spirit up here? What is this doubleness?* These questions obsessed her, and she was sure that no advance in science would ever be able to map or explain the human spirit.

She had to search elsewhere for the knowledge she craved. She would return to California to explore what really interested her: the nature of the soul and its purpose, journey, and development. Her mother, who valued prestige, would be angry about her leaving Yale, but her father, who competed with her mother for her affection, would foot the bill.

She was in a pizza place with Michael the night she told him she had been accepted to CIIS.

"I knew you weren't happy with the program here, but you never told me you were thinking of transferring," he said.

She felt embarrassed that secrecy came so naturally to her. "I never thought I'd get accepted."

He looked surprised, maybe even hurt, by her withholding of information, but that didn't stop him from reaching for another slice.

"And are you going to go?" he asked.

"I'm thinking it over." Robin waited to see whether he'd ask her to stay and look at programs that were geographically nearby.

"What would you study there?" He took his time.

"Different approaches to consciousness, including Asian ones. I thought I wanted to do psychological research, but now I'm thinking of becoming a psychotherapist."

"It sounds interesting. Unconventional, consciousness expanding—right up your alley."

"Yes. The school is only a few years old, but . . . so interesting . . ." She reached for another piece of pizza.

"I think you've already decided to go."

If love was a chess game, she was losing. "I . . . I'm . . ."

"I would never stand in your way," he said.

"I didn't think you would."

"I've enjoyed your company," Michael continued. "And I hope you find whatever you're looking for, wherever it is that you end up."

"Okay," she said, bracing herself.

"I hate long goodbyes."

"You mean," she said, "that we should just end it now and get it over with?" It was early April, and they could have gone on hanging out and screwing for another couple of months. She hadn't expected he'd suggest ending it immediately; she'd imagined their tie would take more time to undo.

"Don't you think so? What's the alternative—to babysit this thing dying while you get ready to leave?"

"Of course. Of course you're right." She wanted to meet his cool, detached tone with the same.

"Hey, we're still going to be friends, okay?" He reached out and put his hand over hers.

"Sure."

Given that she had just gotten involved with someone else and planned on leaving, it made no sense to feel not only wounded in her pride but bereft. Although theirs had not been a big love story, it had been *something*—continuous, affectionate, with moments of sexual passion and connection. Now it was evaporating. No longer hungry, she leaned back against the hard wood of the booth.

Michael, too, had lost his appetite. He pulled out his wallet and put a few bills on the table.

"I guess you can just drop me at my place," she said.

They drove silently through the cold spring night until they reached her Orange Street apartment. He pulled up to the curb and turned off the engine. They looked at each other.

"You're great," he said. "I wish you every happiness."

"You too," she said.

"Hey, I really meant it about wanting to be friends. I'll see you around, right?"

"Of course."

Robin got out of the car thinking, *I never imagined a breakup could be this anticlimactic. Nothing like a train wreck, more like slipping into a muddy puddle. I wonder what he felt for me, really, if anything.*

Upstairs, she found Anna and Doug curled up on the futon in the living room, reading. Doug had taken the train up to New

Haven to take care of Anna, who had a cold and an asthmatic wheeze. He enjoyed keeping track of her inhaler doses, making soup, and bringing her tea.

"Hey," they said, waving.

"Hey." Robin nodded, not stopping to chat. Her pain felt private, and she wanted to be alone.

The rain picked up again, beating loudly on the roof, and it took her hours to fall asleep. She hadn't thought she was in love with Michael, but maybe she had been. Otherwise, she wouldn't be in so much pain now or overwhelmed by so many memories of sweet and sexy moments asking to be mourned. Restless, she shifted in bed until she started thinking of Gloria's large breasts. Kissing and kneading them in her imagination, she masturbated, then fell asleep.

When she opened her eyes the next morning, she felt emotionally drained but peaceful. The sun had come out, and the light reflecting off the wet streets was a soft, silvery gray. She had at times hoped Michael would want to make his happiness with her, but he hadn't. Her face in the mirror was swollen around the eyes although she hadn't cried. Or maybe she had cried in her sleep. She was supposed to meet Gloria later in the day, and she hoped to look normal by then. Thank God for Gloria.

Robin congratulated herself for having someone to fall back on. She should make a point of always doing that. Suddenly, she saw the folly of the romantic quest for happiness. The truth was that all things, including relationships, were changing all the time, and that the search for a single true love—the Master Monogamy Narrative—was a pathetic attempt to deny impermanence by imagining that a one-and-only durable love was possible. But it was not. The realization that there would be no happily ever after, at least not for her, presented itself so brutally that the only response was to strategize methods of coping. And the first was the decision that she would never put all her emotional or libidinal eggs in one basket again.

❄

Robin and Gloria saw each other every day. Robin told her advisor she would continue her studies in San Francisco. His indifference to her departure led her to the conclusion that he was, as she'd suspected, a misogynist who had no use for female graduate students. As for Gloria, she decided she would take some time off from school and think about her next step. Although the conversation was waiting to be had, the two women held off discussing what the end of the school year would mean for their relationship.

"Maybe you should become a massage therapist," Robin suggested one evening. Gloria had given her an excellent rub, and they were having dinner. "You have a healing touch."

"I've actually thought of that," Gloria said. "It might be something I could do while figuring out what I should really be doing." She reached across the table. "Might we drive west together?"

Robin took her hand. "Sure, why wouldn't we?"

They had driven east the previous summer as friends. At the end of May, they would make the return drive as lovers.

"Well, getting me back to Albuquerque means looping south."

"If you're wanting to go home, I don't mind."

"I don't necessarily want to go home," Gloria said, meeting her gaze.

They studied each other across the table.

"Yeah, I imagine going back to Albuquerque would be kinda—"

"Anticlimactic. I don't plan on seeing my parents."

"Why don't you come to San Francisco with me, and we can look for a place to live together?" It was a big question, and it slipped out of Robin's mouth of its own accord.

They smiled at each other happily. "Where would you want to live?" Gloria asked. "I mean, what neighborhood?"

"I've always liked Sunset," Robin said. "The weather is crummy, but I'd like being near the ocean and far from my parents. Though we can stay with them while we're apartment hunting."

"Sunset it is, then," Gloria said, and raised her glass of wine for a toast.

They clinked glasses, and Robin wondered what she'd done.

"Is it okay for me to do this?" Gloria asked, passing her arm through Robin's. They were walking in the cemetery a week later. The ground was moist from recent rain, and the trees were budding. "I don't know how you feel about PDAs. You and Steph were always so discreet at Wellesley."

"That's because she was worried about getting tenure. But you and me, sure, I'm okay with it. What are people going to say? Or do to us?" Robin felt giddy, protected by the new love she was feeling. And being in a couple made it easier to step a little farther out of the closet. "I wouldn't want my parents to know, though."

"No, you don't want that. When my parents found out last summer, it was awful."

"How did they react?"

"My mom said, 'How about you straighten yourself out before your next visit home? We don't need to see you while you're in this phase.'"

"Wow," Robin said. "And that's why you said you don't plan on seeing them."

"Yeah, and that's why I stayed with my sister last summer."

"They'll have to accept it sooner or later."

"Not necessarily. I have four siblings. One child less . . ." Gloria shrugged.

"That's brutal. I'm so sorry." Robin slipped her hand into Gloria's and lifted it for a kiss. "My mother would pretend to be cool about it, then she'd go into the bathroom and have a heart attack."

"And your dad?"

"My dad would be in denial. Or he'd say, 'She's just being a rebel.'"

They laughed, and then Gloria pulled her toward her. "You *are* a rebel. But maybe not enough to kiss me in a Christian cemetery?"

"Oh yeah, but let's stand against that tree over there, to make it more pagan."

Robin pulled her over to the tree where, the previous fall, she and Michael had exchanged their first kiss. Perhaps she wanted to paint over the memory of him by kissing her new partner there. Perhaps she wanted to get back at him for having let her go so easily. Whatever the reason, the tree called to her, and she leaned against it as she drew Gloria toward her. Then, coming up for air, she saw at the other end of the cemetery the very man she had hoped to erase. And she saw that he saw her.

He shook his head at her with that bitter frown she knew well. *He's realizing I was two-timing him before we ended it*, Robin thought. *Damn it.* She jolted and stood frozen against the tree as he swung around and walked rapidly away.

"What's wrong?" Gloria asked.

"Nothing, nothing. I remembered something I have to do."

Robin had never told Gloria about Michael, and she decided she wouldn't now. The two relationships should stay separate in reality, as in her head. She would keep all of it to herself—her past involvement with him, his witnessing their kiss, her shame about causing him pain. Talking about the lab assignment she had due the next day, she quickened her pace as they left the cemetery.

Even as she felt guilty about lying to Michael and the way he'd found out about it, she also felt she had her reasons for doing what she'd done, and she wanted him to understand what they were. She didn't want to live in the shadow of his anger.

About an hour after she and Gloria separated, she called him from her apartment. Ben answered.

"Michael's not here," he said.

Robin thought she'd heard the piano in the background when he picked up. "Is that true?" she asked.

"What do you mean?"

"I mean, is that true?"

"No," Ben said.

"So he actually told you to pretend he wasn't there if I called?"

"Yes."

"Fuck. I'm coming over."

And sure enough, when she climbed the stairs to their place fifteen minutes later, she heard the piano. The door was open, and she let herself in.

"Hey, Robin." Michael stopped playing. His expression was closed and impassive.

"Michael, I'm so sorry about what happened. I didn't mean for you to find out that way."

"You're a piece of shit."

"Michael!" She'd never seen him so angry—except that night when he'd told her about how his best friend had slept with his wife. And there she was, another partner who had betrayed him.

"Go ahead, try to defend yourself. This should be amusing. I don't even know what you're doing here."

He was still seated at the piano, his rampart and shield.

"I want us to be amicable; that's what I'm doing here. You're living with my cousin's boyfriend; we have to be amicable."

"Your cousin's boyfriend, as you call him, and I are hardly getting along because I'm not ambitious enough for him, and we're all leaving anyway, so why does it matter?"

"It does matter!" She was crying now.

"Oh, cut the tears. And tell me how long you've been seeing her."

"Very recent. It's not what you think."

"That's right. It's not what I think; it's what I saw."

It was her turn to get angry. "You never once said, 'I love you.' And Gloria does. Gloria loves me."

"So things have to be labeled neatly for you, is that it? I should have gotten one of those plastic label makers and punched out 'I love you' and stuck it to my forehead?"

"Come on!"

Michael stood up, and she thought he might strike her. But he swung into the kitchen and came back with a bottle of whiskey and a couple of glasses he set on the coffee table. He sat down in the armchair across from her.

Robin sat on the couch. "Sit next to me. Please."

He grunted, moved to her side, and poured them drinks.

"I'm sorry," she repeated.

"The two of you going to live in San Francisco together?"

"Yes."

"What happened? Did you want me to try to convince you to stay here with me instead of going to California? Or you just don't like men?"

"I really liked hanging out with you, and I loved having sex with you, but you didn't make me feel loved."

His eyes filled with tears. "Maybe I've forgotten how to do that. Or don't know how."

"Of course you know how. We weren't right for each other, that's all."

"You know, I did and do love you, kinda sorta."

"And I do love you still—as a friend—and I can't stand the idea of you hating me."

"I'll try not to," he said.

"Give me a hug."

He hugged her sideways, then raised his glass for a toast. "To you and Gloria," he said. "May you be happy together." And he threw it back.

14

GRADUATION PARTY

(Anna)

The commencement ceremony for the class of '77 had ended; diplomas were securely in hand. As Anna lifted her gown over her head, a breeze came up and made it balloon out around her as though to help her out of it. She and Julia handed their robes back to their mothers, who stood by with shopping bags. Doug engulfed Anna in a bear hug, and Ben picked Julia up and twirled her around while the two sets of proud parents stood by. Euphoria was in the air. Intoxicated with their liberation, students rolled on the grass, laughing and tackling each other like lion cubs, as though to defer their entry into adulthood.

The graduates returned their rented gowns and were headed off campus with their parents and boyfriends when Anna saw her advisor and future employer, Leila Behrens. Wearing a 1940s-red lipstick that lifted the darkness of her pantsuit, she looked chic and ready for Paris.

Leila congratulated and hugged her.

"Now we can focus on getting ready for our adventure," Leila said.

"I'm so excited."

The plan was for them to go in early September. Leila would send ahead boxes of books and necessary materials for her research project. They already had passports. Only the living arrangements had to be worked out.

"I have a couple of apartment leads," Leila said.

"Where?" Anna liked to nurture her fantasies with research and map study. She felt giddy at the prospect of returning to France.

"One of them is on the Left Bank, *bien sûr!*" Leila said, and as she giggled, also intoxicated by the adventure ahead, she seemed closer to Anna's age than to the forty-plus years she was. But the silliness was fleeting. "The other is near the Bibliothèque Nationale. Less fun but more convenient." The French National Library was in the second arrondissement, not far from the stock market and financial district.

"You're the famous Leila?" Anna's mother asked. Linda, who rarely left home and her sculptor's studio, had tried to clean the clay out from under her fingernails for her daughter's graduation but without complete success. However, she looked sharp in jeans and a black silk shirt with giant white polka dots. She had three strands of pearls around her neck and her wild auburn-and-gray hair was clipped back. Anna hoped she would behave respectably.

"I am. And you're Anna's mother?"

The two women shook hands.

"You'll keep an eye on her? Make sure she doesn't get into trouble?" Linda asked anxiously.

"Anna's a sensible girl, unlikely to get into too much trouble, I think."

"Young women abroad—don't they always get into trouble?" Linda gazed at her daughter.

Disgusted by her mother's concern, which she thought a sham, Anna didn't respond. Leila touched her shoulder.

"I have to go. We'll keep in touch over the summer," Leila said, and disappeared into the crowd.

"She seems nice enough," Linda said. "I'm hungry. Let's get going."

It was eleven thirty, the beginning of the pre-lunch cocktail hour, and Anna knew her mother was thirsty, not hungry, but she played along.

"Robin will have lunch ready for us," she said.

"Doug! Where's that man of yours?" Linda asked. "There you are!" She grabbed his arm and walked ahead rapidly, impatient for a drink.

Anna's father extended an arm, which she took gratefully.

"I'm glad to have this moment alone with you," Carl said. He looked tired. "I'm so proud of you."

"I don't know why. I've just done what everyone else has done." She gestured toward the other graduates streaming away from the stage with their families.

"But you did it without much support. Moral support, I mean."

Her father's awareness surprised her.

"Me in the lab all the time," he continued, "and your mother . . ."

"Have things been bad?"

"They've been worse." He stopped. "Maybe I made a mistake."

"In marrying her?"

"No." He laughed. "That was too long ago. I meant in intercepting the letter you wrote her last summer."

The memory of the episode sparked Anna's anger again. She frowned. "Why are you telling me this now?"

He shrugged. "I work like the devil at the lab, but I'm lazy about everything else in life. I've always wanted to avoid conflict to keep my head clear for science, but the problems I avoid always catch up with me. Things at home have been intolerable. She never stops screaming at me."

"Dad, you could . . . you could *do something.*"

"Like what?"

"Like leave her. You could leave her."

"Leave your mother? Never. She needs me too much."

"She needs me too much"? Where did that come from? What crazy ethical system?

"How can you put up with her when she makes you so unhappy?" Anna asked.

"Because you can chase after 'happiness' all you want, but what counts in the end is having a meaningful life. And there are two meaningful things in my life: doing scientific research and taking care of your mother. You and your sister constitute a third, of course."

When Doug and Linda reached the car, Carl held back to have an extra minute with his daughter.

"I don't know if you can understand what I'm saying," he said. "When you're young, you want happiness. When you're old, you want it all to add up to something. Something meaningful."

"So you'll never leave her, but you won't make her dry out either."

"You mean have her do a program? I think she'd crumble like a house of cards if they took her drink away and forced her to face the realities."

"What realities?"

"Her failures. That she didn't turn out to be another Rodin."

"Maybe they'd help her realize that her idea of success is ridiculous."

Carl watched Doug open the car door for Linda.

"You weren't so lucky with your mother and me," he said, "but you lucked out with Doug. He's a good one. Hold on to him."

When they arrived back at the apartment, there was pizza on the table, and the room was decorated with holiday lights for the celebration. A cake Robin had made that morning sat on the kitchen counter. She added brandy, sliced oranges, and ice to the wine in a baker's bread bowl. It was a warm day in late May, and the sangria looked refreshing. Anna hoped her mother would control herself, but if not, so be it.

Ben ladled out a glass of punch for Anna. "I'm envious. You're going to live in my favorite city," he said.

"That's right." Anna liked Ben and thought Julia had chosen well. "Any advice?"

"I have an old friend there I can put you in touch with," he said.

"Those things never work out."

"In Paris they do. People are very sociable there, you'll see."

"What's his or her name?"

"Dominique. She's artsy, like you. She'll take you to events."

"Dominique—your ex."

Ben laughed. "Of course, the three cousins tell each other everything. Yes, my ex."

The older generation had settled around the table, so the younger sat on the floor. Anna's mood dropped as she watched her mother take a second cup of sangria. Julia leaned in toward Ben, who stroked her hair and whispered in her ear. Anna and Doug were no longer so affectionate with each other, but she would have liked him sitting next to her. He was talking to Robin as though to console her for being single that afternoon: Robin hadn't invited Gloria, probably because they weren't about to reveal their relationship to the older generation. Michael was supposed to show up, and maybe he didn't know about Gloria either; Anna wasn't sure. Approving of Doug's gallant attention to her cousin, she focused on the pizza; the combination of salt and fat felt sweet in her mouth.

The door opened, and Michael came in. Robin detached herself from Doug and went to greet him. They exchanged the perfunctory hug of two exes meeting again, and Doug, free now, came and sat down next to Anna. He gave her hand a quick squeeze before reaching for a slice of pizza.

"I guess we still have a lot of packing to do," he said. Anna had packed her clothes, but her paintings, art supplies, and kitchen items still had to be boxed up. The plan was to take most of her stuff back to her parents' place, then drive up to the Cambridge apartment he would live in while studying architecture at MIT. Anna would spend the summer with him there. How much of the summer, she hadn't yet decided.

"The past few days have been crazy," she said. "A lot of running around to say goodbye to people."

"Not too many parties, I hope."

Anna gave his arm a reassuring squeeze. Doug tried to keep his jealousy in check, but the specter of parties and what might happen at them kept him vigilant.

"Not parties exactly. More like open suites with drinks available. Kind of emotionally exhausting, actually." For two days she had wandered in and out of senior residences across campus, saying goodbyes and signing yearbooks.

"I saw you talking to Leila." He frowned.

"Doug, I'm not changing my mind. I'm going to Paris."

"Okay, okay. We'll have the summer together. And I'll visit you at Christmas. You still want me to visit, don't you?"

"Of course I want you to visit." She didn't know whether she was speaking the truth or not. And there was something they still had to talk about but had avoided; remembering the violence of his January temper tantrum, she didn't care for another confrontation. Anna put her pizza down and poured herself some more wine. There were screeches coming from the dining table. Glancing in that direction, she saw her mother and Mariel seated next to each other, laughing hysterically.

"Oh, Brooklyn!" Linda hollered. "How I miss thee!"

"Bring it all back, baby!"

Flatbush was still yesterday for these two ladies.

"Brooklyn, city of lights! City of dreams!" Linda yelled.

"Let's hear it for Brooklyn!" Mariel took off a shoe and struck the table with it. "Brooklyn that birthed us!"

"That raised us!" Linda took off her shoe and did the same.

"Educated us!" *Bang!* went Mariel's shoe.

"Formed us!" *Bang!*

"And married us! For better or for worse!"

"Long live Brooklyn!" *Bang! Bang!* went the shoes in a frenzy.

"Long live the Mothers," Julia whispered to Anna in their traditional baritone.

"Whether we like it or not." Anna grimaced and rolled her eyes in return.

Julia turned toward Michael, who raised his eyebrows in the secret language of friends who know when to come to each other's aid. Anna had noticed their alliance before and suffered because of it. It occurred to her that she might never see Michael again, now that they were both leaving Yale; the thought brought back the pain of her unrequited fascination. A familiar, restless irritability came over her. Michael was every-thing Doug wasn't—intense, passionate, and tormented by his own creative energies. Anna kicked herself for being attracted to such a romantic stereotype.

Unaware of her turmoil, Michael gently placed one hand on Mariel's shoulder and the other on Linda's.

"Now, now, ladies, you're drowning everyone out." He could deliver a reproach with total charm when necessary.

"Listen to me, young man," Linda said. "You can't be a real artist of any kind if you haven't passed through the cauldron of Brooklyn."

Mariel stood up. Because she was an actress, it was her job to make speeches.

"Let's drink a toast to the graduates! My lovely niece Anna

and my daughter Julia!" She raised her glass, and Linda banged her shoe on the table again, hooting.

"Mom! What's with the shoe thing?" Anna cried out. She was embarrassed not so much in front of her family or Doug, who knew her mother's drinking well, but in front of Michael, for she valued his high opinion of her, even as they headed toward goodbyes.

Linda stood up and put her arm around Mariel's waist. The two mothers glowed with the tragicomic despair of women in middle age who realize that what they've got is probably all they'll ever get, so they might as well have fun.

"Time for some family history," Linda said. "My sister Sarah and I grew up with just a wall between our apartment and Mariel's. When our mothers wanted to go shopping together, they'd take a shoe off and bang it on the wall. Two taps meant going out in ten minutes, and three taps meant twenty."

"And four taps meant, 'Get me the hell out of here!'" Mariel hollered, and she and Linda started beating the table with their shoes and hooting again. "Because they were desperate for freedom, those poor mothers!" She stood up. "It was only our generation that finally was able to say,"—she yanked the strap of her dress down and with it the cup of her bra, baring her breast like the woman on the barricades in Delacroix's painting—"*Vive la liberté!*"

Linda, exhilarated by her cousin's display, stood up next to her and did the same. Two middle-aged women baring their sagging breasts at the same time.

Sam, used to his wife's performances, held his hands up in front of his eyes. "I'm blinded," he said, "blinded by so much beauty."

Things could only degenerate from there. Anna leaned toward Doug. "I'm the one who needs to get the hell out of here," she whispered, and stood up.

She rushed down the stairs with Doug following her. When they reached the sidewalk, Anna could still hear the mothers hooting and hollering.

"Can you believe Mariel exposing herself like that?" Anna said, fuming. "If I were Julia and had a mother like that, I'd kill myself. And the way my mom imitates her automatically—I've never been so embarrassed in my whole life."

The sound of the mothers' cavorting grew fainter as they headed down the quiet street overhung with spring-green trees. Anna took a deep breath.

"They like being outrageous," Doug said.

"They're trying to prove they are as 'liberated' as we are. They're jealous of us because we were born later, with more freedom."

"Maybe," he said.

"'Maybe'? Don't you see? I need to understand it. I need to understand why she insists on humiliating me. Aunt Mariel, okay, she's an actress, life is one continual theatrical experiment for her, but my mother—what's her excuse?"

"You going to be okay?"

"I don't know. I need to walk around the block."

Anna had learned to escape family dramas by taking the byways of her visual imagination, and a book her parents owned popped into her mind. A collection of photographs of Paris taken in the late 1940s, it featured black-and-white shots of empty, tree-lined streets in quiet neighborhoods, mementos of a postwar city that no longer existed. Nostalgia pleased her, for it was her habit to long for the remote and the unattainable.

She was startled out of her survival daydream by Doug taking her hand. His palm was sticky with perspiration, yet she appreciated the gesture and held on.

"Annie," he said, "I'm so sorry about what your mother puts you through."

She shrugged. It was an old story, and she was already far away, wondering whether she might find a lover in Paris or maybe two. *Why not?* She was twenty-two, and Doug was the only partner she'd ever had.

"I know I was an ass when you first told me about Leila's job offer," he said, "but I want you to follow your dreams. I hope you've forgiven me."

"Of course I have. I didn't expect you to be happy about my going away."

"And you can enjoy your freedom in Paris, and I won't be jealous," he went on, reading her mind. "It won't change our relationship, I promise."

This was the topic that needed to be discussed. After ruminating on it separately, they had reached the same conclusion. Anna stopped. She was a tall girl and had always loved that he was taller than she was, and strong. *I'll never find another hunk like this*, she thought, but what she said was, "And the same goes for you, of course. You should enjoy your freedom too." Inside lurked the thought—no, the hope—that he would find someone else and release her. It would be much easier than her dumping him—which she wasn't ready to do anyway.

"I know that for me, I mean, *I know*, that even if there was someone else, it would be brief, and it would never change my feelings for you and my desire to make my life with you." They had gone around the block and come back to the front gate of her house. "Give me a hug," he said.

Doug drew her to him, and Anna sank her nose into his chest. The white collared shirt he'd put on for graduation felt soft and cool against her skin. Why was she having these fantasies of moving on when his holding her could unwind her nervous system from any shock or stress? "But don't you think," she asked, "that if we have other lovers, it will change us? And if we change, our relationship will change."

"We've changed a lot over the past eight years, and we're still together, and we still love each other. We'll survive the separation and come out better and stronger."

As she touched and smelled him, a permanent break felt inconceivable. And maybe he was correct; their wanderings might draw them closer because other relationships would prove inadequate and superficial in comparison.

"I hope you're right," she said.

"I know I'm right."

A voice interrupted them. "Hey, you guys!" Michael was coming down the stairs. "Nice to see a young couple who can't keep their hands off each other."

"You taking off?" Anna asked.

"Yeah. I'm not family, and the moms are getting kind of wild up there."

"Shit," Anna said. "Are they doing a striptease?"

"Almost. Okay, bye, guys." Michael headed toward his car.

"Hey!" she called out.

"What?"

"I'm leaving later today."

"Oh. A real goodbye then?" He came back toward them. "Anna, the third cousin. What a gang you three beauties have been. May God bless and all that." He hugged her, then shook Doug's hand.

She reveled in his quick squeeze; then it was over. As she watched him get into his car, her chest tightened as though her heart were being stuffed into a plastic bag. Doug waved as Michael honked and pulled away from the curb. He was gone now and forever.

"Come on," Doug said. "Let's face the music."

He was punning, for loud music could be heard from upstairs. When they reached the apartment, they found Linda and Mariel dancing and singing to "Don't Go Breaking My Heart." Anna groaned.

Linda broke away from Mariel, waltzed up to her daughter, and took both her hands in hers.

"*Oh, oh, oh* . . ." Linda sang. "Anna, you are the most beautiful, talented creature in the world!" And, leaning forward, she gave her daughter a wet, brandy-flavored kiss on the mouth.

15

THE CROSSROADS

(Julia)

The day after the older generation left, the cousins emptied and cleaned the apartment. Anna and Doug loaded her furniture and boxes into his car; the plan was to drive to Bridgeport and take the ferry back to Long Island so she could spend a few days at her parents' before they headed up to Boston. Robin had in her car a suitcase she would take to Gloria's.

As for Julia, she had sent some of her stuff home with her parents and moved the rest to Ben's. He had officially asked her to move in with him when Michael moved out, but she hadn't yet decided what to do. As she and Ben loaded his car, she had a moment of emotional vertigo. She had no clear sense of how long she'd stay with him; she might be moving all her belongings back to New York by the end of the summer.

"Hey," he said as he closed the hatchback. "I'm looking forward to the summer together. I'm happy." He kissed her on the lips.

Julia returned his kiss with uncertainty in her heart. She wanted to live with him, but she feared losing herself in her love for him. "Me too," she said, and they went back upstairs.

There was a bottle of wine on the kitchen counter and beer in the fridge. The five of them were sweaty and dirty from packing and carrying boxes, scrubbing, and vacuuming.

"How about Doug and I enjoy a manly beer on the front steps while the three of you say your goodbyes?" Ben said.

The guys stepped out, and the cousins looked at each other.

"I guess it's time to leave our keys," Robin said. They placed their sets on the kitchen counter in an envelope she'd prepared. "Here's to hoping we get our deposit back."

"If he sees how I fucked up the rug, we won't," Anna said.

"You mean, how Michael fucked up the rug," Robin corrected, and laughed. "Hey, let's have our own drink." Grabbing the wine, she led them to the living room, where they sat cross-legged on the floor. She took a swig, then placed the bottle in the middle, between them. All their glasses were packed.

"Oh my god," Anna burst out, "the end of an era."

"I want to congratulate us on living together successfully and not killing each other," Robin said.

"I don't like change," Julia said, and her tears began to roll.

"Hey, hey. Come here." Robin extended her arms, and Julia scooted in sideways for a hug. "For you, not much is changing. You're moving ten blocks from here into Ben's apartment. I'm the one who's moving back to California."

"And I'll be in Boston, then Paris," Anna said. "That's really far."

"I don't like you guys being far," Julia said. "I'm not good at separations." The loneliness of her childhood without siblings, which their cohabitation had assuaged for nine months, had returned and was heavy upon her. She hadn't realized before how sweet the respite had been.

Robin stroked her hair. "We'll write. We'll talk on the phone."

Anna placed a hand on Julia's knee. "And you're coming out to the Island tomorrow, so we'll have a couple days together."

"It won't be the same." Julia wept like a small child separated from her mother in a department store.

"Oh, come on now," Robin said in her most soothing tone. "You have to be brave. You have to grow up."

"I'm so lost," Julia sobbed.

"Ben is terrific."

Julia glanced toward Ben and Doug, who were laughing and talking on the steps. "Yeah, yeah he is."

Robin continued stroking her hair. "I'm sad too. We're all sad. But there's not much we can do about it. Time is like an escalator. It moves forward, or up, or down, and you can't stop it."

Julia wiped her nose on her sleeve. "No, you can't, can you?"

"You'll be fine," Robin said.

"I'll be fine," Julia repeated.

But Julia wasn't sure she'd be fine. She didn't like the idea of remaining in New Haven until Ben finished his doctorate. Job prospects were better in New York, and she knew the motive behind his invitation had been economic as well as romantic. Yes, he didn't want her returning to New York after graduation, but he also needed someone to pay Michael's half of the rent. Julia would stay for the summer as a test run before deciding what to do. In the meantime, they'd stacked her boxes and suitcases in Michael's old bedroom.

Ben's apartment looked tidier but sadly empty without Michael. Gone were the piles of LPs on the floor and the old record player on the bookshelf. The rectangle of wall behind where the piano used to be was a shade brighter than the surface around it. On the windowsill, a fragment of a vinyl record commemorated the crazy dinner party when they had all met. She wondered when she would see Michael again

"Do you think he'll be happy in New York?" she asked Ben, who brought a bottle of brandy over to the couch.

"I don't know. And I don't know why he's still angry with me," Ben said.

"You were pushy, that's why."

Ben shrugged. "I find it hard not to speak my mind when I see something about someone that they don't see themselves."

"And what did you see?"

"A musician who needs to grab his destiny by the horns. Want some?" He poured her a glass without waiting for her answer.

Julia said nothing. The rift between the two guys was unfortunate. She couldn't understand Ben's sacrificing the friendship for an idea of what Michael should or shouldn't be doing, but she didn't want to meddle.

"Why do you have to go to Anna's tomorrow?" Ben interrupted her thoughts. "Why not just stay here for a few days and unpack a bit, then go?"

"Because I want a couple of days with her at the beach, and she'll be heading up to Boston soon. What difference does it make? I can unpack when I get back."

"All right. And then you're still going into the city after seeing her?"

"Yes. We discussed this already. I need to spend time with my parents."

"To have a powwow with your dad."

"Yes."

"I like your dad. And your mom."

"Thanks."

"You think they'll mind your spending the summer here?"

She sighed. "Probably. They want to see me employed and independent."

"You don't have to rush into anything. I can cover the rent until you find a job here."

"You can't afford the whole rent on a graduate student stipend."

"You'll find something quickly," he said.

"My father will probably offer to help in the meantime, then be grumpy about it."

"We don't need his help."

"Okay, we'll see." She felt drained by the emotions of the weekend—graduation, the mothers' outlandish behavior, the many goodbyes. "He'll say something like, 'If you don't find a job by such-and-such date, you have to come home.'"

"If we were married, he wouldn't say that."

Julia was taken aback. Getting married was the last thing an urban, educated woman of twenty-two would rush into.

"But we're not married."

"No, we're not." He stood up. "I'll make us something for dinner."

Ben headed to the kitchen. Gifted with a fast metabolism, he could eat constantly and remain thin. Julia puzzled over this and other mysteries as she went into Michael's old room and rummaged around for some things she wanted to pack for her trip. His ghost was in the room along with his spicy, earthy smell, undoubtedly from some combination of the soaps and deodorants he used. Maybe there was a dash of Tide in the air. She missed the way she could depend on him for advice and support.

She looked forward to her time with Anna, but not to the "serious" conversation with her parents. Given what her father had spent on her fancy education, Julia felt embarrassed about having no job or direction to show for it. Wanting to escape a rising wave of self-criticism, she applied herself to packing.

Ben drove her to Bridgeport the next day, and they walked over to the docks together. The big ferry, rusty but reliable, was nearing shore. They watched as the crew threw ropes and chains over the mooring poles, then lowered the metal plank to dry land. Passengers got off.

"Okay," Ben said.

Julia looked at him. First love performs its particular sorcery, and she was too besotted to think clearly about their future.

"I'll call you," she said.

"Please do."

As they kissed, then hugged, she imagined summer's end and what it would be like if, instead of moving in with him, she established herself in an apartment in New York and changed their relationship to a commuting one. It was unthinkable. Stroking his hair and neck, she pressed herself against him, and he squeezed her slim waist.

"I love your hip bones," he said, caressing them.

He grabbed her for another kiss, and it hurt so much to separate that she knew, *This is my destiny, I can't go very far,* and she pushed him away because the ferry was tooting and went up the plank then the narrow metal staircase to the upper deck. By the time she reached the top and looked out over the railing toward the port, Ben was gone. They'd been apart before, when he'd gone home to London for winter break or when she'd gone into Manhattan without him to visit her parents, and she'd never liked it. There was always the pressure in her chest, the anxiety about interruption—where did that come from? Maybe she feared the possibility that she might, after or during a separation, find him or herself feeling differently. She loved Ben so much that she wanted it to go on forever exactly as it was. *But life doesn't work that way,* she mused, *does it?*

As the ferry approached the opposite shore, she moved to the prow to enjoy the view of Port Jefferson sitting between the sandy cliffs dotted with scruffy, windswept trees. The huge ferry towered over the small marina crowded with sailboats and small yachts. Anna was waiting and waving. The crew moored the boat, and soon the cousins were hugging.

"You smell like the beach," Julia said.

"Shampoo and suntan lotion."

Anna led her to the car.

"That was quite the graduation party, wasn't it?" Julia said.

Anna grimaced. "Yeah. Sometimes I hate it when our moms get together."

"Oh, the Mothers!" Julia said, dropping her voice an octave.

"The Mothers!" Anna repeated, and they laughed.

"I'm sorry mine was the instigator," Julia said.

"I wasn't blaming Mariel. She probably wouldn't act that way if my mom didn't encourage her."

"And the whole Brooklyn thing," Julia said. "They use it as an excuse to put on a show."

"But we'll be different when we're their age, right?"

They got in the car, and Anna drove down roads flanked by dense greenery and occasional houses. There was a vegetable stand with a small farm field behind it. The air coming in through the open car windows smelled of sea, woods, and damp gardens.

"How's your mom doing today?" Julia asked.

"It's amazing, she never gets hungover." Anna shrugged.

"They drink because they're frustrated," Julia said.

"That's no excuse."

"I know."

"It's nearing high tide," Anna said. "We can go swimming."

"Sure, I'd love to."

Julia had visited Anna and her family two or three times a summer every year since they'd moved out to Long Island. Although sometimes embarrassed by Linda's alcoholic performances at dinner, she enjoyed the visits—biking country roads, swimming in the clear waters of the Sound, and the intimate conversations with her cousin. Looking forward to the rest of the day, Julia relaxed and sank back into the seat. They drove through the little town of Setauket with its single main street and white clapboard churches, then past the redbrick post office next to a large pond, and finally down a road running out to the lighthouse.

When they reached Anna's parents' house, the front door was open behind the screen one. It was quiet inside; Aunt Linda was working in her backyard sculptor's studio, and Uncle Carl was at the university lab. The area was isolated and the house never locked. The cousins changed into bathing suits in Anna's room and gathered towels. The way to the beach ran from the backyard along a trail that cut through neighborhood properties, then down a wooden staircase built against the side of the cliff. There was little wind, and the Sound sparkled under the June sun.

They spread their towels on the pebbled beach.

"You wanna go in?" Anna asked.

"I need to get hot first." Julia stretched out in the sun.

"Sure." Anna reached for Julia's hand and squeezed it. "Have you decided yet about moving in with Ben?"

Julia shrugged. "Not yet. It feels so natural when we're together, and so unnatural when we're apart. The practical part of me thinks I should move in with my parents while I look for a job in the city, but another part of me really wants to be with Ben, and all the time. I hate being separated."

"There aren't any jobs in New Haven. You'll be lucky if you get a secretarial position on campus."

"I know. But there are worse things."

"You might want to think this one through carefully," Anna said.

"It's not like I have any clear direction anyway," Julia said, then regretted her words. She sounded negative and dissatisfied with herself, but she wasn't. She simply wanted to be happy, and for the moment Ben was the provider of joy. Maybe not having a direction was what she needed at this point—and with it, at least for a while, freedom from the endless pressure to achieve. After four grueling years of academic life, she craved some time to do other things—to fool around at the piano, learn to cook, and write poetry and stories. People needed time and space to be creative.

"Personally, I couldn't stand staying in New Haven," Anna said.

"You need adventure."

"Maybe. Listen, you should come visit me in Paris."

"I don't know if I'll have the money. I'll see."

"Do you . . . feel sure about Ben? I mean the relationship part, not the living together."

Julia gave Anna a puzzled look. "Of course I'm sure."

Anna sighed. "I guess I'm not sure about Doug. That's why I'm going to Europe. Among other reasons."

"What's that going to look like?" Julia asked.

"What's what going to look like?"

"You and Doug, if you're in Europe."

Anna shrugged. "We'll write, he'll visit. The truth is, what I'm doing is messy, and I know it's not right, but I don't have the courage to make a clean break with him."

"So you're going to let it die a slow death?"

"Maybe. Or maybe I'm just testing it."

"Maybe you'll meet someone over there."

"So many maybe's!" Anna stood up and faced the Sound. "I'm going in."

She dove in and swam. Even though they had lived together for almost a year and shared intimate thoughts and desires, Julia sensed that Anna was keeping something from her. Michael passed through her mind as she remembered how angry Anna had been when he hadn't liked her "orange" painting, and suddenly she wondered whether . . . was it possible . . . had Anna hoped or wanted—? Julia shook off the thought. She and Michael had become so close and shared so many confidences that she felt, in some obscure way, that he "belonged" to her, and if Anna had felt an attraction . . . wouldn't Michael have told her? But then again, maybe he hadn't realized it himself.

Anna, who had swum out some distance, now headed back. She stopped closer to shore and waved. "Aren't you coming in?"

"Sure." Julia walked to the edge of the water. Having spent less time in the sea than Anna, she felt squeamish about the creatures living there. But the water was clear . . . not a single fish over the gleaming pebbles. She dove in. The icy cold made her gasp.

The next couple of days passed peaceably. The two women stopped talking about their men and moved on to gossip about the friends they had left behind, their dreams, and their parents. Julia found dinner with her aunt and uncle to be a more extreme version of dinner with her own parents. When drinking, Aunt Linda had more manic highs, more destructive lows. She could rage one moment, then laugh hysterically the next, and everyone at the table rode up and down with her. It was like being with a toddler.

On the morning before Julia's afternoon train into the city, Anna suggested a longer bike ride.

"I want to show you my secret house," she said. "It's a beautiful old mansion that's been abandoned. You can go in and wander around."

They got the bicycles out of the garage. Anna's parents' house sat on one tip of a fishtail-shaped land mass. They biked back toward the main body of land and out to the other tip called Crane Neck.

The houses in the area were two-story, white clapboard structures in the New England style, set on spacious wooded properties, with modest landscaping. Anna suddenly stopped and got off her bicycle.

"Now what?" Julia asked.

"There's a shortcut here. Follow me."

As they walked their bikes down a narrow path through a patch of woods, Julia looked around nervously for snakes and spiders. They reached a locked gate.

"We have to lift the bikes over the fence," Anna said.

Pushing the overhanging bushes and trees to the side, they managed to get one bicycle, then the other, over the gate.

"Watch out for the poison ivy," Anna said, pointing to some. They continued down the trail until they reached a paved road again. "We're not far."

They rode a bit more, then Anna stopped in front of an old house on a property sloping down to the water. It was overgrown and untended, the front yard strewn with broken branches ripped off by winter storms. They parked their bikes in the driveway, and Anna led the way to the front door.

"You sure it's okay to go in?" Julia asked.

"Doug and I used to come here all the time." Anna swung the door open, and they stepped inside. "I lost my virginity here when I was fifteen."

"It's a landmark then!"

They laughed.

"How come you never brought me here before?"

"I guess I wanted . . . to keep it a secret, but now I don't care so much. Let me show you around."

Julia felt charmed by the old house, the faded wallpaper with little pink flowers in the upstairs bedroom and vertical stripes in the living room, the French doors off the dining room, and the views of the saltwater marsh communicating with the Sound, and farther out, of the other half of the promontory where Anna's parents lived.

Back downstairs, they stepped out onto the front porch facing the marsh.

"It's gorgeous here," Julia said.

"When we were in high school, Doug and I used to fantasize about buying this house one day and renovating it. That might have been the beginning of his architectural dreams." Anna sighed. "I had visions of myself in pretty dresses with lots of adorable children." She laughed. "And a nanny who would take care of them when I went into my painting studio. I saw myself like another Georgia O'Keeffe, but with Mary Poppins to help out."

"Seems like a workable fantasy to me, though obviously you've moved on to other ones."

"The thing about studying the history of art is that you can't get around the sad history of women. As soon as a woman falls in love with a man, her agenda becomes second priority."

Julia was too in love to have feminist preoccupations, but Anna's words were provocative. "I don't think that's always true. Maybe my mom isn't a Hollywood star, but she's had a successful career on stage. And I think things have changed. Ben wants me to live with him, but he's certainly 'liberated' enough to let me follow my own path."

"You'll find out. I thought Doug was liberated, but then he got all conventional on me, wanting me to follow him to Boston and keep house while he goes to graduate school. And everyone I know seems to feel that's okay. I'm starting to think Robin is right. The male-female power imbalance permeates everything in our culture."

"All this feminist theory is good and fine in the classroom, but I just want to live my life."

"Do you want to know what I really think?" Anna asked. "Honestly?"

"Sure."

"I think if you stay in New Haven just to be with Ben, you'll regret it. You won't get to find your path, let alone walk down it."

Julia was ready to receive that kind of prediction from her mother or father, but not from a peer. She didn't want to be judged or told what to do, but she didn't want to fight with Anna either. "I haven't made up my mind yet. And you can't think this one through for me. We're too different."

"Okay."

"I mean, I appreciate your point of view." Julia sensed her own inability to see beyond her obsession with Ben. She stood up. "I have to leave this afternoon. Let's go back."

Waiting on the train platform in Setauket, they talked about whether they'd see each other again before Anna left for Europe. Anna wasn't sure whether she would fly to Paris directly from Boston or go back down to New York after her time with Doug and leave from JFK. Julia's chest tightened as they hugged goodbye.

The old diesel train pulled past little towns and through fields of unripe corn, and Julia thought back on the morning visit to the old house with its flower-wallpapered bedrooms and view of the marsh. She had her own domestic urges and fantasies—a home, a husband, children. One part of her thought, *No, never.* And another, *Yes, as soon as possible.* The decision about living with Ben and the possible ramifications of that decision were huge. And now she would have to deal with her parents. She had told them the white lie that she would spend a few weeks with Ben before coming back to the city to look for work, and her father had agreed she could use some time off. But she hadn't disclosed Ben's invitation to move in with him permanently or her idea that their summer would be a trial run. She wondered how her withholding information might rate on a deceitfulness scale of one to ten.

That night Julia sat with her parents at the little round kitchen table as she had so many times before. Mariel had roasted some chicken and potatoes, sautéed some chopped, defrosted kale, and made a salad. Julia enjoyed her mother's cooking.

"How much do you think you'll need to get you through the month?" her father asked.

Julia could have cited any figure, but she hated to be greedy when her father was so generous. "Not much," she said. "Just my share of Ben's rent, though he's offered to pay it. But the thing is—"

"And then he'll look for a roommate when you come back to the city and start looking for a job?"

"The thing is . . . I'm not sure about coming back to the city. He asked me to move in with him."

Her father put his fork down. She could almost hear his disapproval and her mother's anxiety. They both wanted her to "make something of herself" and be financially independent.

"How romantic," Mariel said dryly.

"What kind of work do you think you might find in New Haven?" Sam asked. "Something on campus?"

"Probably."

"In other words, I worked myself to the bone to pay for your four years at Yale so that you could become a secretary?"

"If I come back to New York, I could end up doing the same thing."

"There are more job possibilities here, and you know it," he said. "There's publishing and journalism, education and business."

He was fuming, and rightfully so, she thought. All that time and money spent on her fine Ivy League education, and there she was, not particularly motivated to do anything stellar with it and consequently a failure. A sense of just wanting to do what she wanted to do, which might be nothing for a while, came over Julia, making her irritable. But she still wanted to please her father.

"I need a little time to figure out what I want to do with my life."

"If it's moving in with Ben and straightaway making babies," her mother said, "let me say, I do not approve."

"Who said anything about making babies?"

"Okay, okay. Let's all calm down," Sam said.

The sullen atmosphere hung over them a bit until the conversation turned political. It was the easiest way out of a family jam.

Julia called Ben after dinner. He wasn't there. Probably at the library. She paced her bedroom a bit, then decided to call Michael.

"Hi, Jul."

"Hi."

"What's going on over there? You doing some deep thinking about Ben?"

"Yeah. Well, thinking anyway. Not particularly deep. What are you up to?"

"Nothing much. No gigs till Friday. You want to get together tomorrow? I bet you'd like to talk about things."

"Do you mind?"

"Of course not. Especially since it's partly my fault. I mean, by moving out."

Julia laughed. "Yeah, if you hadn't moved out, Ben wouldn't have asked me to move in."

"Let's meet at five at the fountain in Lincoln Plaza. We can go get a drink and kick it around."

The next day, Julia took the crosstown bus at Sixty-Seventh Street and got off at Lincoln Center. It was hot out, and as she approached the big fountain in the middle of the plaza, a bit of spray came her way on a breeze, cooling her face and bare arms. Michael was already there, wearing a short-sleeved collared shirt over a T-shirt. He stood with his back to her, gazing at the jets of water, perhaps dreaming of his compositions being performed at the Philharmonic one day. She, at least, imagined that possibility as an uncomfortable excitement mixed with a sad sense that he would no longer be part of her life the way he'd once been. She touched him on the shoulder, and he turned around.

"Hey, Jul." He kissed her on the cheek, rather close to her mouth, as though stumbling awake from a daydream. "There's this bar nearby."

Because Julia didn't drink much, she couldn't relate to bar culture. But when she was with Michael, it seemed like the right thing to do, and she enjoyed the escape provided by alcohol and conversation in whatever dimly lit venue he selected.

They walked uptown on Broadway until he took a right on a side street.

"This is it," he said.

A clean, relatively new establishment, it didn't smell like beer . . . a choice made out of consideration for her, perhaps. They sat at a little table by the window.

"How was your visit with Anna?" he asked.

They gossiped a bit about Anna, her parents, and Doug, then of course about the drunken mothers' behavior at the commencement party.

Finally, he said, "That cousin of yours really did a number on me."

"You miss her?" Julia asked. Thinking he might still not know about Gloria, she decided to tread carefully.

"Of course I miss her," he said. "At least on a physical level. Emotionally less so because there was something off from the beginning." Michael shrugged, then gave her a sharp look. "You know, I have a bone to pick with you."

"About what?"

"I saw her kissing Gloria in the cemetery. How come you didn't tell me about them?"

"Robin didn't want us to."

"You should've told me. I mean, I get why you didn't, but I thought we were close. Like, I don't know, best friends."

"We *are* close!" Julia tried not to tear up. "And I hated keeping it from you."

"Sorry, Jul, didn't mean to get you worked up. And I know now, so it doesn't matter. But wow, they were all over each other. It was a real shock and a big ouch. I was furious with her for two-timing me and I felt humiliated, yada yada, but now the fact that she's with a woman somehow makes it easier. Less personal."

"I can see that." Julia looked at him searchingly. "So you've been angry with me all this time for not telling you?"

"No, I wasn't happy about it, but I figured she'd sworn you to secrecy." He sighed. "She came over to apologize."

"And?"

He shrugged. "I'm old enough to want endings to be civil. Okay. Now that we've gone through your whole family, what about you? Hey, how about a cocktail instead of another beer? What about a martini? A classy drink for a classy lady."

Michael waved at the bartender and ordered a couple of martinis, then wanted to talk about her writing and music. Was she only interested in writing poetry? Did she ever write lyrics for songs? Maybe they could collaborate on something some time, some songs or—wouldn't it be fun—even an opera. He seemed antsy, waiting for the martinis. Finally, the waiter brought them over, and he relaxed. Julia took a couple of sips and felt a buzz coming on.

He leaned forward across the table. "You're going to stay with Ben for the summer as a kind of experiment, if I understand correctly."

"I'm thinking of it as time off after graduation," she said.

"No more bars, no more martinis if you move in with Mr. Serious."

She smiled. "He's not a teetotaler. He likes wine and brandy. But for martinis, I guess I'll just have to make periodic trips into the city to see you." Suddenly—was it the drink, or the idea of occasionally escaping New Haven to see her handsome and interesting friend?—she felt flirtatious and aroused.

"There you go!" he said. "That's what I call creative thinking. It'll make the hot, sticky summer fly by. Hey, we could even go to the beach sometime."

"Sure," she said. She didn't know how she could escape Ben long enough to take a whole day at the beach with his ex-roommate, but she certainly liked the idea.

He always registered her mood shifts, however small, and

reached across the table to touch her forearm. "Don't worry, Jul. We'll find a way to make it work. Our friendship, I mean."

Julia looked away. "I hate New Haven," she said.

"But you love Ben."

"Yes. Yes, I do." She stared down at the ugly green olive in her glass.

"And love trumps everything else, doesn't it?"

She couldn't tell if he was being sarcastic. She looked back up at him. "Sometimes I can't make you out, Michael."

He speared his olive with a toothpick and popped it in his mouth. "Me neither, Jul," he said, and spit the pit into a little dish.

16

ROAD TRIP

(Robin)

Robin and Gloria stopped at motels in Ohio and Missouri, but in New Mexico the plan was to stay with Skye, at her parents' house in the North Valley of Albuquerque. Skye was Gloria's ex-girlfriend from her high school days.

"You sure she'll be okay with me?" Robin asked as they pulled in next to the rose adobe house shaded by cottonwoods and a single, tall sycamore. "I mean, with the fact of me."

"Of course. We broke up at the end of high school. That was four years ago."

"And you don't regret it?"

"Of course I don't." Gloria reached for her hand and kissed it. "She was much too wild for me, kind of insatiable for sex and booze, and she did drugs. A lot of drugs."

"Sounds pretty normal to me. For our generation, anyway."

"She was always getting into trouble."

"Like?"

"Parties so wild that the neighbors would call the police. And she got busted once. Then there was the time she got in a fist-fight with another girl." Gloria laughed. "Seems funny now, but at the time the drama drove me crazy."

Getting out of the car, they were met by a blistering sun softened by a breeze. They followed the flagstone walkway that cut through a garden of succulents to the front door, and Gloria knocked.

A young woman with long brown hair opened the door. She was in full southwest hippie garb: a long flowered skirt, cropped tank top, and big leather belt; she had turquoise jewelry wound around her neck and silver bangles up both arms. Her face and shoulders were tanned almost to a burn. Robin was rarely destabilized by another woman's beauty, but she was thrown by Skye's seductive appearance, which made her feel inadequate in her own cutoffs and faded black T-shirt.

"Gloria!" Skye opened her arms, and Gloria ran into them.

"Skye!"

Robin stood by as the exes embraced. Then Skye turned to her. "So you're Robin. Welcome."

As Skye squeezed her against her braless breasts a little too hard, Robin experienced a wave of arousal.

"Come on in. We're so lucky. My parents are away."

The interior was whitewashed, with high ceilings supported by horizontal wooden beams. To the right was an earthen fireplace, and out back was a view of a southwest garden with cacti, pebbles, and dry bushes.

"You living with your parents?" Robin asked.

"Temporarily." Skye shook her head. "I broke up with someone I was living with and decided to come home. I'll tell you all about it later. Anyway, it's fine. My parents are cool. But it's even cooler when they're gone. And you can have their bed. Let me take you to their room."

They followed her down a hall. The master bedroom had a huge bed and big windows.

"It's a king and a waterbed," Skye said. "Hope you're okay with that."

"Yeah, sure." Robin sat on the edge of the bed, triggering a big wave that rolled across. She laughed. "I've never slept in a waterbed before."

"You'll either love it or hate it. Odds are you'll love it. Why don't you take a moment, and I'll go make margaritas. You can't stop in New Mexico and not have a margarita, right?" she said, and headed toward the kitchen.

"Wow," Robin whispered. "She's something."

"Meaning?"

"Gorgeous and sexy. I understand why you were attracted."

Gloria looked puzzled. "Oh, well, she didn't look that way in high school. Just old jeans and a T-shirt back then." She dropped her voice. "The southwest look is kind of overdone, don't you think?"

"Nah, I love it," Robin said. "I'm going to go out and buy some silver bangles as soon as I can."

They found Skye in the open kitchen rolling the rims of coupe glasses in a plate of salt. "I'm an anarchist," she said, "but I believe in doing some things right. And I gotta get you guys in the proper frame of mind for my sob story."

Gloria went over to her and passed an arm around her waist. "I'm so sorry about you guys breaking up."

Skye leaned on Gloria's shoulder. "Gloria, Gloria, you live up to your name. Always a glorious vision of beauty. An angel." She leaned over and kissed Gloria lightly on the lips.

Robin's stomach roiled.

Skye turned toward her. "Ouch, I sense something—a jealous vibe."

Robin laughed awkwardly. "Oh no, not at all."

Skye walked over and kissed her lightly on the lips. Robin tasted cannabis on her breath. "Now we're all even, right?" Skye said. She looked out the window. "It's cooling off. Let's go have a drink and a smoke outside."

They went out to the patio, and Skye lit a joint, which they passed around. There was the sound of cicadas and the rustling of leaves in the early evening breeze. The margarita was refreshing, and Robin settled into the cushioned garden chair as a spacious state of well-being came on.

"Tell me about your trip so far," Skye said.

It was small talk, warming up for the breakup story to come. Robin and Gloria talked about how they'd packed up together, then stopped in Pittsburgh and Columbus. When they described a picnic in St. Louis, tears ran down Skye's face.

"What's wrong?" Gloria asked, moving to her side.

"Naomi was from St. Louis."

This should be interesting, Robin thought. Another crazy relationship story for the mental filing cabinet.

"Go ahead. Tell us about it," Gloria said soothingly, stroking her arm.

"There's not that much to tell, really. Naomi and I decided when we met that we'd have an open relationship. But we were so in love that we ended up being monogamous for the first year. We rented a casita near campus and were very domestic. You know, making bread and yogurt and all that shit. Then she met this other woman, Mae, and got interested and asked me again for permission, and I said, 'Sure, why not? That's what we agreed on, right? As long as I'm your main gal and you're home for dinner.' And she said, 'You'll always be my main gal, and I'll always be home for dinner.' And I was stupid enough to believe her until one time she didn't come home for dinner, and night fell, and she still wasn't home." Skye's right hand moved the silver bangles up and down her other forearm. "I was in a state, of course. I kept on stepping outside, looking up and down the street, wondering when she was going to show up. At one point, I saw a blue car and thought, *That's her, that's her*, and then it wasn't." She broke into sobs.

"Did she come back?" Gloria asked.

"At two in the morning. I didn't fall asleep until she came in."

"And then?"

"I wasn't going to admit that I'd stayed up waiting. I pretended to be sleeping when she came in. And the next morning, I pretended I didn't mind. I wasn't about to throw a scene after having agreed to an open relationship. So I decided I was never going to say anything, no matter how many nights she came home late. And so, like two or three times a week, I didn't get to sleep until two in the morning. Then one night she didn't come home at all."

Robin listened, spellbound, for Skye had lived out the alternate ending of her own relationship with Stephanie. If she'd stayed with Steph, she would have been like Naomi, a wild woman, inconsiderate and unfaithful, staying out till two in the morning with the secondary lover of the moment. Robin knew her own nature and had even thought of asking Gloria for an open relationship, but she hadn't yet mustered the courage. The memory of how things had ended with Stephanie was still too fresh. And she was ashamed of how she'd two-timed Michael at the end. Were honor and desire destined to be incompatible?

"You couldn't avoid being jealous after all," Robin said.

"I don't even know what the word jealousy means," Skye said. "Does it mean feeling abandoned? Or rejected? Or simply no longer wanted, used and discarded, like you're just not enough? Or all of the above? Whatever."

"You think it's impossible, then?" Robin asked. "I mean, an open relationship."

"I'm not going to generalize from that one experience," Skye said. "If she'd come home for dinner every night, according to the terms of our agreement, it might have worked."

Robin glanced at Gloria, who stared at the ground. They were so close, still in the honeymoon phase, yet there was much unsaid between them.

Skye relit the joint and took a long puff. "But enough of my whining. Why don't you guys help me make dinner?" She stood up and led them back inside.

The somber mood changed over dinner, wine, and a second joint. By the time they'd finished eating, they were all high, laughing at each other's stories about their friends' love affairs, crazy professors, and even crazier parties. Robin and Gloria told stories about the lesbian dormitory, Cazenove, where they'd lived their senior year at Wellesley.

"There was a lesbian threesome that kept everyone fascinated," Robin said.

Gloria laughed. "You mean it kept *you* fascinated."

"Nah. Everyone," Robin insisted. "You too. Admit it. You wondered what they did, and how they did it with three."

Gloria blushed.

"Did they all live in the same room?" Skye asked.

"Two of them shared a room and the third had her own room, but they were definitely a threesome. They were always together at breakfast and dinner. They'd walk around campus all holding hands and lie with their heads in each other's laps at outdoor concerts. Trust me, it was obvious."

"Geez. I mean, sharing Naomi didn't work for me, but maybe if it's three ways, well then—far out!" Skye said. "And I can see how you'd all be wondering how it worked. I mean, three gals in a bed. It makes you imagine things. Especially when you haven't had sex in a couple of months." She stood up, and her nipples danced forward inside her cropped tank. She went over and sat next to Gloria. "Gloria, Gloria, want to share your lover with me tonight?"

Robin watched, mesmerized. Gloria struck her as cautious, and it was hard to predict how she'd react.

"Is that something you'd like?" Gloria asked Robin shyly.

Robin was eager to try it. "Sure."

Skye went over to her and took her hand. "Follow me, girls."
She led them into her parents' bedroom and onto the big
waterbed. "Wait a second." Skye danced out of the room and
came back with a bottle of white wine and the joint. "Want to
keep the happiness going." She stopped. "Hey, it's not like I've
ever done this before." She froze.

Robin took the lead. She went over to Skye and kissed
her and lifted her tank top over her head. Skye had beautiful
breasts, larger than Gloria's, and Robin fell into stroking them
worshipfully.

"This is so comforting," Skye said, and she reached an arm
out toward Gloria. "Sweetie, come here."

The night was one long flight into pleasure. They fumbled
for a bit, exchanging kisses. Then a rhythm set in as they took
turns receiving and giving in tides of arousal that rose and fell
with intermissions for rest and cuddles. The sex fest went on for
hours, but the pot jumbled Robin's sense of time and sequence,
so that the next morning it felt like one conflated rush. The
sexual energy still coursing through her body overrode her hang-
over headache, and she was euphoric. Gloria rolled over next to
her, and a wave surged across the waterbed as a delicious, warm
breeze came in through the screened window. Robin glanced at
Skye on her other side, then the clock. It was almost noon. The
movement of the bed unsettled her stomach, and she slid out
from between her companions and put her clothes on.

"Hey, maybe you can set up the coffee maker," Skye
murmured.

"Sure."

Robin attended to the coffee and poked around in the kitchen
cabinets for crackers. Now that she was sober, her mind was full
of thoughts and questions. Gloria's openness to the threesome
raised Robin's hopes that their living together might not end in
the claustrophobia she expected from being in a settled couple.

Her mood was hopeful and happy as she made toast and prepared a tray to take into the bedroom.

Later, Skye drove them to the Sandia Mountains, where they took a short hike over hard ground dotted with scrub brush. They experienced the excitement of hearing a rattlesnake, but never saw it. The dry heat bit Robin in the nose, and it felt pleasant to sweat. On the way back, they stopped at a Mexican restaurant and had more margaritas and chimichangas topped with guacamole. For Robin, who'd been to Albuquerque only once before, it was a taste of the exotic. As they sat on a flagstone patio with a view of the mountains in the distance, Gloria looked very relaxed, and Robin reflected on the ease of the situation. They'd dropped their defenses the night before while smoking pot and having sex. To be so very comfortable the next day was a surprise and a pleasure. Gloria's laid-back manner confirmed to Robin her expectation that, once they hit San Francisco, the good times would continue. Two young women in a non-possessive relationship could have all kinds of interesting encounters and experiences.

That second night they made a light dinner, a salad topped with canned tuna and salsa and cheese.

"Find me something interesting in the fridge," Skye said.

Poking around, Robin saw a jar of artichoke hearts from Italy, olives from Spain, and preserved lemons from Morocco.

"Where did you get this stuff?" she asked, opening the lemons and giving them a sniff.

"My parents travel a lot and bring stuff back."

"Cool."

"I told you: I lucked out and got cool parents."

Skye seemed like the kind of gal who could get along with anyone, even her own parents.

They smoked pot and drank wine on the patio. After the day's drive, Robin had a sense of being held and soothed by the surrounding desert . . . consoled, even. The childhood abuse she wanted to forget faded, as though leaving a lesser mark after being erased. "Boy, do I love getting high," she said, and heard herself laugh. The sound was open and free, either who she really was or some other person entirely. *Basically*, she thought, *I was raped as an adolescent, and here I am now trying to lead a normal life, which is impossible.* Robin didn't usually use the word "rape" when remembering her uncle—"molest," "incest," and "forced" were preferable. But no matter what language she used in her head, her suffering would always be surreal, and survival came with a lot of pretending. When she looked at Gloria, she was amazed at her good fortune: Gloria showed up with absolute love, without reservation or ambivalence, yet her passion was not so outsized as to be overwhelming.

As the sky above them swirled with streaks of pink and orange light that caressed the neon ochre desert, they cleared the table, laughing about nothing in particular, then left the dishes piled up in the sink, joking that elves would wash them during the night. There was a wave of giggling as they moved back into the bedroom.

"And now, since we all know each other a bit, it's time for dessert," Skye said. Robin and Gloria sat cross-legged on the mattress while Skye left the room, then came back with a canvas bag. Unzipping it, she took out some objects in red and blue paisley bandannas, which she unwrapped, laughing. "Let's see if we can have even more fun than we did last night." There was a pink dildo and a beige one, as well as a vibrator made of white plastic.

They took turns pleasuring and being pleasured. On this second night, the pot slowed their tempo down, instead of speeding it up. Time was a baggy monster that expanded as they stuffed it with experience. All of Robin's senses were heightened. The skin that touched hers felt warm, the dildos cool; her pot-enhanced orgasms started in her vagina and blossomed at the top of her head, then pulsated like white light inside and around her entire body. Gloria's eyes cradled her with unconditional love. Later, as she fell asleep, a breeze coming in through the open window raised goose bumps on her skin. Propped up on a pillow next to her, Skye smoked a joint and hummed softly.

The next morning, they were hungover and exhausted. The conversation over French toast and fruit was sporadic until Skye talked about the Zuni tribe, their customs and beliefs. She was thinking of doing graduate work in anthropology. Robin talked about how she'd hated Yale and was looking forward to the new master's program she would start in the fall. Gloria was quiet, for she had no plans, and toward the end of the meal, she got up to pack.

"You guys could stay longer if you wanted," Skye said. "My parents won't be back for another few days."

"Gloria wants to get to San Francisco and start looking for an apartment."

"She can be very focused," Skye said.

"Yeah, I guess." Robin glanced toward the bedroom. "Well, I'd better go pack too."

"Okay."

When they parted on the porch an hour later, Skye kissed each of them lightly on the lips.

Robin had taken the first stair down the front steps when she stopped.

"Hey, Skye," she said.

"What?"

"Uh, do you mind my asking, where did you get those toys?"

"The Frisky Rabbit in Albuquerque," Skye said, and gave them the address. "Go check it out."

Skye waved goodbye as Gloria pulled out of the driveway. Robin looked back with a bit of longing. They were quiet until Robin asked, "You didn't want to stay another night or two?"

"Not really. I felt done."

"Okay." Robin turned on the radio. "That was quite a weekend."

Gloria chuckled. "Yeah."

"Hey, you wanna stop at the Frisky Rabbit?"

Gloria shrugged. "If you want that kind of stuff, I'm sure we can find it in San Fran. I'd rather get on the road now."

"Okay, sure," Robin said. "But you liked the toys, right?"

"The toys were great. I just want to get where we're going." She drove toward the highway.

Gloria could either be a whole lot of fun or no fun at all, depending on her mood and schedule. She always wanted to get things done, get there, get back to work, get it—whatever "it" was—over with.

Their original plan was to drive through the night and arrive in San Francisco the next morning, but around 2:00 a.m., neither of them could keep their eyes open, and they stopped in a crummy motel in Bakersfield and crashed.

It was only the next day, when they were on dreary, fast Interstate 5, that the conversation returned to their weekend in Albuquerque.

"So, hey," Robin began, "was that the first time you and Skye ever did it with a third party?"

"The answer is yes, but I wouldn't put it that way. I'd say it was the first time you and I ever did it with a third party." Gloria took one hand off the wheel and reached for Robin's. "Because it's you and me now, and she was the third."

"Thanks, sweetie." Robin squeezed her hand. "It was super exciting," she said. "At least, it was for me. What about you?"

"It was fun, yeah. Sort of a lot going on all the time. Like juggling or something. Like, I kept thinking, 'What am I supposed to be doing now?'"

"You mean, too busy?"

"Yeah."

Disappointed, Robin looked out the window. "Variety can be nice, though, can't it?"

"Theoretically, yes. But—"

"But?"

"You know, when people start doing that, there's always jealousy."

"You think there would be jealousy, even with us?" Robin asked, then thought, *Stupid question*. There she was, literally speeding toward a new life with someone she'd just gotten involved with a couple of months before, without ever having spelled out the terms of their arrangement.

"You mean, with those of us who are trying to dismantle the patriarchy?" Gloria laughed. "If I have a reason to wonder whether you might love someone else more or if I start worrying you might leave me, yeah, sure, of course I'll be jealous."

"Stop the car."

"What?"

"Take that exit and stop the car," Robin said.

"What the hell?"

The turnoff landed them amid the huge fields of Central California. Vineyards and orchards sprawled between irrigation canals under a cloudless sky, without a single house in sight. A hot breeze gently spun an old windmill powering a water pump.

Robin reached for Gloria's hands and held them between hers. "I promise not to leave you no matter what happens."

"You're full of it." Gloria leaned forward and kissed her. "It'll be a miracle if we last a year."

"How can you say that?"

"Because you're crazy. I know you had other partners last summer besides Theo."

"How did you know that?" Robin was genuinely surprised.

"You think I'm an idiot? I know you have a restless side."

"Then what are you doing with me and my restless side? Why would you want to live with me?"

Gloria shrugged. "I don't know. Maybe I find it exciting. And I'm in love with you, I guess. It seems like I make you happy, so maybe I'll be enough for you. Maybe there's a chance of a chance." With the air conditioner off, the car was getting hot, so she cranked open the window. The air outside was even hotter, but at least it was moving. "I mean, if you want to have a career in psychology, eventually you'll have to focus on your work and apply yourself. And you'll have to settle down to do that."

"I'm in love with you too. And you're right, I do need to settle down. I want to make something of myself, and I want to make a life with you."

"We'll give it a go, then," Gloria said. "And if you get restless, just don't tell me about it. Come home for dinner on time and don't tell me about it."

"But I want to tell you everything."

"Nobody tells anybody everything." Gloria started the car up again and sped back onto the highway.

Gloria stayed with Robin in her little room on the top floor of her parents' home while they looked for an apartment. Neither Robin's parents nor Grandma Iris downstairs had any idea they were lovers, and Robin had no plans to tell them. It was one thing to play with being out of the closet on the opposite side of the country but quite another back home with her family.

In the morning, the two young women ate breakfast with Iris. Sarah invariably came downstairs mid-meal and smoked a cigarette while they were eating. One time Gloria and Robin had the classified section of the newspaper open between them and were looking at the Apartments for Rent section when Sarah came in.

"You could stay here and save yourselves rent while you're in school," Sarah said.

"That's a fine idea," Iris said.

"As though you'd know anything about money manage-ment!" Sarah scoffed, then explained to Gloria, "My mother is an expert at squandering fortunes."

"Stop it, Mom."

Iris squeezed Robin's forearm. "You don't have to defend me."

"And I'm not attacking. I've made my peace with it," Sarah said. "One learns from negative examples as well."

"These things happen. My grandmother was gypped out of her inheritance," Gloria said.

"Really?" Sarah squinted at her. Maybe she suspected they were lovers.

"She should have inherited half of her father's ranch," Gloria explained, "but they wrote her out of the will because she was a girl."

"In New Mexico?"

Gloria nodded.

"What do you expect?" Sarah said. "New Mexico—a remote corner of a basically uncivilized country isn't going to treat women fairly. But to get back to my point, the two of you can stay here. We can put a second bed in your room. Gloria, you're totally welcome, as long as you help with the chores, of course."

"Thanks, Mom, but no thanks." Robin stayed focused on the classifieds. "This looks promising." She circled something with her red pen.

"You didn't think that was a generous offer?" Sarah asked Gloria.

"Very generous, and kind too," Gloria said, "but I think Robin is right. We need to . . . we need to stay in the—well, get back into—" She came to a dead stop.

"What Gloria means," Robin said, "is I need to stay in gradu-ate student mode, and she needs to figure out what she's going to do with her life, and living with parents won't support our quest for adulthood."

Sarah took a long puff of her cigarette and exhaled, projecting a stream of smoke above her daughter's head. "I suppose I should be happy you are 'questing for adulthood,' unlike much of your generation, and God forbid I should get in the way."

"I'm glad you understand, Mom. And now I'm going to go call this listing."

"There's some old flatware in the storage room you can have. If it's good enough for the both of you, that is." Sarah squinted again, and Robin knew her mother was onto them.

The fourth apartment Robin and Gloria looked at was adequate, and with the pressure of the school year about to begin, they took it. It was the attic floor of a Victorian, with a ceiling that had no insulation, which might make it cold and damp in the winter. But with windows in three directions, it was bright and had a big bedroom and a decent living area.

They signed the lease on the spot, then walked around the neighborhood and over to Clement Street, a wide avenue flanked by Asian groceries and restaurants. Gloria stopped, intrigued, in front of a Chinese herb store, and motioned for Robin to follow her. Inside were jars and open boxes of dried substances, mostly vegetal, some animal. Robin recognized some desiccated seahorses and mushrooms but couldn't identify the rest.

"I love the smell," Gloria said.

"It's okay." Robin was not sure she loved it.

"And just to think that everything here supposedly has some healing property. Look at this—sliced roots or branches of some kind. Fascinating." Gloria moved over to a shelf with some tea canisters and picked up a small one. "Oolong. Probably safe," she whispered to Robin, and took it to the cashier.

They moved into their new apartment a few days later. They didn't have much furniture, only a futon they'd picked up in a shop on Geary Street. For the kitchen, they had some odds and ends Sarah had gifted them and equipment they'd picked up at a Chinese hardware store.

Gloria was big on organization.

"The short glasses go on the right because we're both right-handed and we use them the most," she said, rearranging the way Robin had put them on the shelf. "And the bowls—I think it's better to stack the smaller ones separately from the bigger ones."

"You have a system for everything, don't you?" Robin aimed for a gently teasing tone, but Gloria stiffened.

"I've never lived with anyone before," Gloria said, "so I'm not experienced in these things. But I think if we make certain rules at the outset, there will be less conflict later on. Especially since you're a bit of a—a—"

"Slob?"

"No, an anarchist."

"Maybe, but you're the one dictator I'll obey." She stroked Gloria's neck.

"You think I'm neurotic, don't you?"

"I sure think you're something, but I haven't figured out what yet."

Gloria laughed. "Serves me right for moving in with a psychology student."

They quickly settled into a routine. Robin started school at CIIS, and her schedule was dictated by courses and lectures. She was finally studying what she wanted to: Eastern thought, Indigenous spirituality, Carl Jung, and archetypal mythology. She didn't know what she would do with the mix of ideas she was absorbing, but that didn't trouble her; for the moment, she would simply enjoy being on an exciting adventure in consciousness to parts unknown. Eventually, she would use it all to be a healer and helper to those who, like herself, were in perpetual rebellion against "normal."

Gloria found a job waitressing at a health food restaurant; she

234 234 THREE COUSINS

loathed it and on workdays skated in and out of depression. Her salvation came in the form of her new fascination with Chinese medicine, and she spent her spare time at the public library, reading everything she could find about acupuncture and Chinese herbalism. She was beginning to think she had found her direction, but she feared setting out to do something that was so new in the American context of the time.

With Gloria being moody and confused, Robin found herself taking care of her emotionally when they were home together. But it was a relief to go from the turbulence of the previous two years to this settled domesticity, and she was basically happy, if haunted by their wild weekend with Skye and the conversation they'd had on the road afterward. Now that Robin was back in San Francisco, she thought about Theo a lot. She missed his boyish spark, surprising conversation, and creativity in bed. It was hard to pack up her longing and stick it in a drawer, so she didn't know whether she could satisfy Gloria's desire for a monogamous relationship. Robin imagined herself as loyal but not necessarily faithful. In her mind, those were two different things. Loyalty implied being constant in one's affections whatever the ups and downs of a relationship, whereas fidelity meant not allowing oneself to enjoy sexual love with anyone else. The truth was she'd lied in moving in with Gloria: she had implied exclusivity when she didn't want it, and in the process, she had defined herself as gay, when she was bisexual.

But hadn't their conversation in the car in the Central Valley suggested that Gloria understood her and was okay with what she saw?

One morning, Robin heard Gloria mumbling to herself as she did the dishes before going to work.

"What's wrong?"

"This damn silverware your mother gave us," Gloria said. "Nothing matches."

"Of course it doesn't. That's the remains of four different sets. She wouldn't have given it to us if everything matched."

"It bugs me."

"Why? It's not like we're going to be giving fancy dinner parties."

"It's confusing to look at. It hurts my brain."

"How about you just go to work and let me finish up?"

Gloria untied the apron strings around her waist. "Be my guest." And she stormed out.

Alone in their empty apartment, Robin was seized by anguish. Gloria's oddities were tolerable, but these moments when she became a control freak worried her. Might Gloria have some personality disorder she wasn't seeing? Or was she just stressed? It can be hard to be objective when you're in love. Robin finished breakfast staring out the window. The morning light was muted by the fog rolling in from the Pacific. It was Saturday, so no classes, and she'd be alone all day, waiting for her grumpy partner to return from her hateful job. Robin thought about Theo and wondered how and why she had relinquished so rapidly something so dear to her—her freedom. She had an urge to call him. Was she wanting to prove to herself that she was invulnerable, and that no matter what happened with Gloria, no matter who got hurt, she'd always be able to find someone else? She wrestled with herself for a moment—not a long one—then reached for the phone. She didn't know if he was at the same number or in the same apartment; maybe he'd gone to Mexico or was living with his girlfriend or on the road with his band.

"Hello," he answered.

"Theo, it's me, Robin."

"Hey you."

"Hey you."

"You back for good?" he asked.

"I am. And I'm living with someone, a new girlfriend. What about you?"

"I was living with Lizzie, but she left. Well, not completely. I mean, she comes and goes. That's what she does. Right now she's gone."

"'Right now'?"

"She left a week ago. I bet she'll be back, though."

"But in the meantime you're free?"

"In the meantime I'm free."

"Like now?"

"Now, as in right now?"

"Yeah," she said.

He let out a peal of laughter. "Robin, you're somethin' else. Yeah, I can get it up on command. Come on over."

"Same place?"

"Yup. I'll be waiting with bells on."

Robin hung up, feeling pleased with herself. To hell with conventional morality. She'd go out, she'd come back, she wouldn't tell Gloria. And no harm would be done.

"How long you got?" Theo asked after they'd had sex.

"Till late evening. Gloria's working through the dinner shift."

"We could take a walk on the beach, then make dinner together."

"I'd like that."

They lay on their sides, looking at each other.

"I like this. I mean, just lying here and looking at you this way," she said.

"I call it soul gazing," he said. "I'm gazing into your soul, and you're gazing into mine."

Robin smiled. "That's surprisingly poetic, coming from a sarcastic musician like you."

"You see me as a sarcastic musician?"

"Yup, when I look into your soul, that's what I see." She laughed; then it occurred to her that she and Gloria never did soul gazing. Maybe they had the first few times they'd made love, but then Gloria had started holding her so close that Robin couldn't pull back enough to look into her eyes.

"Sarcastic about some things, maybe. But not about you."

"I love the way you stroke my face," she said. Theo was affectionate and sensual in a way most men weren't. She wondered if she was falling in love with him. Having more than one sexual partner at a time was something she could handle. But two love objects—maybe not.

"And you, you're delicious." He gave her a long kiss, his hand in her curly hair. "But let's go out and buy food for dinner. If we go out now, we'll have time to get back in bed again."

They put a leash on Lobo and went to a Chinese restaurant in the neighborhood where they bought one of the roasted ducks hanging in the window; then they stepped into the grocery store next door for salad ingredients. With a six-pack of beer, they had enough for dinner. His little kitchen had a table next to a big window, and Lobo sat at their feet as they ate. Now and then, Theo fed him a piece of duck. Lobo was a well-behaved dog, as affectionate as his master, and Robin felt a little in love with him too. Maybe someday she and Gloria would have a dog, though it was hard to imagine Gloria agreeing to that.

Being with Theo was destabilizing. He seemed open to everything, a man without rules, taking life as it came. And although Gloria purported to be a fun girl, curious and daring, she was in the end more driven by a need for order and control. Robin recalled her upset over their mismatched silverware as she and Theo did the dishes. She noticed that nothing, absolutely nothing, in his kitchen matched.

"Every single one of these plates is different," she said.

"It's on purpose. I like it that way."

The phone in the bedroom rang. Theo put down his dishcloth and went to answer it.

"Hey," he said, and she knew from how he'd dropped his voice that it was Lizzie. He closed the door to the bedroom, and Robin continued to dry the dishes and put them away. She wanted to hear what he was saying, but he was talking softly, and the door was solid wood.

"Hey, Lobo," she said, and the dog looked up at her with his beautiful blue eyes. "What do you think's going on in there?"

Lobo gave a soft yowl, and she went over and scratched him, then sat back down at the little table. Suddenly, being there felt wrong. She liked the idea of free love and exploration, but the good feelings were receding as she heard Theo talking on the other side of the door. Outside the light was falling and with it, her mood. Robin heard him say goodbye and hang up, and then he came out of the bedroom.

"That was Lizzie, I'm guessing," she said.

"Yup."

"And?"

"She's been in Mexico at her parents', and she's decided to come back. I mean, to live with me."

"Oh, okay."

He gave her an apologetic smile. She shrugged.

"What's she—what's she interested in?" She needed to keep talking. "I mean, what does she do or want to do? You've never told me."

"She's kind of all over the place. She took some acting classes and was working as an usher in a movie theater, but now she's talking about going back to school in special education."

"She sounds interesting."

"Oh, Lizzie, she's one interesting gal, that's for sure."

Robin stood up. "Maybe I should leave."

He seemed surprised. "Why?"

"If she's coming back."

"She's in Mexico. She won't be back for a couple of days."

He came up to her and put his hand gently between her legs. "I was looking forward to another round."

She was immediately aroused and thought to herself, *Why not? What's the difference between once or twice?* And he was the best kisser she'd ever met. "Okay," she said.

And he led her back into the bedroom.

The clock said 10:00 p.m. It was dark out. Time to leave because Gloria would be home by 11:00.

"When Lizzie gets back," Theo said, "it might be hard to get together."

They were standing by his front door with their arms around each other's necks, and she thought, *This doesn't sound like a permanent goodbye, but it isn't a continuance signal either.*

"You mean how would it work logistically, where would we meet—"

"I mean there are motels," he said, "but maybe that would be too 1950s adultery, film noirish for us."

"With neither of us married, it wouldn't be adultery," she said, "but yeah, I've never done anything like that before." The idea of checking into a motel just to have sex both excited and repulsed her.

When he stroked her face again, it felt like his hand was inside her chest mixing things around, a spatula blending chocolate fudge into her heart.

"I don't know. I'm confused now," he said.

"Me too."

"We'll see then."

"We'll see."

He offered to walk her to her car, but she said it wasn't necessary. Once outside, she felt grief landing. It was unlikely she'd see Theo again for a while.

Needing a moment outdoors before going home, she drove toward Ocean Beach. She parked and got out. The sea air was cold and damp, San Francisco style. A big moon shining through the fog reflected on the ocean. A sense of anticlimax fell upon her. Lizzie was coming back, so Theo would be unavailable. Skye was in New Mexico, and more adventures of that kind were, practically as well as emotionally, out of reach because Gloria wasn't that kind of girl. Neither an open relationship nor experiments, like group sex, were likely as long as they were together.

As Robin leaned on the parapet and gazed at the water, the phrase *You can't argue with reality* repeated itself inside her brain like a mantra. Most of the time she didn't care much for reality. She disconnected from it when stressed, and she could only reconnect with it by altering her perceptions of the facts with pot, alcohol, sex, or some combination of the three. The result was that she didn't know what "reality" was because she'd had very little experience of it.

But Theo's disappearing, like the breakups with Stephanie and Michael, was an unquestionable reality. Stupidly, she'd let herself be seduced and charmed by him. Stupidly, she'd fallen in love with him. She felt crushed by the repeated endings, and ashamed and foolish for having risked her relationship with Gloria for someone who could send her packing so easily. Her judgment, which wasn't great to begin with, was further compromised by her own desire for adventure.

Maybe I'm a sex addict, she thought, *and I've got to go cold turkey on fooling around.* A craving for peace of mind came over her, and the decision that had weighed on her was suddenly easy. She would be faithful to Gloria and give their relationship an honest shot because she had to, because it made sense. And she would define herself as gay, not bisexual, to make it easier. And this choice, in giving her existence shape and structure, would guide her toward a meaningful and honorable life.

THE LIBRARY
STEPS

(Michael)

Michael had turned down his mother's invitations to dinner
for two months because his father had cursed him out for
leaving graduate school, and the old man's contempt hurt. But
his mother continued to call, and finally he went over with amicable intentions. After a fierce argument, Michael and his father
could sometimes pretend it hadn't happened. Tonight, however,
might be different. When they sat down to eat, he waited for his
father to lead the conversation as his mother served them and his
brother stared out the window.

Finally, his father spoke. "You could change your mind," he
said. "I'm sure they'd take you back."

Michael glanced sideways at his mother. She pushed the cold
chicken salad she'd made for this hot evening around on her plate
with a silver fork. She was proud of using silver in the age of con-
venience. She looked up and gave her son a pleading look.

"I will," he said to his father. "I will think about it." He had
no intention of doing so, but it was the easiest way for them to get
back to normal footing.

His father nodded approvingly. "Even if you don't want an academic career, a PhD is a handy thing to have under your belt."

It was the tenth or twelfth time Michael had heard that. "I did get the terminal master's," he said.

"Everybody has a master's these days. And it's just another small step for the doctorate. You know how to compose; you know how to write. It's not a big deal."

"Okay, I'll think about it."

His father leaned toward him. "You know, pressure can be good once you learn how to deal with it. It kicks the brain into high gear."

Michael gave him a hard look. "I do know. I grew up with pressure, Dad. From you."

"Yeah, and that's why you're a man capable of great things. Grace under pressure, as Ernest said." Michael's dad was literary as well as musical.

"Well, Ernest cracked in the end, as I recall. Small matter of a bullet in the mouth."

"You have to decide what life is about, that's all. You're thirty—don't you think it's about time to do that?"

"My life is about music. Just like yours. But in a different way."

"All right then."

There was a long silence. "I made a pie, and there's vanilla ice cream," his mother said. "Leave room for that." She smiled and put her hand over Michael's. "I'm so happy to have you back in the city, honey."

He picked up her hand and kissed it. "Keep on making those pies, Mom, and I'll never leave again."

After dinner, he drifted into Nick's room, closing the door behind him.

"How you holding up?" Michael asked him.

Nick shrugged. "I gave in. I'm going back to school."

"Yeah? For what?"

"Early childhood ed. So I can give little kids the love I never got myself."

"I like that idea. Hey, you wanna come out for a walk and a smoke?"

Nick shook his head. "I'm off everything now. Weed too. It's the only way out of here."

"I'm impressed."

"He's getting worse, have you noticed?"

"Not particularly."

"The way he controls and manipulates Mom—it's painful to watch. And she doesn't fight back. She just lets herself be his . . . *thing*."

"Sometimes giving up is the path of least resistance."

"I've gotta get out of here," Nick said.

"Yes, you do. And graduate school is the ticket." Michael chuckled.

A breeze was coming in over the Hudson. Michael had eaten too much and felt uncomfortable. He crossed West End Avenue to Riverside Park, where he sat on a bench and lit a joint he had in his wallet. He felt disturbed by Nick's words about their parents; he wondered how long his mother could continue with the subservience and self-erasure before it impacted her mental and physical well-being. He loathed his father for oppressing her, but thankfully the weed softened his anger. He finished the joint and started walking home.

There was a message on his answering machine.

"Hey, can I come over and hang out?" It was his friend Louise, who'd been a fellow graduate student at Yale. She'd also been in the composition program, and he'd enjoyed her critiques and quirky style. She cut her hair short and wore gigantic earrings with hoops and beads.

He called her back. "You sounded down in the message."

"Yeah, kind of. But I'll try not to be a drag."

"You're never a drag, Louise. Come on over."

Michael tidied up and rolled another joint. Seeing his father always triggered self-loathing, and dinner had left him feeling like a disaster survivor, the disasters being his father, his early marriage, graduate school, his fight with Ben, and every woman from his wife through Robin. Getting stoned with a friend seemed like a good way to end the evening.

Twenty minutes later, the doorbell rang. Louise came in. Her hair was shorter than usual and her earrings so long that they brushed the straps of the tank top she wore. He kissed her on the cheek. She slumped down in his big secondhand armchair, and he sat on the couch across from her. They started to smoke.

"What's going on?" he asked. He liked being distracted from his own problems by those of his friends.

"School's starting next week. I'm wondering if I shouldn't do like you and drop out."

"Nah. If anybody's PhD material, it's you. Louise—composer at large, composer *extraordinaire*."

"You think so?"

"You know I love your work."

"Your support has been so important to me. I don't know what I'm going to do without you."

"Hey, I'll always listen to your work. And you got Professor Peterson." Michael laughed. "He'll get you to the moon."

Louise grimaced. "I hate it. Always being pushed to tweak things this way or that way."

"I know, that's why I dropped out." The memory of the critique groups was unpleasant. Most of the students had less musical experience and talent than he did but acted as though they had more . . . except for Louise, who had been constructive, modest, and kind. He stood up, went into the kitchen, and came back with a bottle of rum. "Want some? Straight or mixed?"

"Mixed, with cubes."

He made them two long drinks with orange juice and returned to the couch. When she leaned forward to grab her glass, her earrings swung forward, brushing her bare collarbones.

"What's with the haircut?" he asked. "Even shorter than last time. You coming out of the closet or something?"

"No, I'm not gay. It's what I do when I hate myself. I chop off more hair."

"Must be nice to have that as an outlet." Michael was already losing his hair.

"You think it makes me more attractive or less?"

He considered her against the light coming through the window, a thousand apartment and streetlights giving off a glow as cold as the moon's.

"More. It gives you a kind of fuck-you mystique."

"A fuck-you mystique? I like that." She laughed. Then the dark look came over her again. "Michael," she said, "let's go to bed."

"Oh no, please, don't! Oh shit. I shouldn't have given you the joint and the rum."

"Yeah, I'm high, but it has nothing to do with that. It's how I feel."

She got up and went to sit by him on the couch. He smelled her fragrance as she landed next to him.

"Aw, Louise, can't we just be friends? We have a great connection as fellow composers and Yale survivors. Let's leave it at that."

"But why? I mean, why not? If you're attracted to me—"

"Because I'm tired of creating messes—"

"I don't mind your messes." She sat up straight and lifted her tank top up over her head. Her breasts were small, her nipples hard, her torso slim and delicate.

"Aw, come on." He looked away.

"Just as a one-time thing." She moved closer.

He looked back, reached over, stroked her breast, and felt the flux of arousal. "It'll fuck up our friendship."

"No, it won't. I promise."

He thought about it in the way that people think about things when they're stoned, meaning not much.

"Why don't we remove these?" He leaned in and removed her earrings, then kissed her.

He didn't feel too bad about it the next morning. Louise knew how to strike the right note, friendly but slightly disengaged, not holding out any expectation of repeat. In any case, she was going back up to Yale in a few days for the beginning of term.

"Thanks for the moral support," she said as they kissed goodbye at the front door. "I feel much better this morning."

"Hey, keep in touch," he said. "Let's keep exchanging work."

"You're my number one composer pal." She gave him a thumbs-up and disappeared where the corridor turned toward the elevator.

He walked to Frank Music on Fifty-Fourth Street. Labor Day was coming up, and that meant the beginning of the school term. He had to collect sheet music and make calls to reconnect with old clients. He loved working with children, and the prospect of returning to teaching filled him with joy. Whether they were five years old or fifteen, naturally gifted or not, kids brought their curiosities and rewards. And he prided himself for making music fun using little games and compositions he wrote to help his students overcome hurdles.

Michael took the IRT downtown, then strolled to the store. After the heat of the subway and the street, the air-conditioned interior was refreshing. The night with Louise had erased his dinner with his family, and he noted the healing power of sex: he felt relaxed and okay. Okay in a way that was more philosophical than emotional. There was the usual anxious restlessness, but he knew he'd made the right decision coming back to the city. All his decisions, even the wrong ones, were right. He thought of the wrong ones as "necessary mistakes"—the mistakes people made when all their choices were impossible.

As he fingered through Scarlatti, he thought of Julia. He'd seen her at the piano, and he thought her technique would benefit from some Scarlatti. Structure, flow, momentum—the big S had it all. Michael was struck by how much he missed her, and he stared off into space, wondering what they might have been together, if it had been possible. But it hadn't been and couldn't be, and not only because of Ben. There was too much disparity between them. Julia was young, fresh in the sense of having an unscarred heart, and he was ten years older than her numerically, maybe twenty emotionally. He was a trash heap, jaded and fucked-up in countless ways. Still, he missed her company.

He'd imagined, when he'd seen her over the summer, that they would continue to be friends. In theory he could suggest, "Let's go out for a drink next time you're in the city," or, "Hey, you want to come over and do some songs together?" or, "Wanna catch a movie?" But the reality was that the fight with Ben made it awkward to get in touch with her. Her phone number was Ben's number now. And he didn't want to deal with Ben.

He could call Julia's parents' home on the weekend, on the chance that she might be visiting. Of course, if Ben came down with her, that would be awkward too. No, he'd just have to wait for her to call him.

Loneliness came over him, threatening his fragile sense of well-being. He went back to perusing Scarlatti.

A few days later, as though he had willed it, Julia called. She'd come to the city by herself to see her parents.

"I'm just staying overnight," she said, "going back tomorrow. Can I see you?"

"We could have dinner at one of the sushi places on Thirty-Ninth, before you catch your train."

"Yeah, sure."

Sushi was in its second American wave at the time, popular but mostly found in the neighborhood just east of the train station, and Michael sought it out when possible. He got to the restaurant first and waited for her.

Julia came in wearing an old pair of jeans and a T-shirt under a smart-looking linen jacket. The outfit was casual with a little polish. Her hair pulled back in a high ponytail exposed her thin neck, and she wore no makeup, as usual. He enjoyed her style. She put her big shoulder bag down on the chair next to hers.

"Hey," was the mutual greeting.

He caught a shadow of distress in her expression as she sat down across from him.

"I ordered some plum wine," he said. "May I?" He poured her some.

"I've never had that before."

"I bet you've never had sushi either."

She smiled. "No, I haven't."

He asked about her parents. She told him Mariel was preparing for an audition. "There's always a lot of drama around it," she said. "Every time, it's like her first time."

Michael laughed. "Some people like drama."

"I don't."

"I got that about you, Jul," he said. "It's like you're drama-phobic. A drama-phobe."

"Is that a good thing or a bad thing? What do you think?"

"Neither. It's just a character trait. You're risk averse; you like security." Michael read people the way he read music—instantly.

He could look at someone and feel him or her in his brain. "Any kind of scene shakes you up." The waiter took their order, then he continued. "I was glad you called because I feel uncomfortable calling the apartment now."

She grimaced. "It would make things easier," she said, "if you guys made up."

"It's awkward. Ben's like another version of my father. I can't do relationships like that anymore, where every move I make I'm being judged or told what to do."

"Okay."

"We'll figure it out. I mean, how to stay friends."

"Will we?" Julia asked. "How?"

"When you come into the city without Ben, like you did this time, call me. If that's not too sneaky for you."

"Okay."

"'Okay'? Is that the password of the day? What's going on?"

"I'm confused."

The first little dish of sushi came, and they started eating.

"I gather you've decided to stay in New Haven so you can be with Ben."

She nodded. "We've had a lovely summer together, so I want to continue living with him. Is that stupid?"

He was touched his opinion mattered to her. "Not necessarily. You're in love with him. As long as you don't forget who you are."

"You think I'm at risk for that?"

"Possibly. He has a lot of ego, that man. He might not like living with a poet."

"Well, I'm not a poet yet and may never be one." She sighed, then grimaced. "I interviewed for a job in the math department. It's secretarial. I'll probably get it. My father isn't thrilled."

"Down with the fathers! You do what you want, Jul."

She poked her sushi with her chopsticks. "What's this?" She played with the little red dots on the rice.

"Fish roe."

"It's good. Juicy the way it explodes in the mouth."

"It'll be okay, Jul. Unless you have a big plan, like med school or like Anna going to Paris, the year after graduation tends to be unfocused. It's normal."

She got a funny expression on her face. For once he didn't know how to read it. He wanted it to be love or desire, and maybe it was, but not for him. For something or someone else.

"Enough about me and Ben," she said. "Tell me about you."

"Getting ready for the new year." He wasn't going to tell her about his night with Louise, so he talked about restarting his teaching business, and maybe he could even get a job in a high school as a music teacher, but it would have to be a private school because he wasn't state certified. "A master's from Yale might open doors." He chuckled. "It should be good for something, don't you think?"

He ordered another round of plum wine, and they continued to talk. He paid, and they stepped out of the restaurant and into the dusk of a September night, when the temperature drops from hot to a warm that seems cool in comparison. They headed up Fifth Avenue.

"When's your train?" he asked.

She glanced at her watch. "In a half hour, or an hour and a half, if I catch the one after."

"In an hour and a half, then," he said.

"I'd better call Ben."

Michael watched her step into a booth and dial her home number. He knew that number because it had been his a few months before. He admired her figure; she was lean, a little leaner than he generally liked his women, but attractive. He was often with attractive women, and though he had given into temptation a few nights before with Louise, he knew he could refrain from acting on every impulse.

Julia hung up and came out of the booth.

"Let's go sit on the library steps," he said, and they started walking again.

"I guess I won't be seeing you much anymore," she said, looping back to their conversation in the restaurant.

"I thought we settled that. You'll call me when you come to the city by yourself."

"But now I'm thinking . . . it might feel sneaky to do that, after all."

"I see. Okay." The prospect of losing her filled him with loneliness. She had become his best friend and confidante, and now, because of his argument with Ben and her decision to stay in New Haven, their alliance was coming to an end. "You have more of a moral compass than I do."

"No, I don't think I do."

"Of course you do. You can't imagine keeping a secret from Ben." He heard the reproach in his voice and hated himself for it. He had no right to reproach her.

"That part is true," she said. "I don't like secrets because I'm not good at keeping them, and I don't like complication, even when it's unavoidable."

"And I'm a complication?"

"Of course you are."

Suddenly, he felt his hand in hers. Had she taken his, or had he taken hers? He grasped it more firmly, and she returned the squeeze.

Still holding hands, they sat down under the lion statue. She had tears in her eyes.

"I'd order you to make up with Ben, but that would be dishonest too," she said.

"Hey, Jul, Jul. Don't cry. I'll always treasure our friendship. You know that." Their friendship being impossible and less than what they needed, he should have said. *I'll always treasure the memory of our friendship.* But the words were too sad to say. He wanted desperately to take her to his apartment, but he computed the time on the subway uptown and back—even a quickie would be impossible. And a quickie wasn't what he wanted with her anyway.

"Kiss me," she said, and he did.

They kissed for a long time, and he thought to himself, *This is the sweetest woman I have ever met. She is so young and her heart so pure—why the fuck am I messing with it?* But he kept kissing her, wanting the complete, intimate sense of union that her love gave him. "A curse upon Ben for finding you first," he said, caressing her face. "Let's go back in time and do it differently."

And then—was it ten or twenty or thirty minutes later?—he came back to reality. "You'll miss your train," he said.

They began running toward Grand Central and kept running, across the traffic, down Forty-Second Street, into the station, looking at the big board for the track number, then galloping down the platform. She leapt onto the train, and he stood with the rubber door bouncing against his back as it tried to close on him, and they had one last kiss.

"Stand back from the doors," boomed the conductor's voice over the loudspeaker.

Stepping back on the platform, he felt like he was falling. It was himself he was falling into, the lonely place of his being. The doors slammed closed. She was sitting by the window now, looking at him, crying.

"Jul," he said, though she couldn't hear him. "Jul, don't go."

The train pulled away from the platform, and Michael stood, unable to move as his best friend, his support, his point of reference, his muse disappeared in the tunnel, and the light of the last car trailed off to the size of a quarter, then a dime, then a dot—then nothing. Suddenly, he felt faint because he'd stopped breathing. Bending over with his hands on his knees, he gasped for air.

NICE WORK

(Julia)

There was nothing outside the train window except the play of city lights in the black night. Julia leaned her head against the glass as tears streamed down her face. The ride to New Haven was about an hour and a half, enough time to weep, then compose herself. She couldn't understand what she'd done given how happy she'd been with Ben all summer. Happy sleeping in his big bed with him, having breakfast together, even looking for a job. Happy when they'd taken a summer break at a beach house in Nantucket and played in the ocean together and eaten fried fish by the water and had sex every day. After their holiday, they'd returned and settled even more comfortably into their life together. How then was it possible that now, after one kiss with Michael, it all seemed so fragile? Perhaps her happiness had been the product of make-believe, and Michael held the key to what she truly needed. She couldn't bear the thought of being separated from him, and the memory of their kiss threw her into misery. She longed to be back on the steps of the New York Public Library, to have another hour with him, and more.

Ben had expressed his discontent over the phone when she'd told him she was having dinner with Michael. Since the two men had had a falling out, it was indeed a betrayal and one she'd sealed with a kiss. What a mess. When the conductor announced Fairfield, she dried her eyes and ran her fingers through her hair. She didn't carry a compact mirror, so she had no idea how she looked. If Ben said anything about her eyes being red, she could say it was from allergies or Manhattan pollution.

The train pulled into New Haven, and she got off with her heart pounding. Ben stood in the lobby area, waiting. She barely noticed the homeless, the trash, or the stench that she hated so much as they walked out to his car parked in the curbside waiting area.

"That was an awfully long dinner you had with Michael," Ben said, walking quickly.

"We took a walk and chewed the fat for a long time," she said.

They got in the car, not speaking. Glancing at him as he drove, she saw his jaw was set.

"'Chewed the fat'? And what did you talk about?"

"Not much. His getting students, going back to his old life."

Entering the apartment, which had once been Michael's home and was now hers, she thought she could still smell him, as though the trace of his presence had been reactivated by her contact with him.

"Want some tea?" Ben asked. Without waiting for an answer, he went into the kitchen and put the kettle on.

Julia went into the bathroom and looked at herself. Her eyes were swollen and red.

When she came out, she was startled by him standing outside the door. He grabbed her shoulders, pulled her closer, and stared into her puffy eyes. "Did you do something with Michael?" he asked.

"Yes. I kissed him." It was in her nature to confess immediately.

"Nice work, Julia. Fuck him, and fuck you."

"It was just a kiss."

"Was it? Was it really? Or did you go back to his apartment with him?"

"No, and how could I have, anyway? I told you, we ate near Grand Central."

"Knowing him, he could have taken you to a hotel room for a quickie. Or not so quickie, since you came home two hours later than planned."

"No! No!"

"This is the thing," Ben said. "I suspected all year that you had a crush on him, that if he hadn't been with your cousin, you might have ended up with him instead of me."

"How can you say that? How many times have I told you that it was love at first sight with you? And I've actually stayed in this dump of a town to be with you."

"I should have let you study in the bedroom with me. What an asshole I am. Obviously, when you were studying in the living room with him, the two of you were flirting behind my back."

"No! We were just friends."

"Friends who fell in love, obviously."

"No!" She wept uncontrollably, guilt and grief colliding.

"Fuck," he said, and marched off toward the bedroom.

She leaned against the wall, sobbing.

They made up, as young lovers do. Julia went into the bedroom where Ben was lying down, staring at the ceiling. She got on her knees next to him. "Please, please forgive me." She climbed up on the bed and unbuttoned his shirt. He kept staring at the ceiling.

"Fuck Michael," he said. She took off her shirt and reached for his hand and put it on her breast. "I love you so much," she said. "Please forgive me. Please forgive me." She repeated it like a mantra. He squeezed her breast and rolled toward her. "I don't want you ever to see him again," he said. He was frowning and angry and had an erection. Full of remorse, self-loathing, and a passionate desire to reconnect, she let him make love to her.

Ben was writing his dissertation now and liked to do research and writing after dinner. One Saturday morning he said to her, "I think Michael's old room should be my study, and our bedroom should be your room. That way I can stay up late and not disturb you."

"Yeah, that makes sense." She went to bed earlier than him because she had to be up at seven for her new job in the math department.

"I'd like to move my books in there."

"Okay, let's."

At twenty-six, Ben already had a lot of books: the ones from Oxford that he'd shipped to America, the ones he'd gathered at Yale, the used ones he'd bought at the Strand in New York, and the dozens he had taken out from the library and was perpetually renewing. His books were his friends, and he liked to keep them close about him. Julia was a reader too, but as Gladys had said, she was also a poet who needed to live in the world and collect raw experiences, and her library was smaller and more selective.

"We should swap the clothes too," he said, nodding toward the dresser. It was hot out, and there was perspiration on his forehead.

She, too, was perspired, but less so. "Okay, I'll wear your underwear, and you can wear mine." She took off her shorts as an invitation. Since the awful night of her confession, they'd been having sex every day, as though to reaffirm their bond. And Ben was quickly aroused, and they did it yet again, amidst the chaos of moving the books around. It was a way of dispelling Michael's ghost, of coming back into what they had. Afterward, they went back to the books. Ben had quantities of poetry. It was as though the oceans written before her had sloshed up into their apartment; it intimidated more than inspired her. She hadn't written a word all summer.

"Now, back to the clothes swap," he said. "I'll bring my clothes into the study and put them in Michael's old dresser"—she couldn't hear his name without a constriction of the heart—"and you can have mine in the bedroom. I think this all makes sense, don't you, since our schedules are different?"

"Sure," she said.

"Maybe tomorrow," he said. "When we're done with the books."

Tomorrow was a Sunday, so that certainly seemed possible. But the next morning she slept in, and when she woke up, Ben was gone. There was a note on the dining table.

Library. Back soon.

She had no idea how long he'd be gone. Perhaps he had an idea he had to follow up on or a book he had to check out. Or perhaps he'd been seduced by esoteric entries in a bibliography. The library was a human rabbit hole, and he might get lost in it for an hour or the whole day. After breakfast, she went into Ben's new study and stared at the old wooden dresser by the window that Michael had used. It had been part of the apartment's minimal furnishings when they'd rented it, so he hadn't taken it on his departure. She opened and closed the drawers, wondering if he'd left anything behind. He hadn't.

She decided she'd move Ben's clothes in there herself. That way she could unpack the suitcases she'd used for clothing storage since graduation. As she put Ben's clothes into Michael's old dresser, the symbolism of the action did not escape her, for the perfect thing would have been to conflate the two men. In a fantasy version of her life, that's what she would have done. Julia was emptying Ben's last, bottom drawer when she found, tucked at the back, a manila envelope. She wasn't a snoop by nature, but she felt immediately that there were letters inside, and she couldn't resist. She sat down on the edge of the bed and pulled them out.

They were from Dominique. Each one was still in its original envelope. She took one out at random. It was written in a mixture of French and English. Julia's French was rudimentary, so only parts were intelligible. Feeling both curious and threatened, she wondered if they were still corresponding, but how could they be when she was living there now and saw Ben's mail as it came in? Unless Dominique sent letters to his English department box.

Julia went through the stack, looking for the last letter Dominique had written. It was from January of that year, probably after Ben's visit to Paris. *Okay, good, Dominique had stopped writing after that.* But if they'd stopped writing, weren't they still friends, as he'd said they were? She started reading the letter.

Je vais toujours me souvenir de notre au revoir. You were a wonderful lover to the very end. But an ocean is an ocean. Je t'aimerai toujours.

Julia knew enough French to understand it. There was more in the same vein, then a list of memories from long ago and more recent. The lines swirled as Julia read them. It was obvious he'd stayed with her in Paris, and not with a male friend as he'd said, and it was obvious he and Dominique had been lovers during their last visit together.

The jealousy swelled up into her chest bitter as bile. She was not metaphysical, yet the pain seemed like a karmic retribution for kissing Michael. Still, there was a difference: she'd told Ben about the kiss, but Ben hadn't told her about his farewell reunion with Dominique. As she sat with the letters on her lap, feeling betrayed and insecure in his affections, she wondered what she was doing there, why she'd given up New York to be in a pit like New Haven with a man she wasn't married to.

Julia put the letters back in the envelope. Now she had a dilemma. Should she tell Ben she'd read them?

She went to the phone in the living room and dialed Michael's number. Ben could walk in at any moment, but he probably wouldn't because he was in the rabbit hole, and she had to take the risk.

Michael answered.

"It's me," Julia said, "I had to talk to you."

"Hey," he said. "I wasn't expecting to hear from you again. Now that you're in your little life with Ben."

There was something about his tone, so cool and distant, that kept her from saying anything about their goodbye, even as the kiss echoed inside her. For the moment, she needed to lean on him as a friend.

"I need your . . . advice. I need to talk to you about something."

"Okay. Go ahead, I'm all ears." He sounded more relaxed, now that she'd signaled she wouldn't mention their kiss.

"I found these letters Dominique wrote Ben, and I read them, and it seems that, you know, when he was in Paris at Christmas, well, they were lovers." She was crying now. "He lied to me."

"Oh, come on, Julia. All is fair in love and war, you know that. Anyway, it's over now between them, right?"

"I guess."

"So what's the big deal?"

"He could have told me."

"Why should he have? Did you tell him about us?"

There it was. Her mind did a somersault. She was a terrible liar, but she didn't want to complicate things or seem stupid or make Michael feel guilty. "No, I didn't."

"Good. I'm glad."

"You don't think I should confront him about Dominique?"

"Goddammit, Julia. Grow up."

She was taken aback by the harshness in his voice, which she'd never heard before. He sounded mean.

"Thanks," she said. "Thanks a lot."

"Okay, I'm sorry. But the thing is, you've got to forget it." He spoke slowly. "Just erase the whole thing from your mind."

"So I shouldn't tell him I read the letters?"

"Again, no! What would be the point of it? He made his decision to break with her, like you made your decision to break with me. It's a done deal."

There was a momentary silence, and she was afraid he was going to hang up on her.

"Michael, I—I want to see you again. I miss you."

"Why? What would the point of *that* be?"

"Why? Why not? I love you."

He snorted. "You moved in with Ben. What's this lovey-dovey stuff all of a sudden?"

"Michael!"

"I can't, Julia. I can't. For a million reasons, I can't. For one thing, I don't want you using me against him."

"What do you mean?"

"Using me to get back at him about Dominique."

"No, it's not that at all, and you know it."

"I can't do this, Julia. We shouldn't talk, we shouldn't communicate. We have to say goodbye. So I'm saying it now. Goodbye, Julia."

He hung up.

She sat on the couch with her head in her hands. She hadn't experienced much loss in her life and wasn't equipped to deal with it. Tears came up at the idea of never seeing Michael again; then she remembered Ben, who might walk in at any moment. Michael was right; she had to conceal the evidence of her nosiness. She would take the contents of the bottom two drawers back to their original location in the bedroom. She would scrub down the kitchen, and when Ben came home, she would say, "Oh, I started to move your stuff, but then I stopped after the second drawer and decided to let you do the rest because I wanted to clean the oven." He'd see her with rubber gloves and an apron on and a scrub pad in hand. And he'd believe her.

19

PARIS

(Anna)

Doug drove Anna to the Boston airport. When they stood at the Air France gate, she was shocked to see tears in his eyes. She'd never seen him cry before.

"I love you," he said. He always said it first. He could be so wooden and passionate at the same time.

"I love you too," she answered, the way she always did.

The separation hurt more than she'd expected it to. She had expected relief, but she felt herself sinking instead of rising as the plane took off. The ground her heart had rested on was being yanked away from beneath her.

She nodded to the wine when the stewardess came by and after a few sips felt a little better.

Anna was happy with the living arrangement Leila had found. Her professor had taken an apartment on a side street off the Boulevard du Montparnasse; included with the rent was an associated maid's room in the sixth-floor attic, known as a *chambre de bonne*, where Anna slept. She took her meals and worked with Leila downstairs, in a living room facing the central courtyard of the building complex. They would sit at the dining table while

Joni, the Persian cat Leila had brought from New York, spent her days basking on the windowsill in the sun's warmth, when there was some.

Landing in Paris for a year was socially difficult at first. Leila was running a Students Abroad center, where she went for part of the day, and she made some acquaintances there. But Anna knew no one and found herself spending many hours alone. There was the cataloging project spread out on the table on index cards, in file folders, and Xerox copies. There were trips to the Bibliothèque Nationale and outings to the neighborhood *marché* and museums.

And there was the mail, which came twice a day.

Doug: *I miss you even more than I thought I would, I guess because our summer together made me happy. I can't wait to see you at Christmas. I have to confess something. I do want you to have a wonderful time in Paris, but sometimes I find myself wishing you'd hate it and come home early. . . .*

Robin: *I'm loving graduate school, and things with Gloria are basically good, though when you live with someone, you find out things about them that can be puzzling. There's some aspect of her that keeps escaping me, that I don't understand. . . .*

Julia: *Funny to think of you embarked on your European adventures while I'm still in New Haven, frozen in time, it sometimes feels like. The math department job is okay. It's kind of mindless, and I wish I could say it was giving me the mental freedom I need to do other things like write poetry and songs. But somehow, I'm blocked, and without knowing what's blocking me. . . .*

There were no letters from Michael. That wasn't a surprise, as they hadn't been close enough for her to expect correspondence. But there were letters from her mother, of course.

Mom: *You're living the dream. Or you think you are. Be aware the cost can be high. You may despise the idea of coming home and doing the detestable "settling down" thing that grown-ups, especially women, are expected to do, but on the other hand, if you keep rolling, like your aunt Doris, you may end up with no family besides a bunch of dogs.*

These voices from the past floated in and out of Anna's head. While she had much to do in her new job, there was little human contact. Sometimes she would carry the last letter she'd received around in her backpack or carefully fold it and stick it in her jeans pocket. Even her mother's letters were comforting. Finally, in need of friendship, Anna took Ben up on his offer of an introduction to his ex. Because Dominique's apartment didn't yet have a phone line, Anna sent her a note. Dominique responded by calling from a phone booth, and they arranged to meet for lunch the following week.

"You'll recognize me," Dominique said. "I'll be carrying a Greek bag and wearing big silver earrings with little birds on them."

The date was something to look forward to.

That night Leila made a suggestion. "How about we go to Le Chapeau Noir after dinner?"

"What's that?"

"It's a lesbian bar I heard about, not far from here. I know you're not gay, but we might meet some people." She smiled from behind her big tortoiseshell glasses.

"Really? Okay, why not?"

"You seem surprised."

Anna studied Leila, her neat haircut and button-down blouse. "It's hard to imagine you in a bar. You seem like . . . like a proper auntie." Anna giggled. They'd had a little wine with dinner. A month into their adventure, their student-teacher relationship had become more familial and relaxed.

Leila laughed. "You mean a spinster auntie? Well, not quite."

After doing the dishes, Anna went up to her room to change into something she thought would mark her as less American— black pants instead of jeans and her one cashmere sweater, also black, that her mother had given her. When she went back down to the apartment, she found Leila had changed into a black pantsuit.

"Here we are, both of us in black, trying to be chic," Leila said. It was the occasion for another round of laughter, then they went out into the cold and dark night, which might have been a deterrent in another city, but here was a bracing invitation to adventure.

The club, in a bohemian neighborhood in the sixth arrondissement, was underground. In the front were a few tables by the bar. Music was playing and women danced in the back. Anna had been to a lesbian club once with Robin in Boston and another time in New York with some friends. She expected the French version to be more elegant, but the women talking and flirting were in blue jeans and casual dress, like home. The only difference was that most were beautifully made up with lots of mascara, and their faces sculpted by a sharpness of attitude.

"Now what?" Anna asked.

"Let's get drinks."

They approached the bar and placed their order. As she admired the petite bartender, a young woman with freckles, short hair, and dark eyeliner, Anna wondered what she'd do if someone tried to pick her up. Then she heard a familiar name.

"Dominique! *Votre boisson est servie!*" the bartender cried out as she placed a cocktail on the counter.

A woman with a Greek bag approached the bar and picked it up. Anna spotted birds in her big silver earrings.

It had to be the same Dominique—Ben's ex.

"I think I know who that is," Anna whispered to Leila.

"Who are you talking about?"

After telling her about Dominique, Anna nodded toward the woman at the bar.

"Go talk to her," Leila said.

"But suppose it isn't the same Dominique? Ben never said Dominique was gay—or bi."

Leila snorted. "He'd be the last one to know, don't you think? Go on, do it."

Anna approached Dominique. "*Pardon*, I think I know you. I'm Anna Stark, Ben's friend."

"*Ah oui*, Anna. We can speak English. I love to practice! Are you here alone?"

"I came with Leila, the professor I'm working for. What are you doing here?" Anna asked, then regretted her blunder. But her new friend took it in stride.

"I like it here. I can really relax." Dominique made a flirtatious little gesture with her shoulders. "Pretty women dancing and no men to bother me, so . . . why not?"

"Okay," Anna said, dubious.

"Let's put it this way: I am open to experimentation." Dominique winked. "Experimentation and variety." The loudness of the music had gone up a notch, and she had to scream over it. "How about we go out to a café? Impossible to talk here. And you can bring your teacher."

Anna squeezed through the crowd back toward Leila at the other end of the counter, only to find her engaging with a middle-aged woman in a matching black pantsuit. Two pantsuits going head-to-head. Anna reached Leila and relayed Dominique's invitation.

Leila waved her hand. "Go ahead without me."

"*Oui.* Can't you see she is *occupée?*" the matching pantsuit said, then passed an arm through Leila's. "*On va danser maintenant.*"

Anna shrugged and nodded to Dominique to join her. The two women squeezed their way out of the bar and into the street.

They went to the café at the corner and sat across from each other in a booth. Dominique ordered two glasses of red wine, then they exchanged some basic facts, with Dominique explaining her studies in classics and the path to a professorship in France, and Anna describing her job as Leila's research assistant and the project itself. "She wants to put together a collection of images of the female figure in the nineteenth-century popular press, mostly engravings, some of them erotic."

"You studied art yourself?"

"Yes, both history of art and studio art. I'm a painter."

"A painter? How wonderful!"

"I don't think I'll be able to paint while I'm in Paris, though. I don't have a studio."

"Ah, but maybe we can find you one," Dominique said. "The first step is to introduce you to some people. Let me think. There's a reception next week for the opening of an exhibit of works by a Slavic French artist named Dimitri Olief. He's a friend of mine. I'll take you!"

This would be an exciting glimpse into the Parisian art world. "What's his medium?"

"Everything, but this exhibit will be drawings. I have to warn you, his sensibility is a little—how should I put it?—twisted. I hope you're not easily shocked."

"Nothing shocks me."

"That's what everybody says because they come to Paris wanting to be shocked. We'll see. In any case, if you're working on the history of erotic drawing, you'll find it fascinating."

Anna felt titillated, both by Dominique—this beautiful woman she'd met in a gay bar—and the prospect of an unusual soirée.

They made a rendezvous to meet outside the Galerie Majeure/Mineure a week later, at *vingt-et-une heures*, or nine in the evening. Anna still had to subtract twelve from French time.

The night of the exhibit, she thought wearing all black to an exhibit opening was cliché, so she put on jeans and a red turtleneck for the event. She arrived to find Dominique in tall boots and a suede miniskirt. An elegant crowd peered at framed etchings and drawings of plastic dolls in odd poses. The artworks were separated by groups of painted Russian dolls displayed on shelves.

Dominique kissed her on both cheeks. "Whatever you think, remember, I warned you. You Americans all have a puritanical streak. You pretend to be open-minded, then the alarm goes off at the slightest provocation, and you call in the witch burners."

"It looks like pictures of dolls, so?"

"Each one is an erotic novel. You'll see."

Anna began looking at the pictures. The drawings were executed in minute detail, in tiny, fine black strokes overlaid with gentle washes of watercolor. The dolls had perfect rosy cheeks, glass eyes, and nylon eyelashes. The first one was fully clothed, the second had an unbuttoned shirt, the third was in a bra and panties. As she moved deeper into the gallery, the striptease continued with the depictions growing more grotesque. Some had fractured skulls, twisted arms, exposed genitalia. Finally, there were breasts oozing milk and gigantic clitorises drooping over large vaginal openings. Anna became increasingly disturbed.

"I can see you're becoming judgmental," Dominique whispered to her.

"I am not!" Anna said defiantly.

"What do you think they're 'about'?"

"I don't know!"

"I think he might be saying something about female sexuality. Like, he understands the importance of the clitoris."

Anna flushed as though she herself were being undressed and exposed.

"I find it disturbing, that's all."

"You see how brilliant it is, then, right? Two things that separately don't shock—dolls and erotic drawing—when combined have a new power." Dominique was excited, perhaps more by her own intellectual somersault than by its object.

"Technically, they're very impressive."

"Oh, look, here's the genius himself."

A tall man with blue eyes in round, deep-set sockets approached. In his late thirties, Dimitri was wearing an Indian tunic over matching baggy pants. The fabric was a pale mint green with a darker, paisley trim. The hippie garb was unusual for a Parisian adult in the 1970s.

He gave Dominique *deux bises* on the cheeks and asked her to introduce him to her friend. When Dominique told him Anna was an American painter, he switched to English.

"We need to find Anna a studio," Dominique said.

"I'll ask around. I'm sure we can find something." Dimitri peered at Anna. "I'm interested in your opinion of my exhibit, as a fellow artist."

"Beautifully executed and very provocative."

"I aim to provoke. I aim to make people think because most people do not."

"And what do you want people to think about?"

"The primacy of the clitoris."

"Aha! You see! I was right!" Dominique exclaimed triumphantly, then noticed that Anna was redder than before. "*Dimitri, tu peux t'arrêter là. Anna est délicate.*"

Dimitri laughed and leaned in toward Anna. "You straight or gay? Or bi?"

"I'm straight," Anna said. On her second glass of wine, she was slipping into a story about someone else.

"That's too bad. You might consider a little experimentation. Because the best sexual education for a young woman can be found in the hands of another woman. Honestly, I cannot see what you girls see in us men. *C'est un mystère.* We are hairy, prone to violence, and have no understanding of the 'tiny organ.' At least, most of us don't. I myself, having studied the matter seriously, know a little more than some."

"Dimitri is a sexonaut," Dominique said, laughing.

"You two should come to my place sometime. I have some good hashish I got in Marrakesh."

Mercifully, another guest snagged him at that point.

"Now what? Another glass of wine?" Dominique asked Anna.

"I think I'm ready to leave."

"It's all too much for you, I can see."

"Not at all. He obviously wants to break every rule in the book, both in life and in art. It's fascinating."

"But you are fascinated to your limits of fascination. I get it. Okay, let's go."

They stepped outside. "So," Anna started tentatively, "you and Dimitri, you're . . . ?"

"We're . . . ?" Dominique imitated her polite tone, taking it up a notch. "You want to know exactly?"

"Sure I do. He seems wild."

"What did you think about his invitation to go to his place and try his hashish?"

"He wants both of us in his bed at once."

"Why not? I mean, would you be willing?"

"I . . . I don't know."

"You could always get up and leave in the middle, if you didn't like it."

"Could I? Or would I get caught up in something that I

couldn't get out of? Especially if I have some hashish."

Dominique laughed. "What if this, what if that—just like an American, to worry about things that are meant to be enjoyed. But who cares about sex when you can go dancing? How about we go to a party?"

"You mean now?"

"Yeah."

The night was getting colder, and Anna hesitated. "I think I'll go home."

"What, is eleven o'clock past your bedtime? Listen, I have some friends from Morocco in Montmartre, they're having a *réunion* tonight, let's go."

Anna hung back. "It's already late, and the metro stops in a couple of hours—"

"The party will go all night, and we can come back when the metro starts again in the morning. Come on, there will be great music and wine and crazy wild dancing—and all kinds of delicacies to eat."

Anna imagined a huge table covered with fragrant tagines, roasted meats, and flaky pastries topped with honey and chopped nuts. Maybe someday, after France and Italy and Asia, she'd go to North Africa and taste the exotic on the spot; maybe she'd go to all the former French colonies and taste not only new foods but also the flavors of rebellion and liberation. Fantasies of travel and adventure proliferated in her head, one out of the other like fireworks, and Anna was wondering how many rules she might be brave enough to break in unfamiliar contexts when she felt her new friend take her hand, and she thought, *If I can't do this now, I won't be able to do any of it, for here is someone I can trust and fly the nest with.*

"Okay, let's go," Anna said.

And, squeezing hands hard, the two women flew toward the metro, hooting and dancing in the crisp night air.

20

MOTHERS AND DAUGHTERS

(Robin, Julia, Anna)

S ix months later, one afternoon in May, Robin had just delivered supplies from the Russian grocery store to Iris when her mother came down with a serious expression on her face.

"Family meeting time," Sarah said. "Both of you, sit down now."

Robin and her grandmother sat next to each other on the little couch.

"What is it? You're worrying me," Iris said.

"I just spoke to Linda," Sarah said. "And it's been decided. We're going to Paris to get Anna back."

"What do you mean, 'Get her back'?" Iris asked.

"Anna's had her year in Paris, and Linda feels it's time for her to come home, and I agree with her."

"Maybe she doesn't want to come back," Robin said.

"She's twenty-two. How can she possibly know what she wants?" Sarah drew deeply on her cigarette, then flicked the ashes into a gold-rimmed ashtray. "And I'm going with Linda. To provide moral support."

273

Iris snorted. "As though you needed an excuse to go to Paris."

"My sister has a right to get her daughter back."

"That's the most ridiculous thing I've ever heard," Robin said. "Why can't you just let Anna do what she wants?"

"I'll pay for your plane ticket if you come with me," Sarah said, giving her an arch look.

"Really?" Robin was willing to be bribed.

"Yes, really. I want company. But you have to promise not to undermine me."

"I won't promise any such thing!"

"And I'm not buying *you* a ticket," Sarah said to her mother. Agitated, she tapped her cigarette again, but this time the ashes missed their mark and fell by the side of the ashtray. "Because if I did, you'd probably lose it, the way you did all your money."

"Enough already!" Iris said. "How many times do I have to say I'm sorry?"

Ignoring her, Sarah refocused on Robin. "It's settled then. We'll go together. We'll meet Linda in Paris and help her convince Anna to stop this European foolishness."

"What about Mariel and Julia?" Robin asked.

"I'm not paying for *their* tickets either!"

"I mean, are they invited?"

"We ought to invite them, I suppose. But Mariel won't come. She'll have a show or an audition or something."

"She won't come," Iris said, "because she's not about to pressure her niece to come back from Europe. Mariel's a free spirit, the way you were, once upon a time. Remember?"

Sarah squirmed at this reference to her wild phase In LA. "I was never a free spirit," she said, smoothing her sheer stockings.

"Oh?" Iris arched her eyebrows. "Those crazy tie-dyed outfits? The going to shul half naked?"

"Mariel gave me those blouses, and I never went to shul half naked. I didn't wear a bra a few times. No one was wearing bras ten years ago."

Iris snorted.

"The point is, freedom isn't all it's cracked up to be," Sarah said, "and it's reasonable of Linda to be concerned."

When Robin got back to her apartment, Gloria was studying. To prepare for a graduate program in acupuncture, Gloria was reading everything she could find about Chinese medicine. Robin reflected that her current partner was another version of Stephanie: she soothed herself by continually stuffing more facts into her brain. Another fact, in it goes—yum! Gloria had the kind of relationship to knowledge that Robin had to sex: enough was always of brief duration, and more was never enough. If given a choice between facts and sex, Gloria would have chosen facts. Given the same choice, Robin would have chosen sex.

This disparity between their libidos had been a big surprise to Robin. When they'd become lovers, she'd thought Gloria was as sexually needy as she was. That misimpression had been reinforced by the crazy weekend in Albuquerque with Skye. But after the first few months of living together, Gloria's interest diminished; rejected and frustrated, Robin had reversed her decision to be faithful to her and gone back to Theo to get what she wasn't getting at home. Theo, now living with his girlfriend, rented them rooms at the local Motel 6.

After doing this for a while, Robin had confessed to Gloria, who first said she wasn't jealous and "understood," then said she was uncomfortable about it—even jealous. The divide opened up with her adding, "How about we just take a break for a bit, and let things shake out? But we can continue living together in the meantime."

Now they slept separately and didn't know if they could even still call themselves a couple, but there was still much love and friendship. Neither was interested in labeling themselves or their relationships.

"How was your visit home?" Gloria asked, lifting her head from her book.

Robin related the plan to "rescue" Anna. Of course, Gloria wasn't invited, and she didn't have the means to go on her own. Robin would go to Paris without her.

"We'll be separated for the first time," Gloria said.

"Only a week or two. Or maybe three."

"Or maybe four?"

"You're okay with me going without you, aren't you?" Asking the question, Robin felt that they were indeed still a couple.

"Of course I'm okay." Gloria sharpened her pencil. She always had one in hand when she read. "And of course, I wish I could go with you."

"I know. But someday we'll go together."

"I'd like that."

Gloria could be impatient and irritable, but her ability to let go and move on had enabled her to tolerate Robin's seeing Theo, and it had eased other differences as well during their first year of cohabitation. She went back to her books, and Robin called Julia. They'd kept the cousinly East Coast/West Coast connection going by phone ever since graduation.

"Guess what? The Mothers," Robin said in their usual baritone, "are plotting a trip to bring Anna back."

"Oh no," Julia said.

"'Oh no' is right. What is it about them, that they can't mind their own business?"

"I don't know."

"My mother's going to support Linda. And she wants me to go too. You have to come. That way it'll be three against two. Otherwise, Anna won't stand a chance."

"That should be possible. I'm supposed to go to London with Ben."

"That's perfect. You can come over and meet us before or after!"

"Yeah, sure. Does Anna know yet?"

"I don't know. We could write her, but she'll hear soon enough, I'm sure."

A few days later, Julia was visiting her parents when Anna called from Paris. Usually, they wrote letters instead of splurging on a phone call, but this was an emergency.

"Have you heard? My mother's coming!" Anna sounded panicked.

"I know. Robin told me."

"And I have no plans to go back!"

"Are you dependent financially on them?"

The transatlantic line crackled and sputtered as usual.

"No, I'm not. Leila's paying me decently to do research, and I've been able to save up. I don't need my parents' money."

"Then what's the worry?"

"She guilt-trips me, and then I end up doubting my own decisions." Anna sounded stressed. "And it seems Sarah's coming too. With the two of them twisting my arm, I might not be able to resist. Because they're wicked and powerful, you know. Your mom's different, she's cool, but my mom and Sarah, they're the evil sisters. They're scary together."

"They're not evil, they're just—"

"Evil."

"Maybe."

"You and Robin have to come. I need you guys here."

"We'll come."

"Thank you."

"Are you okay?" Julia asked. "I mean, besides this."

"I'm great. I'm having the time of my life, and I'm thinking about going to Italy next."

"Italy?"

"Aunt Doris invited me."

"Doris! Everyone says she's crazy." None of the three cousins had ever met the infamous Doris, who had exiled herself to Rome before they were born. And no one in the rest of the family had visited her in years because she was difficult. Or so the mothers said.

"Yeah, well, who's crazy and who's not in our family is a matter of debate," Anna said. "There may be reasons why Doris made her life abroad. She wrote me a letter saying she wanted to get to know me and invited me to visit her. Maybe I could extend my stay to take an Italian language course and then . . . who knows. I might find a way to live there for a while."

"Your mother will have a fit."

"Please don't tell your mother about Doris because she'll pass it along to mine."

"Of course I won't tell her."

When Julia hung up, she saw her mother on the kitchen threshold.

"Of course you won't tell me what?" Mariel asked.

"I'm not going to tell you something she asked me not to tell you."

"You don't have to be secretive with me. I'm on Anna's side. I heard about Linda's plan, and I disapprove." Mariel looked indignant. "I love her, she's my cousin, and I grew up with her, but I've always thought she wasn't meant to be a mother. She did a decent job with Evelyn, but by the time Anna came along . . . Jesus, what a disaster. And now, poor Anna. They should let her do what she wants."

"That's how Robin and I feel too."

"And I disapprove of Sarah going. She's a special case. If I'd had her as a big sister, I'd have turned out like Linda too."

"And how did Linda turn out?"

"You know. The drinking."

"And how was Sarah responsible for that?" Julia saw an opening for more family history, the darker segments of which her mother wasn't always willing to share.

Mariel went to the stove and put the kettle up, as though to indicate a preference for tea over alcohol. "The problem with Sarah was that her husband didn't go to Yale. I married a Yalie, and Linda married a Yalie. But Sarah married a nothing-ie. And what with her obsession with status and prestige, she's never forgiven us. So she puts Linda's sculpting down at every opportunity. And Linda doesn't even see it."

"Uncle Herb may be a 'nothing-ie,' but he's a rich nothing-ie."

"True, so Sarah can justify her existence with philanthropy. Nothing wrong with that. And not much else to do in San Francisco." Mariel kissed her daughter on the forehead. "You go to Paris, and *vive la liberté*, that's what I have to say. Anna's *liberté*, that is."

"I will."

Back in New Haven, Julia shared everything with Ben.

"My aunt Linda is crazy," she said as they had their ritual after-dinner cuddle on the couch. "Anna's always wanted to live abroad, so why shouldn't she stay a while longer?"

"There will be drama, but . . . it gives us an excuse to hop over to Paris together for a bit after we see my parents," Ben said. "You'll go over first for the family conference, then I'll join you."

"I'm so excited."

"You kinda lucked out with your British boyfriend, didn't you?"

"And you kinda lucked out with your American girlfriend, didn't you?"

"You bet I did."

They liked to congratulate each other on their happiness. Of course, it wasn't a perfect relationship. Julia sometimes thought Ben was too serious, not enough fun. But she worshipped him—his intellect, his kindness, and his commitment to her. She didn't think she would ever find anyone better. When the kiss with Michael came back, she dismissed it as an emotional accident—she'd had a moment of doubt about Ben, and that second of flailing had lit a match under her friendship with Michael. She could see now, very clearly, that there had been nothing to it.

Mothers and daughters arrived in Paris a couple of weeks later. Anna was dressing for the family reunion when Leila came into her room. "Let's have an aperitif before you go out. How about a kir?" she asked.

"That's an idea."

It was easy to make—two dashes of crème de cassis in two glasses of white wine. They sat in the living room.

"I hope you'll come back after visiting your aunt," Leila said. "I still need your help. The project is far from done."

She gestured toward the heavily notated index cards and xeroxed copies of lithographs from nineteenth-century magazines covering the dining table. After nine months of research, they'd given up eating there; they ate off their laps in the living room instead.

"I want to leave things open. Do you mind?"

"You could travel, then come back. You don't have to let your mother disrupt your life here," Leila said.

"You're right, I do have a life here." Anna reflected on her work as Leila's assistant, the friendships she'd made, her intermittent affairs with Dominique and Dimitri, and her many Parisian pleasures and routines. "Maybe I'll just go to Italy for a few weeks, then come back. I don't know."

"Try to tell me by the end of July what you decide. If you stay there, I'll need to find another assistant."

Anna gave her advisor a fond look. Levelheaded and supportive, Leila was her mentor and substitute mother, and they'd become close after almost a year of living together. "Of course I'll tell you. The thing is, I'd love to be fluent in Italian," Anna went on. "You can only really learn a language by living there."

"If that's what you want, you should stand up to your mother, instead of running away from her."

"I don't know if I can. She's like a volcano or a tidal wave. I just have to stay away until I get stronger." It had been such a relief *not* to see her mother for a year. But now she had to. The cousins planned to meet Linda and Sarah at Le Procope for dinner that evening. Anticipating the reunion, Anna felt an internal shiver.

In the grayish pink light of a Paris spring evening, soft as a Bonnard painting, she walked to the Latin Quarter hotel where her cousins were staying. The younger and older generations had taken separate lodgings. Julia and Robin's one-star place wouldn't have been good enough for the mothers, who had chosen a fancier hotel on the Right Bank, not far from good shopping and fine restaurants.

Anna climbed the four flights to her cousins' room. It was tiny, with a foot's width between the foot of the bed and the armoire on the facing wall. The window opened up on a cobblestone side street; red geraniums grew in pots and window boxes across the way. The walls were scuffed up, and the stuffing of the upholstered chair in the corner bulged out at the worn seams, but everything looked clean enough.

There were hugs and small talk about the flight and the hotel, then Anna sat down on the bed and covered her face with her hands. "Thank God you're here. She should leave me alone. I'm so angry, I don't know whether to scream or cry. Or kick something."

"We need a strategy," Julia said.

"It's easy," Robin said. "We just let them talk, pretending to listen, then we change the subject."

"We let them talk, then change the subject." Anna felt like a spy memorizing instructions for a secret mission. "But change the subject to what?"

"To anything. To what we're going to do tomorrow. It doesn't matter."

Restless, Anna stood up. "Why don't we go sit in the park till dinner?"

They walked out and headed into the Luxembourg Garden. The light had dimmed to a dusty mauve, and the air was a perfect springtime temperature. Anna's dread was softened by sharing the beauty of the place with two people she cared about.

"It's working out with Gloria, then?" Anna asked, to distract herself.

"Well, it's a little complicated at the moment. We're still living together, but not as lovers."

"How come?"

"I did something she didn't like. Remember that musician guy I had the fling with? Theo? I ended up going back to him again, and she found out. Well, I told her. And then there was someone else . . . a woman . . . ugh, I'm awful."

"Yikes," Julia said. "Was she very angry?"

"Not really. Just hurt and confused, but then she kind of forgave me, because she doesn't like sex as much as I do, and after the first few months she stopped being so interested, so she understood she was partly responsible for my stepping out."

"But you function as a couple day-to-day?" Anna asked.

"Sometimes it feels like we're a couple; sometimes it doesn't. But she's my rock. I love her to bits, so I'm not going anywhere. I think of us as a kind of mini-commune."

They reached the central circle of the gardens in front of the palace, where short palm trees in big wooden boxes had been rolled in for the warm weather. The park was regal, manicured, orderly—a mini-Versailles. They grabbed three metal chairs and arranged them in a triangle.

"You guys are very cool," Julia said. "I don't know how you do it."

"Between her and Theo, your dance card sounds pretty full. So you probably wouldn't be interested in going to any lesbian bars while you're here." Anna laughed.

Robin raised her eyebrows. "You know some?"

"Leila took me to one, and uh, I have this on-and-off thing with this woman, Dominique—"

"Yikes!" Robin's jaw dropped. "Congratulations! My cousin, the adventuress!"

"I'm not gay, Robin."

"Does Doug know? He visited at Christmas, right?"

"Yeah, he was here. For two weeks. I didn't tell him then, and he hasn't been here for a while, and when he's not here, well, we're on pause," Anna said. "In other words, he doesn't know and doesn't need to know."

"You said her name was Dominique?" Julia asked. "Ben's Parisian ex was named Dominique."

"Oh, shit. Yeah. One and the same. Shit," Anna repeated. "I shouldn't have told you."

"No, you should have! But how weird." Julia grew pale. "What a coincidence."

"Well, not really. Ben gave me her contact info."

"He never told me that," Julia said.

"No big deal, just her address, so why would he have? Oh God, I'm sorry."

"And how did it go?" Robin asked.

"Again, I'm not gay, but it was fun . . . It was liberating." Anna looked at Julia nervously. "And then I got involved with this weird artist named Dimitri that she was also involved with, so we're this loose threesome. It's all been kind of casual, but ongoing." Anna shrugged. "I'll tell you more about it some other time. It'll come out in drips and drabs."

Julia stood up. "I don't know why, but I find this really disturbing. What was she like? Very beautiful, I imagine."

"Not as beautiful as you." Anna reached for her hand. "And kind of crazy, promiscuous. Obviously not what Ben needed or wanted. I can see why he broke up with her."

"Yuck, this feels incestuous or something."

"He didn't choose her," Robin said. "He chose you."

"And you and Ben are good, right?" Anna asked.

"Ben and I are fine, yeah." Julia sat back down. She looked at the children running around the garden. "It's late. Shouldn't they be in bed?"

"Are you still writing poetry?" Anna asked.

"Not so much." Julia shrugged. "I think my poetry was an elevated form of whining. I'd write when I was really depressed or frustrated. Now that I'm happy with Ben, I'm not inspired."

"I'm glad you're happy because just think, I brought you two together!" Robin said.

The three of them laughed, remembering the night of the infamous party when they threw the records out the window.

"And Michael? Anyone heard from Michael?" Anna asked. She thought she saw Julia flush, but it was hard to tell in the light of dusk.

"Michael has disappeared," Julia said.

"I thought the two of you were close," Anna said.

"We were, but you know, he had that fight with Ben . . ."

"I really didn't behave well with him," Robin said. "The way I got involved with Gloria before breaking up with him—I'm not proud of that. Messy."

They sat in silence, each in their memories of Michael.

"You're well out of it," Julia said. "You wouldn't have been happy with Michael. He has a real depressive streak."

"That's the thing. I never should have gotten involved in the first place."

"All's well that ends well," Anna said, standing up. "Come on, let's go get this over with." It pained her to think about Michael.

The cousins went around the palace and exited through the tall iron gates at the top of the garden. When they reached Le Procope, Linda and Sarah were standing outside the entrance, smoking cigarettes. Linda was in upgraded artist garb: jeans, a black silk shirt with big white polka dots, and gold cameo earrings. Sarah was in her usual sheath dress with an expensive-looking handbag over her shoulder. The mothers waved at the cousins. When Linda grabbed Anna in a hug, Anna had to fight her impulse to free herself as rapidly as possible.

"You're the French speaker among us," Linda said to her daughter, "so we thought we'd let you take us inside."

The maître d' seated them upstairs at a table by the window. The white tablecloths, the chandeliers, and the view of the cream-colored stone buildings across the way spoke of old-world luxury and elegance. The cousins took the wooden chairs opposite the mothers, who had occupied the quilted leather banquette, with Linda and Sarah across from their daughters, and Julia at the end facing no one. The menu was expensive; when Anna had eaten there before, she'd had the only thing she could afford— onion soup. Now she could order anything she wanted.

"I don't know why we've never had a family reunion in Paris," Linda said. "This is paradise."

"Maybe because it's expensive?" Anna asked, staring at her mother's hands. No matter how hard Linda tried, she couldn't get the clay out from under her nails. Anna had paint under her own. Hating this similarity between them, she put her hands under the table.

"Money! You can always dig more up somewhere," Sarah said.

"That's what husbands are for!" Linda laughed, then stopped herself. "For women of our generation, anyway. For you young women today, it's completely different."

"It sure is," Robin said.

"You're all going to be self-sufficient," Linda said.

"My mother has always worked," Julia said. "That's why she isn't here now. She has a part in a Broadway show."

"And you're still with that young man, Ben, is that right? I've heard he's brilliant and destined for great things," Sarah said. "Maybe he'll be a college president one day."

"Mariel was always very driven," Linda said, her train of thought undeterred. "When we were growing up in Flatbush—"

"Flatbush again," Anna muttered.

Linda gave her daughter a sharp look, then continued. "As I was saying, when Sarah and I were growing up in Flatbush, going next door to play with Mariel was so special."

"That's right," Sarah said. "There she'd be with her costumes, makeup, and records. We'd dress up, and she'd give us parts. It was basically improvisational theater from the age of four."

"Mom, all kids do that," Robin said. "It's called 'pretend.'"

"This was at a higher level than 'all kids' or 'pretend,'" Sarah insisted. "Mariel was a shooting star."

"And shooting upward! She'll be famous one day, mark my words. But let's be here now, as the young say," Linda said, gesturing with her cigarette to the big paintings, the gauze curtains, and the balconies outside. "I love this place. How did you hear about it?"

"It's famous," Anna said.

"Thank God!" Linda said, and for a moment Anna thought her mother capable of self-irony.

The waiter came, and Anna ordered in French for everyone.

"*Mademoiselle parle français très bien,*" the waiter said.

"*Merci. J'adore la France—et les français.*" Anna loved speaking French in front of her mother. It asserted her comfort in a separate realm.

"Well," Linda said after the waiter disappeared, "I don't know what you're going to do with your life, but at least you can speak French. Maybe you could get a job in international business, like with an import/export company. A lot of those operations are based in New York."

"Here we go." Anna rolled her eyes.

"You didn't think I came all this way just to see the Eiffel Tower, did you?"

Robin leaned forward. "How about we leave the big questions until after we've had some food and wine?"

"She's right. Let's talk about what we're going to do in Paris instead," Sarah said, and the subject of Anna's future was dropped. "And let me taste the wine when it comes. Wine is one thing I know something about."

"Only little museums for me this time," Linda announced after a couple of glasses. "I refuse to go back to the Louvre. It's too overwhelming. I start thinking, if I look at one more thing, I'll never sculpt again."

"I know, sweetheart," Sarah said. "All that history, all that competition. We'll go to the small museums, and you'll take it all in in small doses the way you always do."

"And all the art is by men, or almost all of it."

"Just remember, even if you've had no worldly success, you are still a great sculptress." Sarah rubbed her sister's arm in sympathy.

Linda leaned her head on Sarah's shoulder. "And you, you are the only one who understands me."

"I do understand you. I *feel* you."

"Jesus, Mom," Anna said, "you don't have to go to museums at all if you don't want to. There are other things to do in Paris. Like eating and shopping and music, or just walking around."

"Don't be ridiculous," Linda said, then looked across the room. "Where's our food? What's taking them so long?"

There was onion soup and fish in butter sauce, lamb stew and steak frites. The pace of conversation slowed with dessert and more wine.

"Now, you know why we're here," Linda finally said to her daughter.

"I do." Anna had had enough wine by this time that she could take her mother on.

"Yes, we all know why I'm here. I'm uncomfortable—your father and I are uncomfortable—with this free-form wandering you're doing—"

"I'm not wandering! I'm in Paris! Working!"

"But what's next? You don't communicate, so I imagine the worst."

"What's next is that I'm going to visit Doris."

"And the worst is true! Doris? *Our* Doris? Whom you've never met?"

"She wrote me," Anna said. "And invited me to visit her."

"How did she get your address?" her mother asked.

"I bet she got it from Mariel," Sarah said. "Listen, Anna. Doris is crazy. You can't visit her."

"Why shouldn't I visit her?"

"She has dogs," Sarah said, "and she loves them more than her own flesh and blood. Last time I visited her in Rome—1962 I think it was, Robin you were little, your father and I left you with Iris—Doris would promise to take us somewhere, then she'd cancel at the last minute because she had to walk the fucking dogs. Or I'd have to twiddle my thumbs in her living room while she went to the butcher for their special food—"

"You need a plan for your life," Linda said, "that's the issue we need to be talking about. One day you'll come home, and you'll have to make a living. How are you going to do that?"

"Not in the import/export business, that much I know." Anna waved to the waiter. *"Garçon, l'addition, s'il vous plaît."*

Robin and Julia gathered their bags.

"Wait," Linda said, "we're not done here."

"Enough for today, Mom," Anna said.

The cousins stood up, and Linda and Sarah had no choice but to follow them out onto the street, where they could still smell roasted meat and wine sauce. Linda drew her daughter away from the group. "I worry about you." She stroked Anna's auburn hair, and Anna cringed at her touch. "Though I do have to say, Paris has made you more beautiful. I love your hair, and that's a gorgeous blouse."

"Thanks, Mom."

"Still and *however*, you realize this is all an escape from reality. And Doug, what about Doug? Are you guys together or not?"

"I don't want to talk about it."

"He's a nice young man. You shouldn't be jerking him around."

Anna didn't understand her parents' obsession with Doug. After a year abroad, she saw clearly that he was destined one day to fall into that sad category, Early Unsatisfactory Boyfriends.

"I'm going to do what I want to do," she said. "And right now, that's going to Italy. And you have to let me go."

"I miss you so much. I love you and I need you."

Anna saw her mother as a bundle of failures, artistic, marital, and maternal, and was embarrassed by her pathetic pleading. But compassion gave way to rage as she felt the injustice of the situation. Her mother, who had preferred alcohol to taking care of her, now had the gall to ask for her love and support. There was something obscene about this reversal.

"We can talk about it more tomorrow," Anna said, turning to get away.

Linda grabbed her arm. "I don't want you to ever, ever be

economically dependent on a man, the way I am on your father. That's why I want you to think about money and how you're going to make it."

Anna saw the tears in her mother's eyes. She felt sorry for her, then anger and disgust. Then compassion again. "Rest assured, I'm going to do my best not to take after you, Mom."

Thankfully, Julia called out, "Hey, you walking us back to our hotel or not?"

Anna pecked her mother on the cheek. "We can meet for lunch tomorrow and go to a museum if you like. One of the small ones."

"I can go to museums with Sarah," her mother said with a pout.

"Come on!" Robin yelled.

Anna caught up and pulled ahead of them.

"You okay?" Julia asked, speeding up to match Anna's pace.

"I'm angry and confused," Anna said. "And I don't know what to do."

"That's why we're here," Robin said. "To help you figure it out."

"And I'm so appreciative, you have no idea."

Concerned about Anna, Julia suggested she come in when they reached the hotel. Upstairs, the three young women sat on the bed. It was dark outside, and the tiny lamps on the night tables made the room seem shabbier than before.

"Guess what I smuggled in," Robin said, pulling out a joint.

"Oh, you shouldn't have. You could get thrown in prison here for that," Julia said

"She's right," Anna added. "And the American embassy wouldn't help you out. Anyway, I don't want to smoke. I want to stay clear so I can decide what I'm going to do."

"I spoke to my mother about it before I left," Julia said, "and she thinks you should go to Italy. Live your life, have your adventures."

"Mariel is great," Anna said, "and it helps to know that, because now I hear my mother's voice in my head, and I'm wondering how *am* I going to make a living when I go back to the States, and maybe she's right, maybe I should go home tomorrow and look for a real job?"

"But when we were at dinner," Julia said, "it sounded like you really want to go to Italy."

"She put me in a fighting mood. But the truth is, I don't know if I can handle it—the anxiety that comes up around going against her wishes. And if I do, I'll get in trouble with my dad."

"I'm rooting for you," Julia said.

After Anna left, Robin stepped into the shower, and Julia reached for her diary. She wanted to capture the pearl gray and ivory tones of Paris, the way they fostered a sense of internal equilibrium and harmony. Equanimity was much needed in this time when each of them was incurring parental disapproval. Anna wanted to live abroad, and Linda had come to stop her. Robin wanted to enjoy the sexual revolution, but if Sarah had known Robin was bisexual, she'd have banished her. As for Julia, she carried the burden of knowing that her parents couldn't reconcile themselves to her lack of ambition.

Julia admired Anna, who had just spent a year in one foreign country and might move on to another. She was in awe of Robin, who followed her impulses and desires without fear of the consequences. In comparison—and it was impossible for Julia not to compare—she herself was following the tamest of paths. Staying in New Haven, working as a secretary in the math department at her alma mater, not writing poetry—it all added up to a sense of stagnation. When she was separated from Ben for more than a few days, an uncertainty came up, not so much about him but about the way her path had been muddied by moving in with him. Maybe her parents were right to be concerned.

Robin came out of the bathroom. "Why the grim face?" she asked.

"I feel stuck, compared to you guys."

"Nah," Robin said. "You're fine. You're just figuring things out."

"Both of you are having so many adventures."

Robin shrugged. "Well, Anna is. But me, I'm just fucking around, risking my happiness with Gloria because I can't keep myself under control."

"But at least you're on track for a career."

"You'll figure it all out eventually." Robin toweled her curls dry energetically. "You know, it takes courage to commit to a relationship. And that's what you've done with Ben. You're just not looking at things the right way."

"And what would the right way be?"

"That you have the gifts of loyalty and commitment. You used your freedom to choose a meaningful relationship, and now you're doing what you need to do to take care of it. And you're willing to make the necessary sacrifices. I call that being very adult and having sound values."

Julia nodded. The words were comforting, but she felt a wanting. For what, she didn't know; she could only wonder and grope for it. The only certainty was that it was out there, waiting for her. Whether Ben would be an ally or an obstacle in her quest, she couldn't yet know.

As the week went by, Robin became increasingly annoyed as Linda pressured Anna to return home and Anna resisted without clearly stating that she wouldn't do so. Robin didn't want crazy freedom only for herself. She wanted it for her cousins, her friends—her entire generation of women. As she saw it, the three of them were battling not just the patriarchy but their mothers too. Robin, who saw herself as a modern-day suffragette, thought going home would be a disaster for Anna's growth and development. And she intended to use this Paris spring week to help Anna out of her bind.

At the end of every day, the cousins went back to Julia and Robin's hotel to do a postmortem of the evening.

"I'm going to cave if I keep seeing her," Anna said. "Like I did with my father, when I wrote her that letter and he made me tear it up. I can't seem to stand up to either one of them."

"Enough! You need to leave," Robin said. "Just leave! Soon, maybe tomorrow. Just get on a train and go."

"Don't be angry at me!"

"I'm not angry, but you need a good kick in the pants. You should leave without saying goodbye."

"That's crazy."

"You have to because if you spend another week with your mother, your momentum will go down the drain."

"I'd like to, but I can't!"

"Listen," Robin said. "Take my boots." She yanked off her Frye boots and pushed them toward Anna. "Gimme your sneakers."

"Your beloved boots!"

"You need them more than I do at this point."

"My feet are bigger than yours," Anna protested.

"Not by much, and these boots are big in the toes. You can wear them with thin socks or bare feet. They'll make you feel terrific."

Anna unlaced her sneakers, slid on the boots, and stood up. The stacked wooden heels and thick leather soles added a couple of inches to her already considerable height. "Oh my god, they're incredible. They fill me with determination." She punched her fists up toward the ceiling. "Yay! I'm going to Rome! It's decided!"

"You can conquer the world in those things. You can kick ass in them. Literally. Kick your mother's ass, if it comes to that."

Anna walked back and forth. "And you're right. I shouldn't tell her. I'll go to the station tomorrow morning first thing and get a ticket for the night train. We'll have lunch with them and say we're going to have dinner just the three of us without them, and that'll be it."

After Anna left, Julia opened the shutters. "Look at her in those boots," she said. "She must be six foot two in them."

Robin joined her by the window. "She's a powerhouse and doesn't even realize it." And, overcome with protectiveness, she heaved a big sigh as Anna rounded the corner and disappeared.

Striding down the Boulevard Saint-Michel, Anna towered over the crowds on the sidewalk. The streetlights sparkled, and cars and taxis whooshed by. On the terrasse of La Closerie des Lilas, overhung with blossoming wisteria, waiters served oysters and Champagne. Dimitri had taken her there the night he had seduced her. Walking by, she wondered how many other lovers he'd had while seeing her. It didn't really matter. Nothing did now, except moving on. *I'm eloping with myself,* she thought, exhilarated at the idea.

It was late, but Anna knew Dominique would still be up, and she wanted to say goodbye. She was glad to find her alone when she arrived. They sat on her bed by the windowsill with the empty perfume bottles as Anna told her of her decision.

"I want you to have a memento of me." Dominique went over to the little wooden desk chair and grabbed the Greek bag hanging over its back. She dumped its contents on the table and presented it to Anna. "Take this and use it."

"Your bag!" Anna was touched, for Dominique took that bag with her everywhere. "You sure?"

"Absolutely. It'll make me happy to think of you wearing it." Dominique came over and passed the strap over Anna's head. "And what about Dimitri? Will you say goodbye to him?"

"Is it necessary?"

Dominique reflected. "Not really. He won't be offended if you don't. With Dimitri, the door is always open, and you can come and go as you please." She rearranged the strap of the Greek bag across Anna's chest. "I hope you have fun in Italy. Whatever you do, remember, it's okay to fuck Italians, but don't fall in love with one. Too dangerous. I mean, I'm assuming you want to have a life someday and not live cooped up in a little *appartamento* with lots of babies."

Anna laughed. "Uh, no. That's not me."

Dominique gave her a tender kiss. "Just be careful, okay?"

On the day of Anna's departure, the cousins and mothers wandered around the Left Bank, stepping in and out of little stores with toys from around the world, handmade paper, medicinal honey, and radish juice in glass vials. They stopped for lunch at a café with big mirrors and brass lamps, one of those neighborhood places that smell of coffee grounds and cigarettes between meals and coq au vin and flounder in butter sauce at lunch and dinner. They talked about the discoveries of the day till coffee, when the mothers returned to the subject of Anna's future.

"We continue to wait for your decision," her mother said.

"You know you're torturing her," Sarah said. "Okay, we get it, you're in your independence phase, but enough is enough."

The waiter brought Anna chocolate mousse with Chantilly cream on top. She spread the cream into a smooth layer with the back of a spoon. She had her train ticket in her Greek bag, and her suitcase was packed and waiting to be picked up from Leila's. She didn't enjoy the subterfuge of escaping in secret. *But she's forcing my hand.*

"I've decided to go home with you," she said in her sweetest voice. "Maybe I can even get a ticket for the same flight."

"I'm glad you're finally coming to your senses," her mother said.

"I am," Anna said. "You're right, of course, the way you always are. It's time for me to get serious about my life, move in with Doug, and look for a real job." The mothers sat on the leather bench that ran the length of the wall; facing them, Anna and her cousins were reflected in the mirrors so that she could see all five of them at once. She took in the contrast between her own youthful beauty and her mother's dropped face and untended hair. "Maybe it's even time to start a family." A fierce, creative energy came up with the lying, and she wanted to embroider, to see how far she could go with the farce. "I'd like to have a couple of babies by the time I'm thirty."

"Oh, honey," her mother said, extending her hand with its clay-rimmed fingernails across the table, "I've always wanted to be a grandmother!"

That evening the cousins sat at a tiny café table across from the big station clock, and Anna ordered three cognacs.

"That was quite a performance at lunch," Robin said. "I'm proud of you."

"I'm proud of me too," Anna said. "And I couldn't have done it without your support. I can't wait to meet the famous Doris and visit Rome and study Italian."

"I'll come visit you," Robin promised.

Anna looked at Julia. "Maybe I can too," Julia said.

The café was lively with bartenders pouring drinks and drawing espressos for night travelers. The clattering of plates in the back kitchen was punctuated by departure announcements and the screech of trains coming in. Anna loved the bustle and the noise. She breathed a sigh of content as she read the destinations posted by the tracks; they promised a variety of journeys, one of which she would start that night, while others would be made in the future. She looked at Robin, with her bandanna restraining her curls, her big earrings, and her attitude, then Julia, so prudent and tentative about everything, yet always dreaming and wanting more.

"It's time," Robin said. "Let's get you on your way."

With Dominique's Greek bag on one shoulder, Robin's boots on her feet, and a small suitcase in hand, Anna strode out toward the Paris–Rome train, known as the Palatino, that was waiting at the platform under the nineteenth-century glass and wrought iron canopy. They reached Anna's car. There were hugs and I love you's. Anna climbed up the metal stairs and slid into her compartment. She hoisted her bag onto the rack and sat down with the heavy feeling of being alone. But then she saw her cousins on the platform waving to her. The three of them were about to separate, but they would eventually come back together, and they would love and support each other for the rest of their lives—of these things Anna was sure. The spirit of adventure was upon her, and she smiled and waved back.

Slowly the train pulled out from under the station canopy into the maze of rails that shone in the evening floodlights.

"She's off! A job well done, if I do say so myself," Robin said.

"I hope she'll be okay," Julia said.

"You worry too much." Robin rubbed Julia's shoulder. "Though the truth is, I'm a little worried too. But she must live. It would be a mistake for her not to."

"Aunt Linda will be furious," Julia said.

"Oh yeah, she'll have a fit when we tell her. It'll be fun to watch."

"Just think, the moms came all this way to get Anna back, and she resisted," Julia said.

"Their mission failed, but it was a noble battle," Robin said.

"We'll be just like them one day, you know."

"In that case," Robin said in her baritone, "long live the Mothers!"

"Long live the Mothers!"

And with that joint cheer, the two cousins locked arms and headed back to the hotel.

ACKNOWLEDGMENTS

I am indebted to those who read versions or chapters of this manuscript: Shams Kairys, Richard Devore, Veronica Reilly-Granach, Kristene Cristobal, Linda Wright, and Leoncia Flynn. Thank you, Roger Clark, for providing the lyrics of "Crazy Free." A special thank-you goes to Andrea Hurst, editor and book doctor, for her many suggestions. I am also grateful to my family, Tim, Emily, and Sophia Hampton, for their love and support.

A thanks goes to the *New English Review* for publishing an earlier version of the chapter "Harlem Afternoon." Additionally, I was fortunate to have a wonderful team at She Writes Press: many thanks to publisher Brooke Warner, project director Shannon Green, copy editor extraordinaire Lorraine Fico-White, and designer Julie Metz, for a job well done.

TO BE CONTINUED . . .

To fast-forward to Julia in her early thirties and see what happens in her relationship with Ben and her friendship with Michael, read *The Geometry of Love.*

If you'd like to learn about Anna's adventures in Italy, read *Nothing Forgotten.*

And yes, there will be a book about Robin, her relationship with Gloria, and the family they create together!

The novels in The Cousins Series are interconnected but can be read in any order as standalones.

ABOUT THE AUTHOR

Photo credit: Chris Loomis

Jessica Levine is the author of *The Geometry of Love* (She Writes Press, 2014), a top-ten women's fiction title in the American Library Association's *Booklist* in 2015, and *Nothing Forgotten* (She Writes Press, 2018), which won the Next Generation Indie Book Award. She is also the author of *Delicate Pursuit: Discretion in Henry James and Edith Wharton* (Routledge, 2002). Her essays, short stories, and poetry have appeared in many publications including *The Southern Review* and *The Huffington Post*. She has translated several books from French and Italian into English.

Jessica holds a PhD in English literature from the University of California at Berkeley, where she was a Mellon Fellow. She was born in New York City and now lives in Northern California. You can find her at www.jessicalevine.com. Jessica has been a practicing hypnotherapist since 2005. You can learn about her work at www.levinehypnotherapy.com.

Looking for your next great read?

We can help!

Visit www.shewritespress.com/next-read
or scan the QR code below for a list
of our recommended titles.

She Writes Press is an award-winning
independent publishing company founded to
serve women writers everywhere.